THE EMERALD CROSS

A THRILLER

Other Titles by
KEN CRUICKSHANK

Eagle Bay

Stand Up: a memoir of disease, family, faith & hope

THE EMERALD CROSS

A THRILLER

KEN CRUICKSHANK

Glendoveer Press LLC

Phoenix, Arizona

Copyright © 2024 Ken Cruickshank | kencruickshank.com

All rights reserved. No part or any portion of this book may be reproduced in any form, mechanical, digital, or transmitted without the author's prior written permission, except for the use of brief quotations in a book review.

This novel is a work of fiction. Names, characters, places, and incidents are the product of the author's imagination and do not depict real persons or events. Any resemblance to actual people or incidents is entirely coincidental.

For information about this title or to order other books and/or electronic media, contact the publisher:

Glendoveer Press LLC
31237 N. 124th Dr.
Peoria, AZ 85383
info@glendoveerpress.com

Cover and interior design by The Book Cover Whisperer:
OpenBookDesign.biz

978-1-960981-14-1 Hardcover
978-1-960981-13-4 Paperback
978-1-960981-12-7 eBook

Printed in the United States of America

FIRST EDITION

For Karen Marie

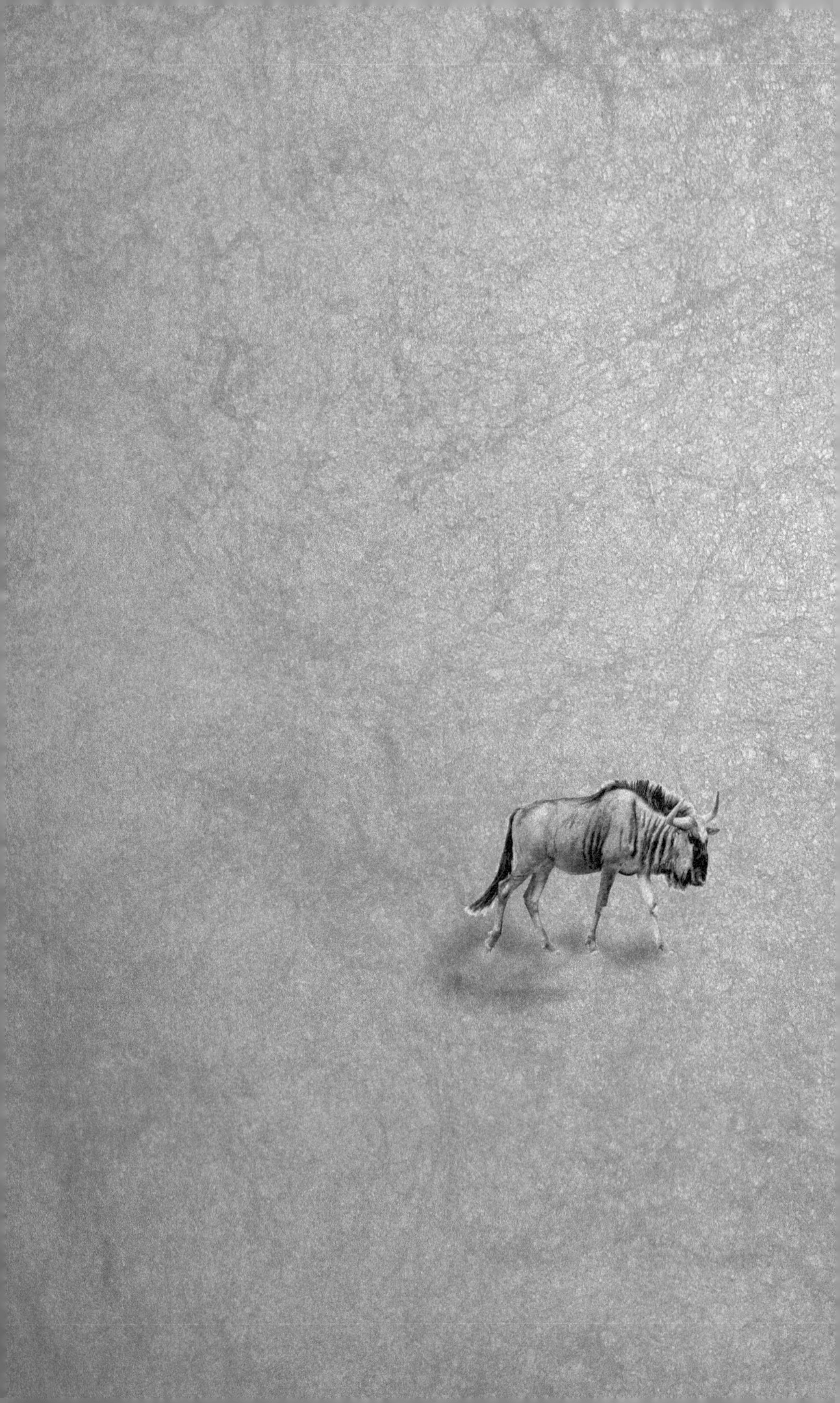

THE
EMERALD
CROSS

CHAPTER 1

On a balmy Mexico City evening in 1991, Samuel Morales lay in bed contentedly beside his wife, Maria. Barely conscious, he hadn't noticed the approaching shadow reaching from the hall into their bedroom. Sensing the presence of another human, he turned his head and opened his eyes, finding himself face-to-face with an expressionless little man.

"Papi," the two-year-old whispered, "you sleep with me." With full lips and almond eyes, adorable Jaime Morales extended an arm, imploring his father to join him for slumber on the boy's mattress.

"Honey, if you get out of bed whenever he asks you to, he'll never accept sleeping alone." Maria rolled onto her side and caressed her husband's arm while releasing an exaggerated yawn. "And it's a critical evening for you to get rest, don't you think?"

Samuel smiled at a boy dressed in Ninja Turtle pajamas, gesturing to rouse him from bed. Sure, Jaime needed boundaries, but that could wait. He kissed Maria on the cheek, grasped their son's hand, and walked down the hall to a tiny bedroom, convincing himself five hours of slumber should suffice for the biggest day of his life.

Sitting in the kitchen at daybreak, clean-shaven with a head of wet black hair, Samuel sipped coffee from an old mug adorned with a heart.

Maria pressed her hand to his warm neck and wiped a touch of milk from the edge of his mustache.

"I'm so proud of you," she said from a chair beside her husband. "I've always admired your integrity." *But your obsession with justice sometimes terrifies me*, she silently pleaded.

Samuel and Maria shared their favorite traditional breakfast, *chilaquiles*. Watching her eyes fill with tears, he pulled her in for an embrace. "Stop fretting, Maria. Please. It'll all be over in hours. Jaime will wake us again tonight, demanding to snuggle with his favorite parent." Gazing into admiring eyes, he smiled tenderly while forcing trepidations from his consciousness. Revealing anxieties would have shaken her.

Samuel gripped an ornate metal handrail and descended the outside stairs of their *departamento*. Reaching the sidewalk, he whistled and waved at a passing taxi. He gazed out a passenger window and measured the controlled chaos of bustling urban streets. The aromas of cooked breakfasts wafted through the streets into the green Volkswagen, a *Vochito*.

The clock has started. I've made it to the floor of Congress. Whatever happens next is out of my control. Before exiting the car, he handed the driver his fare with a generous tip.

Samuel Morales was about to set the wheels of justice in motion. His tireless efforts as a journalist for Mexico's *El Universal* newspaper led to this pivotal moment. The exposé he was about to present would offer damning information uncovered through probes into government corruption binding five Mexican senators to the country's most notorious drug cartel, *La Buena Familia*.

President of Mexico Antonio Cornesa had reviewed Samuel's findings weeks earlier, leading to today's special session. Samuel had detailed for Cornesa evidence of extortion and payoffs, including testimonies from imprisoned traffickers and sicarios—trained assassins. He hoped a coordinated government response might challenge and topple Mexico's fastest-growing and most brutal illicit drug enterprise. He'd demand that political leaders get publicly held to task. These were not times for lawmakers' dithering or indecision.

President Cornesa informed Samuel he had ordered a thorough investigation. The journalist knew senators' careers would soon end in disgrace, their reputations destroyed. But the country would not heal unless those perpetrators spent appropriate time behind bars, the necessary penance for accepting millions from drug empires in exchange for disregarding or enabling the cartels' drug wars and killing.

Samuel sat alone and organized his thoughts inside Senado de la República, the meeting place for Mexico's Senate, upper chamber of the country's bicameral congress. President Cornesa delivered a subdued introduction, and Samuel ambled from his seat to the flag-adorned platform from which he would present. Attendees inhaled tension-filled air on a humid day. The cavernous room fell silent, and Samuel stared into their collective gazes.

He counted backward from three to calm his shaking hands. "I am a proud Mexican, a doting husband and father. I want the same things for my family and country as you. But our society and government are encountering unique challenges today, perpetuated by abusive pursuits of power and wealth. What I have uncovered will, I ardently hope, trigger an avalanche of change necessary to save our beloved nation from bowing to the rule of terrifying drug cartels. Here are the facts . . ."

Samuel finished his ninety-minute address and hoped he'd done enough to spur real action. Opening his briefcase, he grew comforted glancing at a photo of Maria and Jaime. He gazed at his hands and noticed they had stopped trembling. Sweat dripped down his neck and drenched his shirt.

Legislators remained seated, stunned into guarded murmurings. No one applauded. Per President Cornesa's instructions, Samuel did not name the five senators he contended were La Buena Familia puppets. But it wouldn't take politicians and the public long to connect the dots.

After several officials offered tentative handshakes and nervous compliments, Samuel walked to a courtyard beside the building. His pulse rose again as he contemplated the magnitude of unknown events he had just triggered. He held no regrets. In minutes, an essential next step would begin, an overview of his speech for Mexican and international media. The public deserved to hear a summary direct from the source, unfiltered by bureaucrats.

Roberto Enriquez, the Attorney General of Mexico, greeted Samuel as he stepped from the building. Samuel hoped Enriquez's presence implied a commitment to helping transform the republic through broader policing and legislation. Gilberto Herrera, the head of the country's federal police, was among the eager crowd gathered around the courtyard.

Four Chevrolet Suburban SUVs with government plates were parked curbside sixty feet away. Eleven members of the *Policía Federal Preventiva*, referred to as *Federales* by Mexicans and Americans, assembled nearby in black uniforms. Ski masks concealed their identities, thus protecting themselves and loved ones from retaliation—an unsettling but familiar reality. The Federales scanned the crowd, each man armed with a customized version of the AR-15 American troops used and a holstered Beretta 92F sidearm.

Maria watched the proceedings on television from home, proud of her husband's diligence in exposing La Buena Familia's links to crooked politicians but constantly fearing for his safety. Three grisly executions of reporters and media executives nine months earlier had revived her worries. Samuel told her if he and other journalists hid from the public or cartels, it would be tantamount to surrender, precisely what the drug lords wanted.

Samuel glanced at his notes. A dozen microphones from the news outlets snaked in and around a podium. Lawmakers and their aides stood nearby, and Samuel assumed he could read their thoughts. *Which senators were guilty? Will government forces storm La Buena Familia compounds?*

Attorney General Enriquez spoke with what some considered orchestrated bravado about the government's commitment to eradicating drug empires. He reminded people that the insatiable demand for marijuana, opioids, and methamphetamines in the United States drove the drug trade—the amount of illicit wealth involved was staggering. That was true.

While the attorney continued, three more dark SUVs with tinted windows and government plates pulled up. Two Federales, with firm grips on their weapons and experienced fingers resting upon triggers, asked the new arrivals for identification. An officer in charge adjusted his earpiece while reviewing IDs, then turned his head to speak into a mic clipped to his left shoulder sleeve. *Who requested the backups?* Simultaneously, the Federales monitored developments and subtly lifted their weapons to more readied positions. The scheduled government and media proceedings continued.

Rays of late afternoon sunshine draped the gathering. Enriquez shook Samuel's hand as he approached the podium wearing a turquoise tie that brought a smile to Maria's lips. She recognized the coded tribute.

Samuel laid three typed pages upon the console and breathed deeply. An image of kissing Jaime on the forehead flashed through his mind. The vision felt slightly ominous, but he convinced himself it was not. After twisting a gold wedding band, he cleared his throat.

Flocks of gray pigeons glided through trees and landed among the bystanders. Samuel began speaking just as the doors of the three late-arriving SUVs opened a second time, and six different Federales offered badges identical to those of the other forces. Three words lay tattooed under the wrists of their muscular, uniform-covered forearms: La Buena Familia.

A woman screamed. Urgent shrieks echoed across buildings and through an adjoining plaza. Automatic machine gun fire exploded and reverberated. Panic stretched in every direction. People scrambled and knocked each other down, bewildered. The sickening sounds of human bodies getting penetrated by 39mm AK-47 rounds blended with whizzing noises of ricocheted bullets hitting cement, buildings, and vehicles. The fake Federales tossed smoke grenades over streets and walkways, magnifying the confusion.

Seven loyal Federales were the first to die. It was impossible to save themselves, let alone the lives of unarmed men and women slain while standing in the crossfire of La Buena Familia's seemingly indiscriminate firing. The four legitimate officers who survived the initial gunfire paused for only seconds, assessing which uniformed men were comrades. That hesitation resulted in their deaths.

A journalist beside Samuel was thrown to the ground and moaned after being shot in the chest by an approaching triggerman. Samuel flung himself next to the victim and watched his eyes close forever. He assumed the worst, that life with Jaime and Maria was over. Instead, strong hands clutched his biceps and thrust him upward. Strangers aggressively wrenched a bag over his head. He saw only darkness. Rushed from the scene toward an idling SUV, he was shoved inside. The vehicle rattled as doors slammed shut, then it roared south on Avenida de los Insurgentes and through the streets of Mexico City, part of a three-car caravan.

Gang members had meticulously planned and executed the brazen attack, turning the government's day of hope and purpose into a spectacle of carnage and heartbreak. The drug lords had won yet again.

Marco Delgado, kingpin of La Buena Familia, watched the onslaught from a television inside his lavish Sinaloa Mountains hacienda two hundred fifty miles away. He calmly puffed on his cigar and sipped tequila. Glancing at his gold watch, he noted the time before reaching for a tissue to clean the crystal of his timepiece. His rugged and determined face showed little emotion.

Within minutes of the ambush, Maria's neighbors rushed to her residence in a quiet district of Mexico City. AK-47 gunfire had obliterated news cameras when the violence erupted, so she and the public remained in the dark. She had no idea Samuel had been kidnapped.

Ninety minutes later, the authorities informed Maria her missing husband and his abductors had vanished. But he's alive, the Federales insisted. They told her Delgado spared him for a reason, so there was hope. It felt illogical to believe that, but she tried.

She always understood her husband's investigations were fraught with risks. Even so, she felt betrayed.

CHAPTER 2

Over the next two weeks, increasingly hostile police officials confirmed that La Buena Familia remained silent while authorities followed leads. Maria shouted at the lead investigator, shaking her head, "You keep repeating the same line! This is not progress." Measuring their words as indifference, she audibly mumbled, "Just let the men do their jobs, Maria. They'll inform the ignorant and grieving wife when it's warranted." Blatant chauvinism enraged her.

Knowing Samuel was the only person kidnapped set her imagination wild. It was impossible to keep herself from reading accounts of the cartels' torturing tactics, especially of those daring to expose anything detrimental to their empires. Her heart broke for the bystanders killed during the attack, especially the families of Samuel's journalist associates.

"Papi come eat?" Jaime asked.

It had been a tradition for Samuel to walk from his *El Universal* office many afternoons to share lunch with his son and wife. "Papi loves you, Jaime." Nine days later, she tasted salty anguish after realizing the boy had not asked about his father that afternoon or evening. Stepping into the bathroom late at night, she stared into the mirror and gently rubbed her swollen eyes.

The government's lack of meaningful updates felt like it was intentionally pain-inflicting. She wondered if the people she relied on to locate Samuel might be aligned with La Buena Familia. Neither Marco Delgado nor his lieutenants had delivered any demands for her husband's release. Authorities awaited contact from La Buena Familia. Just more evidence officials were clueless, Maria decided. Or afraid to aggressively pursue and expose anything that might trigger reprisal against their families; he was a terrifyingly vengeful drug lord. Her fears were crippling. She wound a rosary around her wrist as if to ward off a vampire.

Comisario Pérez, Federale Commissioner, arrived at the Morales's home with two heavily armed officers. She pressed Pérez hard for an update on casualties. "Señora, the final tally from the attack is a staggering fourteen dead and seven badly injured."

"How could three SUVs with fake plates roll right up to the press conference? Then present fake IDs to legitimate Federales before mowing down innocent people with machine guns? Why couldn't this massacre be prevented? *Give me answers!*"

"We will learn much from this tragic slaughter, of course. It is regrettable."

"Regrettable? That's an oblivious and hurtful word choice."

"It is not the word I should have used. My apologies."

He appeared sincere, and her tone softened. "Please, put yourself in my shoes," she said like someone dealing with unspeakable tragedy. "And consider the other families dealing with death or horrific injuries."

After days of pushing for answers to reasonable questions, the authorities stopped supplying Maria updates, and every Federale assigned to her security detail repeated the same line: *The investigation is ongoing, and the very public drama will end well.* She insisted it was an absurd proclamation.

"It is what we are instructed to say, Señora," said one of the Federales guarding her door. "I am so sorry for your anguish and the uncertainty."

She stood with a face reflecting his genuineness, then glanced at the name on his uniform. "Thank you, Officer Hernandez."

Finally, a break in the case. A courier delivered an unsigned letter to Attorney General Enriquez. The communiqué urged the government to get its facts straight: La Buena Familia was a legitimate family enterprise revered by rural communities, which it supported through farming, health care, and education services. The note included the line: *"Señor Marco Delgado expresses heartfelt condolences for the deaths and casualties outside the Senate chambers, and he hopes authorities locate and prosecute those responsible."* The AG and President Cornesa's eyes squinted in contempt.

The message then advised: *"If you find Samuel Morales, ask him about the Emerald Cross."* No one in Mexico's investigative agencies knew what the baffling statement meant, and authorities deemed it immaterial to the urgent task of saving Samuel.

Senior investigators agreed the note was likely scribed or dictated by Delgado. Justifications, irrelevancies, and riddles—they'd read similar ramblings from the young and powerful madman. Those prior dealings never ended without him exacting further revenge and shedding more blood.

"This is likely a death warrant for Señor Morales, Mr. President," said Attorney General Enriquez.

President Cornesa agreed and decided there was no benefit to sharing that opinion with Maria. Then he demanded all updated police and military intelligence for a review with cabinet members.

Cornesa chaired the meeting with leaders of the Federales, Army, and Mexican Marines. The officials concluded a quick strike on a presumed Delgado compound in Sinaloa State was their best of meager options. Army intel established a high likelihood the narco boss currently occupied a rambling property nestled in the hills of heroin country. They hoped to apprehend the drug lord and negotiate Samuel Morales's release on the slim chance he was still alive.

Six Mexican Marines helicopters descended upon a walled estate in the mountains eight hours later. Three Army Special Forces assault vehicles and thirty Federales and Ejército Mexicano soldiers stormed the vast compound. An intense battle ensued throughout the acres abutting the hilltop hacienda. Government troops penetrated the fortified residence, defeating narcos and Delgado lieutenants committed to never surrendering.

Infuriatingly, their target eluded capture, though his brothers Jesús and Rico were killed during the attack. Police and joint branch commanders informed President Cornesa that interrogation of the wounded traffickers suggested Delgado fled just prior to the assault. Cornesa nervously believed he knew what to expect next.

Everyone's worst nightmares turned real. Two days after the assault on the drug kingpin's lair, Maria received word from Cornesa that a farmer discovered Samuel's body along a roadside trench. His appendages had been severed and hideously scattered in what had become a typical La Buena Familia signature. The point was to intimidate and paralyze. A stretch of masking tape across his forehead read *Samuel Morales, liar and thief.*

While the victim shared Samuel's appearance and body measurements, bruising and swelling of the face complicated definitive identification. President Cornesa demanded expedited forensics and DNA analysis. Science confirmed it was Samuel. Later, adding to Maria's agony, the defaced body was mistakenly cremated due to administrative ineptitude. "*No damn way!*" she pleaded. After hiring lawyers to scrutinize the government's seemingly absurd claim, their investigation concluded the government's account was truthful. Cornesa appeared genuinely affected as he visited Maria to apologize for the incineration debacle.

Samuel Morales's ashes arrived at Mexico City's most famous cemetery, the Panteón Civil de Dolores. Wet and dreary skies blanketed mourners and echoed the mood of the ceremony. During the service, Maria stared at a crucifix, pondering how God could allow heartless criminals to take such an exceptional man.

Weeks of personal reflection passed, during which Maria debated a life-altering decision. She loved her country and the people within it but struggled to trust those responsible for investigating Samuel's murder. She feared Delgado and La Buena Familia might never pay for their horrific deeds. Samuel named five senators in his secret report handed to President Cornesa, but Maria grew unconvinced any would serve meaningful time.

Her sole comfort in life was Jaime. Increasingly, she felt like mother and son were living in a shrinking fishbowl, imprisoned spectacles under constant scrutiny. She worried about his long-term safety. Slowly, the once inconceivable grew obvious: She and Jaime needed to leave their homeland.

The US government granted Maria's appeal for emergency asylum.

Upon approval, things moved quickly. One morning, a government SUV shuttled them to the airport from their apartment in Mexico City. The next morning, they awoke in Maria's brother and sister-in-law's spare bedroom in North Tustin, California.

CHAPTER 3

Time moves on. Two decades had passed since Samuel's murder—a staggeringly inadequate word to describe what he endured. In the summer of 2011, the pain of losing her husband sometimes remained excruciating. Maria Morales hid it well.

She missed certain relatives and lifelong friends living in her beloved Mexico. Simple observations would sometimes unexpectedly bridge *what was* with *what is*. Orange and black monarch butterflies, indigenous to California and Mexico, represented bonds to past and present as she watched them flitter across her yard.

Sipping coffee from Samuel's favorite mug in her kitchen, she reflected on all the happenings since relocating to Southern California. Raised in their adopted homeland, Jaime was in many ways more American than Mexican, with a name change to emphasize the point. In sixth grade, he decided he preferred the Americanized version of Jaime. "It's the same letters, Mom. I just like how it sounds." She was uncomfortable with the request but later asked herself, why not? She acceded but drew the line at permanently changing his legal name to *Jamie* Morales. If the nickname stuck, he could deal with the bureaucratic nightmare of modifying myriad government documents as an adult.

Her phone vibrated atop the counter, playing a ringtone melody by Los Caminantes. "What a coincidence—I was reflecting on your happy childhood."

Jamie chuckled. "Don't forget the part about me getting reprimanded for interrupting my teachers too often. Or bringing a king snake to school that promptly got loose and freaked out the girls *and* Mrs. Adair."

"If only you could see the width of my smile." She poured cream into her black coffee and watched the color fade to brown while stirring. "You were an easy child to raise," she said in Spanish. Their conversations switched effortlessly between both languages. "And you're still my best friend."

"Likewise and forever, Mom."

"Brooklyn may have something to say about that."

"Nah, she could never be threatened by an old Mexican woman who's turning gray."

"Hey, I'm not old, cadet. And all I need is a bottle of L'Oreal to make my few gray strands magically disappear forever. But just so you know, my new neighbor told me yesterday I look thirty-five—and that's *with* my budding gray."

Hearty laughter filled both phones. "Thirty-five? That would mean you gave birth to me at thirteen. Seems highly unlikely." He glanced at the time on his phone. "Hate to do this, Mom, but I need to get moving. I just wanted to check that you got flights and a hotel for the ceremony."

"Of course! Did you really think I'd somehow forget? Go to your meeting, and thanks for thinking about your aging mother. Love you. Ciao."

Maria understood that if Jamie had been school-aged after arriving in America, aware that his father had been gruesomely tortured and executed, he might have lived burdened with a lifetime of emotional scars. Because he was barely three when they fled, he mercifully lived his youth oblivious to the agonizing truths.

"*Knock, knock!*" someone bellowed at the front door.

There was no need to glance through the peephole; she knew this man's voice too well. Manuel Jimenez, or Manny, as he was known to friends and family, ran a successful landscaping business creating magazine-worthy hardscapes for clients in wealthy beach and hillside enclaves.

"It's wonderful to see you," she said. The siblings embraced. Manny and his wife, Natalie, had two sons, Manny Junior and Daniel.

"Everything's great, thanks. Natalie's busy with her tennis, charities, and the boys." He lifted his mug in appreciation of the steaming, aromatic coffee. "Business is great—there's a lot of money in California."

Her brows arched, her mouth opened, and she shook her head. "So true! It boggles my mind. It's why most people can't afford to live here. Again, Manny, we never would've been able to buy this house without your generosity."

"Dear sister, that was years ago. Let it go. Stop thanking me. Having you two so close has been a blessing."

"It's been magical since the day we arrived here. Can you believe it's been eighteen years?"

"Honestly, no. Yet here we are." She felt the warmth of his palm pressed to her cheek. "We are *so* excited for Jamie's graduation and commissioning. He's always been an extraordinary young man. Sam would be uncontrollably proud." When the families gathered twenty years earlier, Samuel and Manny had always enjoyed each other's company. "What are you staring at?"

"Just look at the trees out that window," she said. "Towering eucalyptus, palms, and pines. It's just so beautiful here."

"I love seeing you this happy. How are things at your school? Are teachers still trying to find you a potential husband?"

During her initial years in California, it seemed every educator and neighbor she'd befriended tried to match-make her with "a great guy I just know you'll like." Remarriage hadn't happened, but she voiced no regrets. After settling in North Tustin, Maria hadn't expected her degree in history from Universidad Nacional Autónoma de México to help her quickly secure employment. She was thrilled to have been wrong. Bilingual skills and an impressive academic transcript earned her a teaching position at an elite private school.

Reminiscing about life in Orange County brought a pleasant expression to her face. She wished she could somehow relive the precious, entertaining years. Though Jamie continued to earn reprimands for disruptive behavior through sixth grade, Maria's instincts told her the boy might be remarkable. She reminded herself that would be a common opinion for many parents, but other people drew the same conclusion as he matured. He became popular with students and staff, a great student, and unusually wise for his age.

Manny asked, "How is Brooklyn? And why haven't they eloped yet?"

"Please don't give them any ideas." She pantomimed a slap across his face. "I still remember Jamie's words after his first day at Hewes Junior High: 'I met someone who's going to be an awesome friend—I just know it. Her name's Brooklyn, like the city. She's incredible.'"

"You told me back then their infatuation would fade. You were wrong! The precocious thirteen-year-old has remained the center of his universe."

"That's true. But I wasn't the only one with reservations. Brooklyn's parents questioned whether it was healthy for two barely teens to maintain such strong bonds," she said. "Then week by week, year by year, their obsession only strengthened."

"Well, it all seemed to work out. Kudos to you for not squelching it."

"Trust me, I thought about it often. But somehow, those two put the MacDonalds and me at ease. Anyway, here we are."

After chatting a while longer, Manny pecked her on the cheek. "Thanks for the coffee and catch-up. I'm meeting a client for a big job in Newport Beach." He departed, and Maria continued her trip down memory lane.

Jamie lettered in two sports at Foothill High School while garnering national academic honors. He attained the rank of Eagle Scout and earned salutatorian of his class, then received an appointment to the United States Military Academy—West Point. He'd always relished uniforms, military history, and the principles of freedom and democracy. Yes, Maria proudly recalled, his high school teachers and coaches had been right, too: Jamie Morales was a natural leader.

While Jamie achieved his milestones and accolades, Brooklyn did likewise as an accomplished student-athlete. Her ambitions remained unwavering, and her grades or performances never suffered from Jamie's ubiquity in her life. Maria glanced at a photo of the young couple at Disneyland taped to the refrigerator door. Their expressions were colored with limitless adoration.

Unknown to both sets of parents, the lovestruck teenagers began discussing their futures together as spouses during their senior year of high school. When Brooklyn dropped Jamie off at Los Angeles International for a flight to New York, preceding his initial bus ride to West Point, people may have assumed he was heading off to war instead of college based on Brooklyn's emotional farewell.

Maria recalled her son explaining that he savored the physical and mental challenges an institution like West Point demanded. Getting screamed at as a plebe by cows and firsties, being air-horned awake at four-thirty in the morning, marching in stifling humidity or subfreezing air, and studying until his eyes grew bloodshot—Jamie insisted he relished all of it.

Recently, her son spoke of one classmate with the most profound esteem; that man was Wes Berkeley. They'd met as plebes, but lately, Maria realized Wes occupied Jamie's private mantle of honor. She reminded herself she'd meet Wes at the men's impending commencement at The Academy.

Maria glanced at a photo of Jamie in his formal Army dress uniform and grew lightheaded with pride. Five-eleven, thick dark hair, and military fit. He was the mirror image of Samuel, with features that expressed his Spanish and indigenous Mexican heritage. The observation prompted a moment of regret. If only . . .

Walking the West Point campus the day before graduation was a remarkable experience, with every building steeped in fascinating history. Maria's face seemed permanently fixed with a look of unbounded admiration. The ceremony lasted the day and surpassed her expectations, which was predictable since no one—not even her son—told her what to anticipate.

Swiping through photos on her phone, she was filled with appreciation for her and Jamie's beautiful life proceeding Samuel's revolting death. Brooklyn, Uncle Manny, Aunt Natalie, and Jamie's two cousins appeared similarly delighted. Maria glanced at Brooklyn, the woman representing Jamie's future. *Would I remain a fixture in his life?* She caught herself. *Stop! You're already sharing him with the "other" woman.*

And they remain central to your life. You're blessed, Maria. She distractedly shook her head, self-judging a pointless insecurity.

White, gold, and blue visored hats shot upward like an eruption, an Academy tradition that signified the graduation ceremony's conclusion. Freshly commissioned Second Lieutenant Morales faced his family and Brooklyn with glistening eyes. Moments later, he glanced to the skies and whispered, "I love and miss you, Samuel... *Papi.*" Maria had raised him to appreciate the doting father he couldn't remember.

Phase Two of her son's military career deeply unsettled Maria. Without her counsel, he'd decided to train to become a member of the legendary United States Army Special Forces, the Green Berets. Maria wouldn't attempt to squelch his enthusiasm for serving on the elite squad, but she told herself she'd pray—a lot.

Jamie drove her to the airport the next morning, and she again expressed trepidation about the Green Beret decision. He hugged her and smiled. "Mom, it's what I want to do, and it'll all be fine. Please don't fret."

CHAPTER 4

Four years after graduating from West Point, I arrived in Kabul as a first lieutenant. Weeks later, I peeled off part of a platoon to collect and tag eviscerated body parts of Shiite men, women, and children that Sunni rocket launchers had shelled. A group of civilian women desensitized to hardship assisted. What must it feel like to bend over and pick up your spouse's or neighbor's body parts? They glanced at me, conveying pain and heartbreak. I was just another invader American to them, but I sensed we were occasionally aligned: How could humans justify doing this to each other?

Clearing the dead and wounded was more challenging for an eighteen-year-old Army private under my command. He performed his duty as instructed without hesitation. Measuring his gradual transformation, I asked, "Soldier, are you okay?" Of course he's not. Nobody would or should be. The enlistee remained silent, staring, shellshocked. "Private Lincoln, I asked you a question."

The soldier stiffened and faced me, appearing incapable of responding.

"How long have you been on tour?"

He swallowed hard twice and barely squeezed out the words. "Ten days, sir."

No one was prepared to witness this sort of hell. Nightmares weren't supposed to be real. "Private Lincoln, you and I are now bonded forever. What surrounds us is beyond rational people's comprehension. Go inform Master Sergeant Guilford that I want a soldier with at least six months of service to replace you."

I ambled about in contempt of those who'd attacked Shiite families celebrating the end of Ramadan. Their enemies were also Muslims but of a different sect. The violence loosely resembled the Catholic and Protestant uprisings in Northern Ireland during the '60s and '70s, though intensely magnified in these deserts and mountains. More weapons, brutality, death, and destruction. I could never convey the emptiness of purpose and the burdened soul I carried that day.

Time often rendered itself meaningless during Middle East tours. Sometimes, it moved at a snail's pace, other times at breakneck speed—never as expected. Depending on the day and what happened, that was a blessing or curse. It was five years ago that I solemnly gathered fragments of bodies in Afghanistan.

In 2015, the Taliban captured and tortured me in ways I promised never to reveal to friends and family. My Green Beret comrades rescued me. They saved me again in 2017 after a bullet tore through my left thigh, barely missing my femur and arteries. Though I never stepped on an IED, I knew or learned of soldiers who did. Very few survived. Those were real heroes, and their reward was to live scarred forever. Service to Country provided a range of experiences, some difficult. We all knew that before we arrived.

Scores of enemies killed on these tan sands and valleys were conscripted by Islamist lunatics as kids. It is a heartbreaking reality; those forced to live under fanatical rule stand little chance for ordinary lives.

Al Qaeda, the Taliban, and ISIS never cared about Western precepts of justice or religious freedom. Their driving force was jihad. Many of the men and women I fired upon grew up as casualties of a fundamentalist culture embracing rigidity, dogma, retribution, and death. If born in Southern California, they would have been prepping for SATs. Not fighting, killing, or getting killed.

I stopped sleeping solidly through the night a few years ago. After a year of deliberation, I decided not to re-up for another tour. Our CO told me last night he hated to see me go—his final attempt to get me to stay. I'll miss him and the soldiers I've served with. I will forever be impressed by their perseverance, sense of duty, and commitment to making the world a better place. People ask me all the time why I'm checking out. The easy answer, intended to change the topic, is that civilian life had finally beckoned.

The last time I kissed Brooke was in June 2018, the day I proposed. She's the simple reason I'm checking out; she deserves to have me home after all she's endured. Soon, I'll hop aboard a C-130 for the first leg back to Fort Benning. A week later, I will be an ex-Green Beret.

The familiar smells of grilled eggs, hash browns, and bacon snapped me out of my thoughts. Army coffee was another aroma greeting me. Ersatz coffee, diluted coffee, not what I'd call *real* coffee, but technically some sort of morning brew. I also recognized burning JP-8 fuel wafting through my tent from three or four idling Humvees preparing to put soldiers in harm's way. That's what Humvees do.

A very different potent fragrance soon overpowered the odors of food and combat—a Wes Berkeley fart. I thought it was the distant rumblings of Abrams tanks trudging over rough terrain. But no, this was a much more common disturbance, an echoing from the butt of dear Wes. A tear-inducing concoction I'd be excited to inform my fellow West Point grad of after he awakened. I had already tossed fresh white cotton skivvies onto his blanket, convinced he'd need a change. I assumed most of Wes's tighty-whities had stains contrasting the faded white. How could they not? Wes farted more than a cow burped.

Most soldiers would wake their buddies after being victimized by such a pungent assault. I won't be doing that. Wes Berkeley is the noblest man I ever met. The sort of son no mother could ever rationally expect to be gifted with—minus the farting. He exceeds anyone's expectations of what a good human should be. Wes also remained my best friend. Would be for life. A brother who took a round from an AK-47 while covering me during a battle in Anwar province that killed two of our eight-man squad. Wes is my hero. He could float as many god-awful air biscuits as he wanted.

There's one other smell I recognized that morning. It would stick with me all day, as it always did. Most grunts and officers insisted I imagined it. I replied it was as tangible as any real thing could possibly be. It followed me every step of every day during my tours in Afghanistan and Syria. It was the stench of death, and I looked forward to leaving it behind.

Wes turned me into a classical music aficionado. My latest favorite morning tune was Brandenburg Concerto Number 3 in G major—unbelievable stuff. Ours was the only tent not pumping out Zeppelin, Brooks, or Kanye. Wes and I embraced our musical snobbery and enjoyed lecturing soldiers about the splendor of classical music. Fellow warriors typically responded by throwing shit at us.

Midday, Wes and I received orders to tamp down a minor disturbance, possibly our last hurrah together. I was leaving the Army, and

Secretary of Defense Mattis was sending Wes to the War College in three months. It was quite an honor, but it didn't surprise me. My best friend would wow the brass with his keen intellect and leadership skills. With a name like Wes Berkeley, I often joked that he'd grown up destined to become someone notable or rare. A movie star or ethical politician. But Wes was built for the military. A month earlier, I bet him a hundred bucks he'd become Secretary of Defense before age fifty. I aim to collect.

Syrian villagers had reported a small band of real or wannabe ISIS fighters harassing young men at a grade school twenty miles from base camp. It was not something you'd typically assign two senior battle-tested Green Beret captains to, but regional Army support was light that week. Besides, it's the military. They order, you go. That applies to Green Berets.

Islamic revolutionaries recruited kids all the time, filling their heads with bullshit stories of heroism, martyrdom, or their perverse creed of duty to Allah. Hardened warlords often destroyed hopes for normal lives before youths turned fifteen. I met good people in these unstable lands, hopeful men and women just trying to stay alive and care for their families. People who simply wanted to live free. But the good were too often intimidated into silence and inaction. Thus, the bad propagated their wickedness and doctrine. Brutal realities hardened people. Hardened people were more likely to fight. And to kill.

When the Taliban, Al Qaeda, and ISIS realized American forces were approaching, they scattered like ants and disappeared. We'd arrive, and there seemingly wouldn't be an insurgent within miles. Too often, the locals requesting protection disclosed nothing: direction of the terrorists' escape, number of fighters, weapons they possessed—not a damn thing. It was hard to blame them; even rumors of aiding the infidels could get them killed.

We reached the school at the base of a rocky knoll overlooking Ankara. Wes and I jumped out with weapons at the ready. Whether in a crowd or standing in groups of two and three, it was beyond challenging to distinguish friends from foes in these war zones; they often dressed the same. I never forgot that an extra second of hesitation or indecision could get me killed.

Critical decisions made in uncertain situations leaned on instincts. That's not necessarily how instructors taught it, but it was reality. My gut told me there were hostiles in or around the school. I grew more vigilant and unrelenting, with my finger on the trigger. Rules of the war game required a delicate balance of protecting innocents while keeping oneself alive.

Wes was sometimes less suspicious of the locals than I was. My mantra? Low-grade risks have a high potential for bad outcomes. Regardless, as compatriots and experienced soldiers, we trusted one another like blood brothers and respected each other's combat skills.

We dispersed around the school grounds with some battle-tested grunts. I respected the three- or four-tour enlisted soldiers as much as Green Berets. Sometimes more. They'd seen much, survived myriad hellish situations—never just by luck—and possessed something I termed *desert smarts*.

A grizzled sergeant led three soldiers to the school grounds' perimeter to reconnoiter and defend against ambush. Just because any number of unsavory characters skipped town doesn't mean they won't return. Approaching cars or trucks received two rounds in their direction as a warning, followed by a couple of shots into the dirt just below their front grill. If they continued forward, Army guns obliterated tires and wheels. When they advanced further, soldiers assumed the worst. That's when terrible things sometimes happen.

Upon entering the school's main door, a commotion erupted from within, and five boys rushed from a classroom screaming. I trained my M4 on them until it was clear there were no human bombs. Glancing backward to Wes, he gave a hand signal before moving to the right and down the hall. I continued forward. The three soldiers trailing me split away to back up Wes.

Thap thap thap!

AK-47 rounds blasted into the wall that me and two grunts stood behind. The barrier separating us from the onslaught was only inches thick. Every third or fourth bullet penetrated the earthen wall. Dust filled the halls. Our concussed ears filled with high-pitched sounds. The smells of weapons fired in close quarters grew intense.

I extended my field mirror around the corner and found a lone shooter in the shadows of the classroom. The two kids lying on the ground beside him had holes in their foreheads. More shots rang out. I glanced backward and saw that Wes and his men had peeled off. Perhaps they'd found another shooter.

Thap thap thap!

The soldier behind me crumpled to the ground. Blood poured from a neck wound. I inspected the damage and squeezed his shoulder. His eyes widened. "Tell my mom I loved her."

I leaned closer. "Tell her yourself."

No other windows or doors led into the classroom. I heard a distinct sound—the extraction of a magazine from an AK-47. The jihadist was swapping ammo. It was time. Crouching low, I bent around the corner into the room and squeezed off three rounds. Bullets ripped through the enemy's shoulder and chest. Splatters of dark crimson colored the light brown wall and floor.

I advanced to the fallen but still-breathing shooter and watched his dirtied, bearded face transform into a twisted expression of hate. Then he unclenched his right fist, and a trigger device dropped from his clutches, meaning anyone within fifty feet would get blown to hell. *Damnit! We'll all die because I fucked up!* My gut told me it was futile, but I screamed for evacuation. I assumed it was the last command Captain Jamie Morales would ever utter. I flung myself into the hall and draped the bleeding US soldier with my body. Pressed tightly to the grunt's upper torso, I smelled the blood still oozing from his neck wound.

Nothing blew up. No one else died. Not yet.

Soldiers would live to see tomorrow because a hate-filled, dying ISIS terrorist's ignition mechanism failed to detonate a bomb likely hidden in the classroom. I inspected the two kids lying on the ground. Why murder innocent schoolboys? The man's second sneer made me want to finish the bastard off, protocol be damned. I didn't act on my emotions, hoping the terrorist would stop breathing before our medics saved him.

The round missed the upper spine and neck arteries of the injured soldier. Scared to death but alive. I watched him get loaded into a 9 Line medevac Humvee. Wes worked to corral the wandering children. Most appeared shell-shocked. Their parents marched up a dirt road in our direction with purpose. These were dangerous moments—it took time to differentiate who was who. Three war dogs ordered the advancing parties to stop. Reading the American's eyes, they halted. This wasn't the time to challenge the invaders' commands.

We found no other threats besides the now-dead man lying in the classroom. The kids were too agitated to offer much intel, but I directed my Syrian interpreter to keep pushing for information. I walked about eighty feet beyond Wes and the interpreter before someone called out. A soldier informed me one of the children observed a truck with four insurgents depart minutes before we arrived. The kid insisted there had initially been six. The now-dead man in the school made five. Where was the straggler?

I maneuvered back toward Wes and the children. Then I observed a shadow extending over a rock outcropping. I homed in on the distinct profile of a man thumbing the keys of a cell phone. *He's remotely triggering an IED!* I glanced at the school kids and noticed one standing stiffly with arms at his side, fear on his face, and a slight bulge across his back. An unwilling human bomb. *ISIS devils!*

Raising my M4, I riddled the outcropping with bullets. I screamed at Wes and the interpreter to separate themselves from the children. *Now!* I kept firing at the rock and approached the man with the phone, but the shadow of his profile remained steady. I glanced away from my gun sights toward Wes, who pushed the bomb-wired child to the ground at his feet, hoping to shield him as he scanned for Islamists. He had no idea the kid was a human C4 bomb.

It all happened in slow motion, images that would forever torment me. An unknown bomb maker would be proud of his brutally efficient weapon. The interpreter and the young boy no longer existed. Neither did my best friend.

Limbs were torn from torsos. Bomb material flew at me with intention, a torrent of bone and blast. I felt a pain in my eye, then sensed my body getting torn into a thousand pieces. I was dead.

I awoke from death seven days later inside an Army hospital near

Landstuhl, Germany. The intense ringing in my ears numbed my other senses. One eye ached and felt heavy. The surgeon explained a bone fragment from one of the exploded humans had rocketed toward me and decimated my left eyeball. I lay confused because my death felt absolute, flashing before me frame-by-frame. Yet here I was, breathing, alive.

If my death were a mirage, could Wes also still be alive? I demanded answers to that question. People hesitated. People knew the truth. Their expressions slaughtered my hopes. Visions of Wes, the kid, and the interpreter streamed through my consciousness over and over.

Brooke was at my side, crying, loving me. Maria peered into my eye with an anxious gaze. I also recognized hope.

Burdening the people you love never feels good. It felt as if I'd somehow let them down.

I'm wired to never surrender, but I was forced to accept this defeat. It was time to go home.

CHAPTER 5

My physical healing arrived first. Each morning, I lumbered into the bathroom and stared at the mirrored reflection of a fit soldier with one eyeball missing. Pretending it was an amusing look, I'd call out, "Brooke, have you seen my eye?" I doubted she ever bought the act.

Brooke's love and support strengthened our bonds and changed my life. She realized remorse from the battlefield was a heavy burden for Civilian Morales. I shared how images of Wes, the young boy, and the Syrian interpreter disappearing before my eyes plagued me.

Brooke discovered my journal, where every battle I'd engaged in during three tours was reassessed. I questioned whether my role in killing people born into gut-wrenching circumstances and shackled by inane terrorist groups was justified. War was the purest form of hell on earth but also one of those clichéd necessary evils. At least, that's what I wrote. She also learned that I sometimes judged those justifications unconvincing. Her cheeks were wet with tears when I found her perusing my thoughts. Maybe it will be liberating one day, knowing I gave her a glimpse of my burdened soul.

Brooke grew particularly disturbed by me asking God to forgive certain deeds while serving as a Green Beret. She argued that the men and women earning Purple Hearts and combat stars protected our democracy. *"You're a damn hero!"* she insisted, pleading for me to embrace that truth. She learned that reconciling horrors from the battlefield wasn't something any soldier achieved on command.

Life's banalities and our approaching wedding helped widen the mental distance between Orange County and Syria. Six months after my reentry into civilian life, I hoped Brooke and Mom understood how hard I was trying to regain equilibrium. Emotional healing takes time.

For years, I considered it lame when friends moved back to their high school hometowns. *Hey, good luck rekindling those glory days.* Then Brooke suggested we do just that. She didn't care about my stupid reservations, only that we were moving back to a beautiful area with great schools for any future brood.

We could never have afforded a house at the base of the foothills in North Tustin if it weren't for Brooke saving every dollar she earned or me investing in e-commerce and semiconductor stocks while in the Army, on Wes Berkeley's counsel. Before liquidating my stocks to help fund our down payment, I gazed up to the skies and smiled. *Cheers to your great advice, Wes. You're in my thoughts forever, buddy.*

I applied for and earned a prestigious management training position at an aerospace company in Los Angeles. USC accepted me into its MBA program at its Orange County campus. Admissions discounted tuition based on my military record and service to the country. Everyone in Southern California understood USC's alumni network was among the most influential in the country. Naturally, everyone asked who I'd paid off to gain admittance.

We purchased a Mexican ranch-style home with a courtyard. Our agent wryly described the property as having potential, a euphemism for properties in desperate need of renovations. Uncle Manny surprised us with a pre-wedding gift, showing up two days after we'd moved in, ready to tear the outside apart to create one of his company's signature hardscape transformations. The finished project was spectacular, more than what I thought we deserved. Brooke disagreed.

Every day with Brooke grew more amazing and healing. She was a better person than me, though such comments annoyed the hell out of her. On our wedding day, I stood in my blue-gold-white dress uniform with the band of my eyepatch stretched around my head, jaw clenched, measuring life as near perfect while my high school sweetheart floated up the aisle in her streaming white dress. Brooke's sister, Ashley, served as maid of honor. Uncle Manny stood as best man; Wes Berkeley would have if he were alive.

We made a significant decision during our honeymoon in Whistler, Canada. Upon returning home, we'd invite Mom to move onto our property after constructing a casita, enabling her to remain an indelible part of our lives. Later, she interrupted our offer with flushed cheeks while exclaiming, *"Yes!* Thank you." Certain moments stick in your mind forever. That was one.

Months after the wedding, we lay in a deep slumber. Sprawled on my back, Brooke's soothing, warm body partially atop mine, memories suddenly returned. My limbs twitched lightly. Moments later, my arms and legs flailed stiffly, uncontrollably.

She screamed, *"What's wrong!* What is it, Jamie?" I didn't respond, and my thrashing grew more violent. Shooting out of bed, she flipped on the lights. My contorted expression appeared frozen in anguish, and my mouth twisted agape to form and release a silent scream. Completely freaked out, she darted back to the mattress. Squeezing my body with all her might, she called out my name repeatedly. As my torment weakened,

I inhaled and expelled air from my lungs as if I'd been drowning. My body fell limp. She said I projected a curious look she interpreted to be something like defeat.

Finally settling down, realizing what was happening, I placed my arms around her and whispered, "God, Brooke, I've seen so many horrors. So much death." Moments later, I said, "And I desperately miss Wes."

"Of course you do."

We both heard the creaking of Maria's steps slowly retreating to her bedroom down the hall. What did she hear? What must she be thinking? How painful is it for mothers to learn their sons are living terribly scarred? There had been only slight bouts of moodiness in the weeks leading to the recent days of PTSD flashbacks, but demons from the battlefield don't schedule their visits.

CHAPTER 6

Weeks passed since the flashback of Wes disappearing before my eyes. Dr. Penny, my therapist, urged me to connect with other Green Berets and soldiers who'd witnessed death and atrocities. One challenge in sharing burdens with fellow warriors was that I usually judged it selfish to reveal my struggles. So many men and women endured much worse horrors than mine. Others came home in caskets draped with American flags.

Ashley added an entertaining dimension to my life, making me smile whenever she walked through our front door. She was a stark contrast to my practical and unwavering wife. I'd label her the over-generalized California girl: blonde, blue-eyed, and excessively, sometimes annoyingly, carefree. I playfully suggested to Brooke that Ashley acted a bit "self-absorbed," a label she coughed up milk over, chastised me for stating, then jovially conceded might be pretty damn accurate. "But she was a great high school and college student," she reminded me. "I hope she'll eventually put her unwavering confidence and classroom smarts to use. Like, maybe get a steady job." I smiled, convinced she would eventually do just that.

Ashley could also be mulish and brooding at times, contrasting her typically sanguine demeanor, and Brooke and I laughed about that essence being part of her allure. Despite her self-centeredness and quirks, or perhaps because of them—plus her beauty—she was often the most captivating person at any party.

My new job, MBA studies, and home projects slowly distracted me from battlefield recollections. Brooke and I joined a coed softball league with like-minded young professionals. We even recruited high school classmates to play, so it parodied the sort of glory days reunion I had complained about.

Ashley was a teammate and garnered much of the squad's attention. She was a talented player with a rocket arm, but most people grew mesmerized by the fascinating or unexpected things she'd say or do. I once invited a Black Hawk pilot I'd served with in Afghanistan, ex-Army Captain Sylvia Sokolov, to our team's obligatory brew and burgers at a local bar following a game. After introductions and a short conversation, I overheard Sylvia commenting that Ashley's blue eyes were "stunning," to which my wife's sister replied, "Thank you, Sylvia. I hear that a lot." Sylvia peered over Ashley's shoulder and raised her eyebrows at me as if the vain remark were my fault. I curled my lips between my teeth and clamped down hard to avoid losing it. Sylvia flashed me an assassin's stare, wordlessly demanding, *Did your sister-in-law really just say that to me?* Classic Ashley.

Brooke and Ashley's father died when we were in high school, and I maintained fond memories of the man. I considered it ironic that Mr. MacDonald perished from a stroke, as he exercised regularly, appeared incredibly healthy, and had a keen sense of humor coupled with a sharp mind. Other family and friends considered him good-natured and relaxed. It often struck me that Brooke had not only inherited her father's looks but also his demeanor.

Conversely, Mrs. MacDonald was a walking contradiction.

Sometimes pleasant and engaging, other times obstinate and off-putting. She regularly barked at Brooke during high school, which was never justified. Ashley didn't suffer the same fate, and she was clearly her mom's favorite. To Brooke's credit, withstanding the brunt of her mother's mood swings weighed more heavily on me than it ever did on her. "She's my mom. I love her regardless."

One foggy Sunday morning in mid-June, Brooke picked up the *Los Angeles Times* from the end of our driveway, ambling past moistened grass and terra-cotta pots bursting with colorful geraniums. I had just stepped from the shower and looked out our bedroom window while Brooke stopped to smile at a giant green katydid clinging to a textured wall on the front porch.

Brooke plopped the newspaper onto a tan kitchen counter and sat on a stool. Green tea, coffee, and a newspaper were vital parts of her morning ritual. Her brows narrowed as she scanned the *Times*. A crisp bang resounded as she lowered her rose-colored mug to the counter and pushed it to the right, needing more room to study the newsprint. Initially, the words La Buena Familia captured her attention. Years earlier, I had explained the cartel was responsible for my father's execution.

The article coincided with the upcoming thirtieth anniversary of Samuel's kidnapping on the outside steps of the Paseo de la Reforma e Insurgentes Senate building in Mexico City. Brooke instantly recognized the drug lord's name, Marco Delgado, and shook her head with disgust as she pored over the particulars of the ambush and discovery of Samuel's mutilated corpse.

Maria had persevered through that day's madness, but Brooke knew the incident must have forever tormented her mother-in-law. She was convinced the public exposé of the horrors befalling Samuel would wrench mother and son.

She flipped to page A6 just as I strolled into the kitchen with matted hair and a comically centered eyepatch overwritten with the words "Chicks Dig Me"—my signature brand of stupid humor. I kissed her cheek, simultaneously measuring her concentrated stare at an article typeset around a photo of Maria taken thirty years earlier.

"*That's Mom!* What the hell?"

"A journalist is writing about Samuel, the kidnapping, the shoot-out, and why you and Maria ended up in California." She inhaled deeply, studying my expression and reaction.

"Do you mind?" I moved the paper closer, set my arm on Brooke's shoulder, and scanned the ink of each line. "This woman interviewed Delgado! Are you kidding me?"

"Yeah, I thought the same thing. It'll get her readers, but why even talk with a known killer? And she should have asked for Maria's input before dredging things up and printing the psycho's claims."

"She doesn't have to ask," I said. "But she should have." I flipped to another page, then lowered my head to focus on the print. Moments later, I shoved my index finger onto a paragraph. "The Emerald Cross? What kind of bullshit is that? Never heard of it. Mom's never mentioned any cross."

Maria rushed into the kitchen as I yelled out the comment, tightening the sash around her white cotton robe. Her dark hair was pulled back in a ponytail. "Why did you just say that?" she said with authority and a stern gaze. "What made you speak those words, Jamie?" Her eyes grew wide.

Confused by her reaction, I shifted my gaze between her and Brooke.

I paused before explaining more about what the article revealed. Mom slowly turned expressionless, then said, "Marco Delgado's a despicable human who killed your father. My husband." Her eyes teared up. "Nothing else matters."

"Of course, Mom. He's a cold-blooded killer who likes to play head games. I've studied him and La Buena Familia more than you realize. But the reporter insists this "Emerald Cross" is somehow connected to what happened to Samuel. Have you ever heard of it?" She didn't reply. "Why would Delgado mention a cross? What's he trying to prove?"

"Why should you care what he says?" Maria shot back. "This man leads the most ruthless drug cartel in the world, living in luxury while no one holds him accountable for selling drugs and killing people. Any comments about this cross are a distraction. Another of his many mind games."

Perplexed, I persisted. "I'm just trying to understand." I returned to a paragraph on page A6 and scanned the sentences. "He says our family stole the cross. This is news to you?"

"*Stop!* Let it go. Trust your mother. Don't challenge me, Jamie."

"I'm not challenging you. I'm sorry you think I am. Let's drop it . . . for now."

With her face a shade of red, she turned and strode down the narrow hall back to her temporary bedroom. The door closed soundly behind her.

I stared at Brooke in a daze. She stroked my back with her hand and leaned her head against my shoulder.

I gazed into her eyes. "An emerald cross?"

CHAPTER 7

Maria sat on her bed and stared into a full-length mirror, agonizing over what to say or do. She debated disclosing that the Emerald Cross was more than a distraction—it was real, holy, and immeasurably dangerous. Few people, including her and Delgado, knew it existed.

It was a problem having her son challenge her regarding the journalist's reporting. She realized her response could only have mystified Brooklyn and Jamie. The news was unwelcome and required careful deliberation before answering more fully.

Certain truths were better left unspoken. She grew terrified by the prospect of revealing what she knew about the exquisite artifact and its history, especially the part about the Delgado family owning it for centuries. Providing half-answers to Jamie would only pique the ex-soldier's interest. Acknowledging the cross's existence could lead down a path of real peril.

She understood her nemesis was playing nuanced games, as psychotic killers often do. The reason the narco ordered Samuel's execution was because of his 1992 exposé on La Buena Familia, reporting that led Mexican forces to storm his compound. They didn't capture the cartel boss but killed two of his brothers during the intense battle.

The drug lord's interest in the cross was a problem thirty years ago, and the *LA Times* article delving into the past would inevitably heighten risks again. If Delgado learned Maria possessed the bejeweled cross, he wouldn't hesitate to do *whatever* was necessary to reclaim it, she ardently believed. Thus, she protected her perilous truth: The cross had been in her possession since just before Samuel's kidnapping in Mexico City. Samuel disclosed that Marco Delgado's father, Mauricio, gifted it to him. It lay hidden for months in a metal safe below the Morales's bed, concealed in a compartment under four nondescript tiles and a rug. She carried it in her oversized handbag while immigrating to America. Because the horrors of 9/11 had not yet transpired, airport security personnel studied the cross and handed it back to her. Later, she stored it in her bedroom beyond the reach of her young son, hoping he'd remain unaware of its existence forever. That changed with today's article.

The revelation was impossible to ignore. She locked the door to her bedroom and stepped into the shadows of her closet. She pulled a wooden box from the top shelf and placed it in her lap. Opening the lid, she pulled the Emerald Cross from its silk bag.

Whenever alone with the cross, she grew mesmerized by an icon made of Inca gold, with large emeralds adorning the horizontal post and vertical beam. It hypnotized her.

Maria had once considered donating it to a major museum. But she believed Delgado would kill her and Jamie out of spite if he concluded she'd covertly owned "his family's cross" upon emigrating from Mexico. She never got it appraised, afraid its heritage might provoke questions and trigger news of its whereabouts that worked its way back to La Buena Familia. The Emerald Cross was a great secret she wasn't ready to share with anyone. Not even Jamie . . . *especially* not Jamie.

She returned the cross to its box and set it atop the shelf in her closet. Then she stepped into a white-tiled bathroom and turned on the shower. As she shampooed her thick mane, she told herself she might eventually divulge the truth to her son—decades from now.

But her son was an inquisitive man. Now alone at the kitchen counter, he fired up his laptop and typed a search for "Emerald Cross." All he found were jeweled crosses for sale, primarily women's necklaces. He scratched his stubbly chin, stared outside at a mockingbird dive-bombing their cat in a corner of the backyard, and took another sip of coffee. The number of questions grew, but the internet wasn't answering them.

Brooklyn suggested Jamie approach his mother later for another conversation about the cross in a delicate manner that wouldn't threaten or insult her. He'd find time for the discussion over the coming days.

There were no reasons to rush.

CHAPTER 8

I was sure there was something to Delgado's claims, so my imagination ran wild. While Brooke peered out a window to a fountain set inside our flower garden, compliments of Uncle Manny, I joined Mom in the backyard. She inspected the ongoing construction of the casita. I approached with a grin and wrapped her in my arms. "Does your future abode meet your expectations?"

"It's stunning. I love the little private patio; what a perfect spot to drink tea or coffee while reading." She set her palm upon my cheek and stared into my good eye, silently expressing boundless love.

"Everything worked out so well, Mom. We love having you on the property to share our futures. Brooke and I couldn't be happier." I turned on a hose and watered pots containing daisies of various colors.

"Thank you, son. We're all blessed. But I'm guessing you have something else you want to discuss." She winked. "Am I right?"

No reason to beat around the bush. "I do, Mom. But I don't want to make you uncomfortable again. You know, regarding Delgado and the—"

She cut me off. "I knew it was just a matter of time before you followed up. You're nothing if not thorough." She asked for the hose, screwed on an extension, and reached to drench potted spider plants hanging from a white beam spanning the patio. A stretch of comfortable silence passed.

"And?" I finally asked. I'm not as patient as she is.

"It's all a ruse by Delgado. Just another of his bizarre ploys. There is no emerald cross—at least, not that I've ever seen."

"Really? I strongly sensed you knew something. Or maybe a detail related to it?" I adjusted my eyepatch. She smiled, and I continued to study her nonverbal facial and body movements. "So I'm wrong?"

"You are. I'm convinced it doesn't exist. An insecure drug lord is laughing at this little ruse playing out in the media." She turned off the spigot, removed the extension, and wound the hose.

"Mom, hiding anything involving Delgado from me wouldn't be smart. You get that, right?"

"Look, honey, of course I do. But I know nothing about some imaginary cross he wants to make relevant. He's psychotic. You can't let him get into your head."

I stared hard for contradictory clues. If she was lying, she was doing an Oscar-worthy job. I eventually half-smiled. "Okay then, you've sold me. I can see you're not holding anything back. Sorry I doubted or misread you."

"You doubted me. But I still love you."

I hugged her again. "I'd have been concerned if the stupid thing were real. And if you knew anything about its whereabouts." I set my hands on her shoulders. "The guy's a twisted freak."

"You can relax. God knows why he might have concocted the story, but we shouldn't spend another minute trying to figure him out. As you said, we're lucky to be spending our futures together. Speaking of futures, you know what would make your mother particularly excited?"

"We're trying, but there's nothing to report yet. Brooke and I look forward to being parents." I smiled. "Let's get inside. Gourmet lunch on me."

During the first year of my MBA program, I attended classes at the USC Center in Irvine, near John Wayne Airport, where Ashley trained to fly airplanes. Because of the proximity of my studies and her training, we'd occasionally meet for lunch at the airport. While it surprised nobody that I was earning an MBA, it surprised almost everyone that Ashley was taking flight lessons. But she was an adventurous and capable woman who, according to her instructor, was skilled at "making the airplane do what it's supposed to do"—quite the old-school flight skills compliment. Brooke discovered later her mother was paying for Ashley's aviation classes and airplane rental costs. That disclosure surprised no one.

The day Ashley was issued her private pilot license, Mrs. MacDonald died from a brain aneurysm while walking through her neighborhood. Brooke and I offered to plan the ensuing life celebration and burial. Ashley said she couldn't contribute financially, so Brooke and I covered all expenses.

Two days after the funeral, Brooke learned her mother's entire estate—$600,000—was left to Ashley. Brooke made no waves, but I could see it was hurtful. I suggested she ask Ashley to cover portions of their mother's funeral costs since she was now flush with cash. Brooke considered that an unpleasant and ill-timed conversation. She also *insisted* Ashley would eventually volunteer her fair share.

Weeks later, Ashley arrived at our place driving a sparkling Ferrari Portofino. Brooke grew simultaneously impressed and enraged. It wasn't enough for her sister to have received their mother's estate; now she was squandering money on a look-at-me rental.

"So, what do you think?" Ashley said excitedly.

Brooke replied, "Well, it's beautiful. But I'm guessing it was absurdly expensive to rent."

"Can you just be happy for me, Brooklyn? It's not my fault Mom left me the money. I don't know why she did, but she did. And this is something I've always dreamed of owning."

"*Oh my God!* You bought it? Are you frickin' kidding me? How much was it? $80,000? $100,000? Don't you understand how ridiculous and self-indulgent that is?" I placed what I hoped would be a soothing hand on her forearm.

"Please don't," she snapped. "Sometimes it doesn't pay to be calm." She turned back to the shiny red sports car. "I think it's time for you to pay us back for half of the funeral expenses, Ashley. You agree?"

My lips curled into a barely perceptible but extraordinarily satisfying smile.

"Whatever," Ashley said as she turned and walked toward her new car with a temporary dealership plate reading MacPherson Ferrari. She abruptly pivoted. "I planned on offering to take you for a ride, Brooklyn. I'm no longer in the mood." She held the red door open. "By the way, you sound jealous. It's unbecoming. I bought a car, so what? You've got everything: a nice car, a great husband, a beautiful home, and you live in the hills. Pretty sweet life, I'd say."

"*It's a life we earned, Ashley!* We've worked our butts off for everything we have! Not like you and your $100,000 Ferrari."

Ashley shook her head, reached inside to grab a plastic bottle of Perrier, and threw it in Brooklyn's direction. "Thanks for ruining my day, sis. And newsflash—it's none of your business how I spend *my* money, but guess what? This baby cost $150,000. *Chew on that!*"

I put my arm around Brooke. "Let it go. She'll regret buying the stupid thing, and you've spoken the truth." I brushed the hair away from her reddened face.

"Mom shouldn't have left her a dime. She's never tapped into her God-given potential and has always been financially reckless. Unbelievable." She exhaled dramatically. "Nothing's ever boring with her, is it?"

"Speak up, guys!" Ashley yelled from her topless Italian sports car. "I can't hear your rude private conversation!" The capricious blonde shook her head and pressed back into a leather bucket seat embroidered with the classic Ferrari emblem. The roaring sounds of a revved engine merely set the stage. Smoke and squealing erupted as she spun the exotic ride backward off the driveway.

Darting onto Foothill Road, the right rear portion of her dream car slammed into the front right fender of a sturdy Waste Management refuse truck. The sounds of locked-up wheels and scents of burned rubber were instantly and forever embedded in every witness's mind. Two men in the garbage truck jumped out and examined the sparkling new Ferrari, which suddenly appeared less impressive.

Brooke and I rushed to the street and joined the sanitation engineers standing beside the classic Italian auto. We all peered into the car while my sister-in-law spouted a stream of expletives and slammed the leather-trimmed steering wheel with her fists. Talk about great theater.

Ashley turned and glared up at enraptured onlookers, then flipped us all double birds. One of the trashmen commented, "Well, I guess she's okay." The second man opined, "I think she might be nuts. She looks crazy."

"*No one's crazy!*" Brooke barked. "She's my sister. Okay?"

The guy replied apologetically, "I'm sorry, ma'am. I didn't say you're crazy—just her. I mean, uh, never mind. I'll call our tow service to get this mess handled." Bothered by his assertion that Ashley might be mentally imbalanced, the man awkwardly attempted to make amends. "Your sister is *beautiful*."

It was difficult to suppress my emerging grin. Neighbors we hardly knew streamed out of their homes to glimpse the drama, a scene they'd likely describe at cocktail parties for years.

Two weeks later, we all gathered to enjoy homemade guacamole scooped up with thick tortilla chips Mom had baked. Ashley offered Brooke a heartfelt mea culpa. They reestablished their friendly conversational norm, though I assumed future theatrics were inevitable.

Watching the sisters interact over the weekend, I thought: *This is what family's all about. Forgive and move on.*

CHAPTER 9

Ashley sat facing her therapist in an office overlooking trendy South Coast Plaza, dabbing wet eyes, miserable and inconsolable. The psychiatrist leaned forward, offered a second box of tissues, and scribbled notes. Ashley stared out the window at the hazy sunshine.

She turned to the therapist. "I don't know if I can tell them. It's too hard to accept." She lowered her head. "*The money is gone!* I had to sell the Ferrari at a $60,000 loss to help pay my gambling debts. I'm getting evicted from my rental in Laguna." She squirmed atop a plush sofa and shook her head. "I've squandered my inheritance. I owe Caesar's Palace $10,000, which I don't have. And now I might lose my sister and brother-in-law. I'm screwed."

"Brooklyn doesn't sound like someone who would banish you, Ashley. The way you've described her, I think she'll help you through this." The doctor tasted her chamomile tea from a light blue mug that read It's in Your Head. "And Jamie sounds like an exceptional person. You might be surprised by their support."

"$600,000! *Gone!* In six months. Unbelievable. God, why couldn't this be a bad dream? I've made mistakes, but this is so unfair. People have taken advantage of me."

The therapist jotted more notes. "Ashley, again, you need to take responsibility. Yes, Caesar's played you, so to say; that's what casinos do. But the Ferrari, the hillside rental overlooking the ocean, the shopping sprees—those were conscious decisions." Ashley shook her head continuously in slow motion.

The psychiatrist moved beside her. "There is a path back to self-worth and happiness, even if you can't see it now."

On her drive back to the beach inside a borrowed car, Ashley noticed everyone she saw in vehicles, on bikes, or walking the streets appeared happy. That contrast to her misery was unbearable. Unable to disclose the truth about her reckless spending to Brooklyn and Jamie, she considered something brazen that could solve all her problems.

Two weeks earlier, she had stopped by the Morales's on her way to Las Vegas for what she hoped would be a reversal of fortunes during a nasty run of lousy gambling luck. No one responded to her knocking and ringing at the front door, so she pushed open the side gate and strolled into the backyard. Because no one answered, she strode toward the just-finished casita and surprisingly found the entry door open.

A startled Maria shrieked from the edge of her bed, nearly dropping the box set on her lap, desperately attempting to close the lid while obscuring its contents. *"Ashley!"* She set the box on her nightstand. "Honey, you can't just walk into a person's private bedroom unannounced." She regained her composure. "I've been moving belongings into my new residence—this amazing casita." Wanting to pretend the box was inconsequential, she calmly tossed it on the top shelf of her closet. "Have time for coffee?" she asked.

The rest of the morning was ordinary, but Ashley's glimpse inside the box affected every thought stirring in her head. It confirmed the existence of the cross they'd all read about in the *Los Angeles Times* article—the cross Maria ardently declared never existed.

Ashley acted oblivious while drinking coffee and eating cinnamon rolls in the kitchen. She was confident that Maria believed she had seen nothing. Over the next two weeks, she didn't disclose her discovery of the Emerald Cross to anyone.

CHAPTER 10

Ashley's mind drifted further into dangerous prospects as each day passed, and she'd lay in bed analyzing opportunities. Delgado wasn't lying; Maria was. Even after a quick glimpse, the Emerald Cross appeared ancient and spectacular. Her obsession grew unshakable. *Pure gold and giant emeralds? A historical artifact? It's got to be worth at least one million dollars.*

The great secret morphed into her grand plan. This was a time for bold decisions. Any delay would only magnify the mess she'd created for herself. Before her stood a *real* solution.

But how would she contact the reclusive cartel boss?

Ashley was a natural salesperson; people gravitated to her and listened with interest. She'd often gained the confidence of people she'd just met, another of her innate talents. She excelled in her advanced Spanish classes in high school and college and studied abroad in Chile for six months. Her Spanish was impressive.

Upon tracking down the *Los Angeles Times* reporter, Ashley disguised herself as a dual-citizenship crime journalist for Chile's leading newspaper, *El Mercurio*. Lifting a name from the paper's website—Federica Gomez—she informed the reporter her job was to elicit commentary from Marco Delgado about recently overturned trafficking and murder convictions of two members of La Buena Familia incarcerated in Chile. Shockingly, the reporter called Ashley back the next day and provided the narco's number.

Frightened but determined, Ashley calmed herself by downing the last four ounces of no-longer-affordable Macallan Single Malt Whiskey. On the other hand, if she could pull this off—*when, not if!*—Macallan might once again serve as her beverage of choice. The whiskey relieved anxieties and induced the proverbial liquid courage. She took one last swallow before slapping her glass down so hard that droplets scattered across the tabletop. Then she dialed the number of Mexico's most notorious cartel boss.

He answered on the third ring but said nothing. She heard only his steady, deep breathing. His sustained silence was unnerving. Ashley's heart pounded, but her courage did not wane. "Marco Delgado?"

The exhalation through his nose created static. He remained quiet, but she heard a woman's soft voice groggily ask in Spanish, "Who is it?"

Rustling sounds, followed by silence, led her to believe Delgado had covered the phone with his hand. Ashley heard him say, "I've told you before not to ask about my phone calls." His words sounded calm and precise but menacing. He had yet to answer Ashley.

"I want to sell you the Emerald Cross," she blurted. The moment the words left her mouth, darkness and fear enveloped her. *Say nothing else. Stop. Hang up, Ashley!* Her finger was an inch from the disconnect button when he replied.

"I am listening," he said. "The cross means much to me. I will pay handsomely for it."

The impossible was now a disturbing reality. She struggled with what to say next.

"You must be a family member to know of the cross. I have often wondered if Maria smuggled it to California. And now I know. Thank you for that. Are you Jamie Morales's wife? I believe they call you Brooklyn, a uniquely American name."

Suddenly, paralyzing dread consumed her. *What am I doing? How did this wicked freak know Brooklyn's name? Dear God.*

She ended the call.

Awakening at nine a.m., Ashley filled herself with coffee as she watched sailboats tacking north and south beyond the coastline. She showered and borrowed her friend's car to drive to her sister's. Steering through Laguna Canyon, she committed to revealing to Jamie her financial problems, the truth about the Emerald Cross, and her conversation with Delgado.

The Moraleses had organized an afternoon picnic and ultimate frisbee competition at Irvine Park. Just as Brooklyn asked Jamie to rush out for paper plates and red plastic cups, an unfamiliar car entered their driveway. Ashley stepped from the vehicle.

※ ※ ※

WE WATCHED ASHLEY STAND rather indecisively next to a very basic sedan. Brooke said, "Looks like she's traded in the Ferrari! Thank God for common sense." She placed her hand around my bicep and gently squeezed. "Why don't you go meet her? I'm prone to high-five her and yell, "Yay, no Ferrari, sis! You're no longer an idiot." I chuckled and patted her rear while striding toward the front door.

Brooke and Mom peered through a window from the kitchen. My

smile waned because I could sense Ashley was really preoccupied with something. Jogging back into the house, I grabbed my USC baseball cap. "We'll be back in twenty or thirty minutes. She wants to chat. I'm sure it's no big deal. Maybe she further regrets her words to you during 'the great Ferrari debacle,'" I said while flashing finger quotes. "I'll remember to pick up the picnic supplies."

"I'm sorry you're stuck dealing with her drama. And I doubt she'll apologize for anything. It's not like Ashley to be burdened by guilt for *too* long."

I stepped through the front door.

"Hold on," Brooke said, "you'll need these." She tossed my sunglasses. "Don't forget, we need to leave the house *by* twelve-thirty. Invite Ashley; I think she'd have fun."

"I agree and will do." I'm unsure why, but I returned to the kitchen to give Brooke a peck. Maria winked, and I kissed her cheek before darting out of the room.

Just before the front door slammed shut, Brooke called out, "You're a good brother-in-law!"

Jogging to the driveway, I hopped into the ugly sedan. Driving north on Foothill Road, I wanted to probe just a little. "I've never seen these wheels, Ashley."

She flashed a sad glance. "It's a friend's car. There's a lot to tell you, Jamie. I hope we can stop at the Starbucks on 17th Street for fifteen minutes." She paused for a long moment. "To discuss something mentioned in the *Los Angeles Times* article."

"That's strange. But, yes, of course." Ashley's aura seemed absent. Her palpable anxieties filled the cabin, while I remained relaxed, though curious. We cruised into town, and I wondered how anything in the

LA Times article could interest her. Staring closer at her expression, I recognized dread across her face.

What the hell is going on?

CHAPTER 11

Sitting across the Starbucks patio table and listening to Ashley bare her soul was difficult. She lamented gambling losses, selling the Ferrari, and squandering her inheritance, which painfully bypassed Brooke. She accepted responsibility for poor decisions and apologized profusely. I told her she'd receive Brooke's and my full support to get back on her feet.

Ten minutes in, we hadn't yet delved into her comment about the *Los Angeles Times* article. I checked my watch and noted we had only minutes left to chat. And I still needed to pick up the picnic supplies.

Ashley cleared her throat. "Jamie, you need to know I did something terrible and selfish last night. But I hung up before revealing too much."

"Wow, that's one hell of a salvo. Before revealing too much to whom? Let's start there." Seconds ticked by as I tried to make sense of the strange comment. I remained baffled and increasingly perturbed. "Ashley, please, fill in the blanks."

"I almost struck a deal to sell Marco Delgado the Emerald Cross."

Stunned, I pushed my drink away, removed my sunglasses, and squinted. "You're messing with me, right?" She stopped talking and studied my intense glare. "Ashley, tell me this is a bad joke."

"It's no joke, but I hardly spoke. He could never figure things out."

"What are you talking about? Figure what out?"

"I saw the cross, Jamie. It's real!"

"So wait a minute—you *actually* called him? Please tell me the answer is no because that would be insane. And the cross does not exist!"

"*But it does!* Maria's hiding it in the casita. In a cloth bag inside a wooden box. I panicked about my debts and recklessness, and I thought—just for one or two days, Jamie—that I might take and sell it to him."

I scanned the Starbucks, parking lots, and streets. "Mom's been lying? And now he thinks *we* have it?" My head shook in disbelief. "You told *Marco fucking Delgado* the cross is in our home?"

"Of course not! I didn't say *where* it was, and he had no idea *who* I was. He wrongly guessed I was Brooklyn."

She watched me grit my teeth and pace in a tight circle. "He's cunning, Ashley. And you're smarter than this. Brooke, Maria, and I live in the same house! One location provides three potential holders of the cross!"

I reached across the table and grabbed her keys. "He's a cold-blooded killer. With money. Technology. His own damn militia. You insist the cross is real, which means he'll want it." Ashley followed me to the car, her mind surely mired in contrasting thoughts. We jumped inside. I turned the ignition, stuck it in gear, and pushed the pedal to the floor. We drove diagonally through a red light. "Call Brooke. Tell her and my mom to drive to Uncle Manny's." Ashley stared back, frozen with her mouth open. "*Now!*" I shrieked.

"Jamie, slow down and take a deep breath."

"*Make the damn call!*" I watched her struggle and calmed myself.

"Look, I'm sure everything's fine. I'm just not the sort of person to leave things to chance."

She called. Brooke didn't pick up. Then she dialed Maria—no answer.

Dammit, why did I get rid of the guns? My Green Beret brain fired on all cylinders—anticipate, strategize, act. I turned to Ashley. "You essentially implied Brooke has the cross."

"No, I didn't."

"Well, that's what he could have concluded. His men could have popped over the border, driven a couple of hours, and parked in our driveway."

"Jamie, get real. You're inflating things."

"I hope you're right."

"I must be—Delgado's not a mind reader."

"If he thinks Brooke, me, or my mother have the cross, he'll just act." *I'm going easy on you,* I thought. *Please just shut the hell up.*

We sped up Foothill Road and swerved into oncoming traffic to pass a sedan occupied by an older couple. Their horn blasted in protest. Upon arriving home, things appeared normal. Car in the driveway, blinds opened, geraniums freshly watered. But the birdfeeders near the front porch, typically a flurry of sounds and motion, were quiet.

"Stay here, Ashley. If I'm not out in three minutes, drive away and call 911."

I could see she finally internalized my very real fears. She stared at me for words of comfort, but I jumped out and dashed to the front door.

"*Brooke! Mom!*" Food and drinks for the picnic lay on the kitchen counter. My echoed pleas grew increasingly frantic. I kept hollering and ran down the hall, crashing open the doors to bedrooms and bathrooms.

Glancing outside at the casita, I noticed its door cracked open several inches. I darted across the yard.

Ashley never left the driveway. She called 911 and now stood before me. Instantly tormented, she screamed, and her body turned rigid. Her hands froze near her face, fingers splayed.

Brooke and Mom's ankles and wrists were bound with gray duct tape. They sat motionless with their backs against the wall below a windowsill. Legs outstretched over blue and white tile. Tape over their mouths. A single hole had bored through each of their foreheads. Blood trickled down their faces and dripped from their chins.

I placed myself between them, one arm over each of their shoulders. Pulling them tightly to my body, their heads fell limp against me. A strange sound was forced out of my lungs.

The sirens blared louder. Tires soon screeched over asphalt and cement. Heavy footsteps and anxious voices rang out. Police hurried from room to room until they discovered the horror. Ashley pressed her fists against her temples. Her head bowed in Brooke's, Maria's, and my direction. She repeated, "I'm sorry. I'm sorry. I'm . . ."

The Tustin Police Department officers tried calming an inconsolable Ashley. They peeled me away from two dead bodies. The property was cordoned off. I approached my sister-in-law. She was an arrogant, selfish idiot for the risks she'd taken. But never in her wildest self-absorbed dreams would she have guessed she'd put Brooke and Maria in the path of ruthless killers. That's what I forced myself to believe while embracing the heaving body of the woman who put this all in motion.

During the police interrogation, I snapped out of my stupor and asked Ashley to show us where she saw Maria hide the Emerald Cross. It was gone. In its place was a cream-colored envelope with *Jaime Morales* handwritten across the front. Inside was a folded sheet of paper with a message scribed in Spanish. An investigator stepped forward and asked for the letter, deeming it evidence.

    I thrust a rigid arm to create space and then read the note.

CHAPTER 12

My hunch turned out to be agonizingly prophetic. Our family's adversary acted swiftly. I focused on committing each word to memory:

Jaime Morales,

This is Marco Delgado. I am in Mexico, so this note is being transcribed by one of my men. Your father Samuel falsely accused La Buena Familia of crimes and atrocities thirty years ago. Mexican troops then stormed one of my haciendas, and my beloved brothers Rico and Jesús got mercilessly gunned down in a fierce exchange. Later, Samuel was justifiably killed to settle scores. But then your mother emigrated from Mexico with an artifact belonging to my family—the Emerald Cross. I questioned whether Maria knew anything about the relic's whereabouts for three decades. She knew a great deal, it turns out. If you had been home today, you too would have been executed. Fate spared you, and I am a believer in fate. I have had my retribution and reclaimed the cross. You have your life. I consider the matter of our families' disputes settled. Any pursuit of retaliation will result in your death, and there are no longer reasons for you to die.

Without enmity or regrets,
Marco Delgado

"No enmity or regrets?" I said to myself but aloud, walking toward a window and peering outside. My words filled the small room. "This man killed my father. Mutilated his body." I rubbed my eye. "He just executed my wife and mother."

The letter became crucial evidence. I left the casita as officers led Ashley to the patio. She appeared dazed and incapable of internalizing what had happened.

My sympathies suggested her culpability might burden her forever. *She'd deserve that, damnit!* I silently implored. I felt sorry for her but also despised her. Cringing, I pleaded with myself to find compassion. But watching this drama play out before me was crushing thoughts of forgiveness and redemption.

Uncle Manny, Manny Junior, and Daniel arrived on the property. After intense questioning, police cleared them to enter the grounds, stating only that "a woman perished." The family approached, and Uncle Manny embraced me tightly. I lost it.

The coroners wheeled Brooke's body past us. I reached out to clutch a portion of the cart, tearfully whispering, "Forever, Brooke. I love you forever." I lost it again.

Confused by Maria's absence, Uncle Manny asked, "Where is my sister?"

"*What?* You don't? Oh my God, Uncle Manny," I said, my face strained by disbelief. "I'm so sorry. They killed Maria, too. Both of them, gone forever."

"Oh, my dear Maria," Uncle Manny cried aloud. "The police told us a young woman had died, not *two* women." He pulled off his glasses and squinted, his brows knitted, his forehead etched with deep wrinkles. Manny Junior and Daniel shook their heads in shock and sorrow. Making our way to the edge of the front lawn, the four of us watched two body bags get slid into a pair of Orange County Coroner's vans.

"Any idea who did this?" asked Uncle Manny.

"The same man who killed my father."

"Delgado—that bastard," he replied. "More torment for our families." Our emotional desolation affected everyone on the property. Ashley watched from across the yard. She covered her face with her palms while seated next to a female police officer interviewing her.

After explaining everything, Uncle Manny flashed recognition when I mentioned the Emerald Cross, which bothered me. I studied him more cautiously. In a borderline accusatory tone, I asked, "Do you *know* something?" Manny Junior and Daniel glanced at their father, offended by my tone but hesitant to voice that disappointment. I was sickened by my insinuation.

Uncle Manny motioned his two sons away. "I know of the cross, yes. Before leaving Mexico, Maria told me it existed and that the Delgado family had once owned it. Marco Delgado insisted your father had stolen it, but the Delgado family patriarch had gifted it to Samuel. When I lectured Maria on the dangers of possessing it, she told me not to worry because she'd left it with someone unknowable in Mexico."

"All this over a damn relic," I mumbled. "Yours is the only family I have left." I glanced at my grieving sister-in-law and hesitantly said, "And Ashley."

Manny reached for my hand while rubbing his eyes. He, too, appeared dizzy from the pace of the revelations. We navigated wrenching anguish in real-time.

The police chief introduced himself and shared everything he'd learned so far. I'd already moved beyond anything that preceded the murders. "Marco Delgado just killed my entire family. I expect authorities or the military to hunt his ass down."

Chief Younkin nodded and said, "We'll need your help, Mr. Morales. As a first step, I hope you and Ms. MacDonald can join us at the precinct to tell us everything you know. Because of the Delgado angle, the DEA, CIA, and FBI will all want a piece of this case. My job is to help align government resources so you can find the justice you deserve."

"Justice? There is no justice, sir. Delgado's already won. I need our agencies to find him. Life in prison or death."

Chief Younkin said, "I understand you're a Green Beret hero. Distinguished Service Cross. Purple Heart. Rescued half a platoon while battling insurgents. I'm sorry you must deal with yet more tragedy."

My head eventually tipped in the chief's direction. "With all due respect, my service record is irrelevant. It has nothing to do with what's happened today or what needs to happen."

"Of course. But I'm hoping you and Ms. MacDonald can provide your accounts, then step aside to let us do our jobs, Mr. Morales. That you won't try to intervene, exact revenge . . . trained as you are."

I stepped closer. "Six months ago, I promised my wife I'd never pick up another weapon. I've seen enough death to last a hundred lifetimes." I recalled kissing Brooke ninety minutes earlier. My throat tightened. "This day has *crushed* me. I feel mentally and emotionally defeated for the second time in my life." Watching the conversation, Uncle Manny stepped forward and placed an arm over my shoulder. He led me to a quiet part of the yard.

Later, we measured the bustling activity of the police, a coroner team, and the just-arrived FBI investigator. I saw Ashley smoking a cigarette behind the casita. She no longer sobbed, but her face looked vacant, broken, separated from the moment. What must it feel like to know one's actions caused such nightmarish and permanent loss?

She stared blankly as I approached. "I didn't know you smoked."

"Only when I'm completely stressed out. I saw one of the cops pull out a smoke and figured, why not?" She extended the pack. "Want one?"

"No, thanks." It was an odd question since I'd never smoked my entire life. Now didn't seem a reasonable time to start. I got it—she was a wreck and somewhat incoherent. "You okay?" I struggled to keep my damning thoughts to myself. "I mean, this is all so terrible." I'd never seen her face this shade of pale. "I'm worried about you." She shuddered, and I pulled her in for an embrace. Her actions hadn't only irreparably harmed me. She lost her sole sibling and the last remaining family member. Still, part of me wanted to curse her to hell. I couldn't do it. "We'll get through this. We have to."

Her eyes had dried, but she could barely stand straight. "Oh, God, Jamie. How will you ever forgive me?"

I tried to put myself in her shoes. She'd done an epically selfish and stupid thing but also attempted to come clean. To disclose a fateful conversation before it led to an unthinkable tragedy. Delgado acted hurriedly, as I surmised he might. Still struggling to internalize the cause-and-effect and irrevocability of the murder of Brooke and Mom, I said, "Know that I've already forgiven you, Ashley."

I didn't know if I meant it.

CHAPTER 13

Uncle Manny offered me a lift to the Tustin Police Department. Ashley insisted on driving herself, a decision I argued against staunchly because she appeared in need of emotional and physical support. But she could be epically stubborn, so we departed in separate vehicles. Perhaps she needed time to get her head straight before authorities rattled off questions and challenged her responses. Manny and I exchanged few words during the fifteen-minute drive.

Ashley parked her borrowed car in front of the precinct just as we entered the parking lot. When we passed her car, she acknowledged us with a nod from her driver's seat. Uncle Manny parked twenty spaces away. The place was bustling with activity. I adjusted my eyepatch, opened my door, and strode quickly toward Ashley's sedan. She was seated with her head tilted against the steering wheel.

The precinct exterior was a cheap knockoff of California mission-style architecture: white stucco, red roof tiles, brown doors, and wood-beamed walkways. Ashley lifted her gaze and studied the building through a window before I opened the driver's side door. She leaned against me as we stepped toward the precinct entrance.

It's impossible for me not to instinctively scan the goings-on and perimeters of any new area. The habits of battle-tested soldiers are hard to shake. Glancing across the street, I noticed a dark-skinned man peering our direction while opening his sedan door, which he remained behind. Strange. My eyes narrowed like a hawk. The man's gaze appeared to be tracking us. The motion of his left arm instantly transported me.

"*Take cover! Enemy fire!*" I shoved Ashley between two vehicles and heard three sharp pops of a handgun just before I rolled her under the chassis of a Ford pickup. Transported to the Middle East, I reached for my M4 and sidearm that didn't exist, then yelled to no one in particular, "3 o'clock! Single shooter! Black clothes and sunglasses!" Having provided the enemy's location and description, I squinted at my watch and noted the exact time, as I'd done countless times in Afghanistan and Syria. It was 5:03 p.m. It grew difficult to breathe.

My intel prompted a female police officer who'd just exited the precinct to enter a state of spatial awareness. First, she had to determine what caused the commotion, who was at risk, and whether the perp remained dangerous. After watching Ashley and me duck and roll and the shooter across the street bear down on his target—*us*—she crouched and trained her Glock22 on the triggerman. "*Police!* Drop the gun! Do it—*now!*" Instead, the man pivoted and aimed his weapon.

Four successive shots rang out. The stranger collapsed to the pavement beside his dark Mercedes as the officer approached with her weapon trained. Reaching upward for his car door with his right hand, the left-handed shooter steadied himself and fired six more rounds at the policewoman. She snapped off four shots in response, one of them ending the man's life.

Within seconds, four other TPD officers and an FBI agent hurried outside with weapons drawn, measuring the chaos. Splitting into teams, one trio advanced to protect their female comrade. The remaining duo trained their guns on Ashley and me.

Crimson colored the ground next to me as the officers approached, unexpectedly triggering visions of Wes Berkeley's gruesome end. Ashley lay frozen, bewildered, her body trembling. I realized the blood next to us flowed from just above Ashley's temple. I must have thrust her down with too much force.

"I've been shot," she said as her hand moved to her head.

"What?" I inspected her skin. "Jesus, Ashley, the bullet grazed your hairline. It's not deep, but it's bleeding like crazy."

Two TPD officers bellowed, "Stand up slowly with your arms outstretched. No sudden moves. *Let's go!*"

"Lower your weapons!" ordered Chief Younkin. "Get a paramedic for Ms. MacDonald. Get these two inside." He stared across the street at the downed assailant. "Looks like we need the coroner, too." He shook his head at me. "Unbelievable. Your day of horrors continues. That man there," he pointed at Special Agent Dan Forster, "is a heavy within the FBI."

I nodded but said nothing. Things were moving so quickly. I swept bloodied light hair from Ashley's face. "I'm guessing Delgado wanted you dead. The lifeless assassin lying in the street didn't do his job." Measuring her fear, I wondered how much more mayhem she could absorb in half a day.

"*I deserve to be killed!* Look what I've done to your family. To your wife. My sister. How can I go on?"

"Ashley, please. Stop talking bullshit. You don't deserve to die." I embraced her tightly. "Your sister loved you," I said with a glistening eye. "So did Maria." We stepped toward the precinct entrance.

"Stop with the charade!" She shot back, momentarily oblivious to her wounds. "Your wife is dead *because of me!* Stop acting like what I did was just unfortunate."

We stared at each other for a long pause. "Fine, Ashley, here it is. I hate you for scheming behind our backs. For what happened to Brooke and my mother." The words were true, and oddly, she seemed somewhat calmed by them. Or maybe I just cut her heart out. "The hate will fade. Anything positive I've expressed in the past won't suddenly become conditional." Tears welled in the corner of her eyes. "Ashley, I'll have to forgive you because the alternative would separate us forever. And in the end, we may need each other."

A female officer behind us appeared spellbound. Ashley fended off bouts of emotional collapse. The officer nodded at me, took Ashley's hand, and led her indoors. Standing in a scene teeming with motion and sounds, I felt out of place.

Suddenly aware, I realized I hadn't seen Uncle Manny since the shooting. Hustling between cars, I retraced the path he would have walked. "Uncle Manny!" And again. *"Uncle Manny!"*

He approached with a pair of TPD officers. I put my hands on his shoulders. "Where'd you go?"

"I saw the shooter and ran back to grab my Ruger," Manny said. "I tripped and dropped my gun. Scraped my hand on the pavement. I wasn't much help."

"You carry a Ruger?"

"I do . . . sometimes. I've got a concealed weapon license. Before heading to your house earlier, I grabbed the gun and chest holster. Tucked it under the front seat."

Chief Younkin rejoined the group. "Please, let's take this inside."

The chief checked the parking lot and street and counted nine TPD vehicles and eleven officers. He called out to his second-in-command. "Post two men at the entrance and rear exit to the building. We're dealing with La Buena Familia."

"La Buena Familia? What is that?" asked one of the rookies.

"The most dangerous drug cartel in Mexico. Maybe the world," Chief Younkin replied.

CHAPTER 14

Inside the police station, Ashley received medical care for the grazed bullet wound on the side of her head. Meanwhile, FBI Agent Forster and two officers questioned Manny and me, and Police Chief Younkin monitored discussions. Tustin Police Department Officer Beckett informed us our responses would be recorded.

Every detail over the previous twenty-four hours was presented. I told them Ashley would offer critical intel leading up to the murders of Brooke and Maria. Manny and I detailed anything we knew about Marco Delgado, his ordered execution of my father thirty years earlier, and the relevance of the Emerald Cross, which neither of us had ever seen. Darting eyes told me some authorities held doubts, which didn't surprise me, nor did I care.

An officer guided Ashley into the room. The top of her head was wrapped in thick white gauze. She disclosed her conversation with Delgado the night before, including her mindless attempt to sell the Emerald Cross. When finished, she said, "I'm just shocked such a short conversation could lead to . . . well, to everything that's happened."

Her words made me cringe. Wondering how an absurd and ill-conceived plot triggered a madman to deliver unspeakable vengeance only compounded my pain. I struggled to purge unpleasant thoughts of her.

FBI Agent Forster set down a cup of coffee he'd held for thirty minutes but never drank from. "Why would you be surprised? Your plan and conversation with Delgado were unspeakably stupid. You're lucky to be breathing. Two people are dead. Three if you count the guy lying on the street outside."

"She understands the ramifications. What's done is done. Commentary like that doesn't help anyone." After I spoke, the room grew silent. Despite my intervention, I realized that embracing excruciating truths would be part of Ashley's penance. I set my gaze on her. Tears fell once again. She appeared to have aged ten years in a day.

Officer Beckett, whose fingers tapped keys faster than anyone I knew, looked up from his laptop. "There's nothing about an emerald cross with any historical significance posted anywhere online. I mean, literally nothing." We thought Chief Younkin appeared annoyed by his officer's quick bias. "I'm skeptical." Beckett studied Uncle Manny. "Mr. Jimenez, you say your brother-in-law Samuel Morales told you about the cross decades ago. But you never saw it?" Manny and Beckett locked gazes.

I was sure Uncle Manny wondered what he would gain by acknowledging a fact already established and repeated for theatrics. Then Beckett turned to me. "Mr. Morales, you insist you'd never heard of the cross until you read about it in the *LA Times* article? And that your mother subsequently claimed it didn't exist? Chief, we're getting zero details about the cross and conflicting statements about its existence."

"And?" I said.

"And I think the three of you are in cahoots. You're hoping to throw us off the trail of discovery. Maybe you want to misinform for reasons we don't yet understand."

"Believe what you want, sir," I said disinterestedly. "I've devoted my adult life to service for this country. My military record is unblemished. I'm honest and don't play bullshit games. I'll vouch for my uncle. That may not be good enough for you, but it's damn well good enough for me. And I trust Ms. MacDonald's account. She said she saw the cross, so I'm sure she did. I don't know what else you're looking for. My gut says you're too biased or incompetent to be of much help."

"You people..." Beckett glared at me with an expression of contempt.

"Me and my uncle's people? My wife and Ms. MacDonald's people? You're a disgrace. I hope you get pulled off our case."

Chief Younkin pointed to the door. "We'll take it from here, Officer Beckett. Meet me in my office at seven a.m." The chief's arm and index finger remained rigidly extended toward the hall.

Beckett exhaled loudly. "Yes, Chief." He glowered at me as he walked from the table.

The door shut, and Chief Younkin gazed at me intensely. "That was unacceptable. He'll be held to task."

I just nodded.

Two more hours of interviews ensued. All our words grew softer, more reflective, and less succinct. It was gut-wrenching to know that regardless of the nascent investigation and any justice ultimately served, our futures were forever absent of people we loved and needed in our lives. Chief Younkin suggested we go home to cope with our paralyzing grief. Ashley, Manny, and I exited the building, still shell-shocked.

※ ※ ※

IT WAS IMPOSSIBLE TO sleep when I got home. No one falls asleep after their wife gets executed. Ashley slept in a bedroom down the hall. Two cops were parked outside. A precaution. I think I was too exhausted to cry any more tears. I just lay there, depleted. Delgado certainly ordered the attempted hit on Ashley, and he wouldn't stop simply because one of his assassins failed to finish the job. And despite his note stating he didn't need me dead—that killing Brooke and Mom had settled all scores—I would've been an idiot to believe that. The guy was responsible for hundreds of deaths. He probably considered it entertainment.

The following day, the FBI and TPD met with Kirby Washington, Special Agent in Charge at the DEA's Los Angeles Field Division, and Gloria Kirkwood of the CIA. The group deliberated options, prioritized objectives, and put together recommendations before sending them up their chains of command for debate. The scope of the investigation and its relation to Delgado and La Buena Familia quickly pushed the Tustin Police Department out of the way. The case clearly exceeded the scope and capabilities of any police department.

DEA Special Agent in Charge (SAC) Washington argued the investigation and any missions were DEA domain. Delgado had been a critical target of the agency for two decades. He believed the cartel boss's personal vendetta against the Morales family and his emotive interest in the Emerald Cross—if it existed—might provide something compelling to smoke him out. By the end of the week, senior officials inside the FBI, DEA, and CIA agreed Los Angeles-based DEA SAC Kirby Washington would lead efforts to bring Marco Delgado to justice for the killings of Brooklyn and Maria Morales.

Washington promptly recommended Ashley and I enroll in the Witness Protection Program administered by the United States Marshals Service. The program's charter was to guard crucial witnesses before and after trials of powerful criminals, where the risks of harm were real. The probability of capturing Delgado wasn't necessarily high. But the mere prospect the drug lord could be exposed based on information we provided justified putting us into protective custody for at least the time being. While ninety-five percent of those enrolled in the US Marshal Witness Protection Program were criminals, we had inadvertently entered Delgado's domain.

CHAPTER 15

Brooke and Mom were now encased in decorated ceramics. A priest slid the urns into a mausoleum at a cemetery overlooking undeveloped rolling green hills northeast of Tustin. Two US Marshals accompanied the few attendees: Ashley, Uncle Manny, the Franciscan, and me. Manny agreed it would be prudent for his wife and sons to stay home. Ashley pleaded to attend despite the risks. *She got them killed*, I argued to myself. *Let her share the misery of their burial.* I wasn't proud of the sentiment and knew Brooke and Mom would have castigated me. I would have countered that laying a murdered wife and mother to rest prompts harsh judgment.

After explaining the circumstances of the two women's deaths, I told the Franciscan not to feel obligated to preside at the internment. It was a potentially dangerous assignment. But the cleric appeared oddly enthused about officiating the graveside service. "To hell with Marco Delgado." I hoped he and I could share a beer someday.

After twenty minutes of prayer and valedictions, the two urns were placed in the mausoleum. I put my arm around Ashley and led her to an innocuous white sedan. One of the US Marshals scanned the cemetery grounds. His partner opened a door for a woman they were now responsible for protecting.

I never intended to enter witness protection but pleaded with Ashley to accept the offer. Upon consenting, officials informed her she'd get comfortably housed and expertly guarded in an undisclosed location.

Following an extended emotional embrace, after one of the marshals repeated it was time to depart, Ashley let go of me and struggled to say, "I'm so, so—"

"I know you are." Grabbing a tissue from inside my Army dress uniform, I wiped away tears from her eyes and face. "Until we meet again..."

The marshal closed the door, and Ashley stared at me as the car wound its way out of the cemetery. I raised my arm and forced a wave goodbye, damning her actions that left my life in shambles.

While enrolled in witness protection, Ashley would inherit a new life—different name, Social Security number, license, and credit cards. DEA Special Agent in Charge Washington told us that, depending on how the DEA's pursuit of Delgado played out, she might need to live with her assumed identity for years. Delgado was a psychopath, so the list of precautions was necessarily long.

After she left, I focused on assisting the DEA and FBI. I demanded the authorities stop meeting Manny in police or agency buildings. If Delgado deemed him a threat, he and his family could become targets. SAC Washington obliged but strongly opined that only Ashley and I were at elevated risk of retribution by La Buena Familia.

Days later, Washington and I met at his office. "I should have asked you this earlier. You're a military hero. Army captain. I've been calling you Mr. Morales, and you haven't corrected me. But should I be addressing you as Captain Morales?"

"No. That was then, this is now. I'll get called Captain or Captain Morales on base and at military functions, but that's it. Outside the

Army, I prefer Mr. Morales. Or Jamie among friends." I assumed we would never become friends.

"Noted," he replied before swallowing coffee and pushing his chair further from the table. "So you've never seen this Emerald Cross? Not even as a child? I'm surprised your mother was able to keep her secret." The agent slid a bag of Doritos across the table. I nodded and pulled the bag open. "Agents are surprised you never saw the cross Ms. MacDonald swears she saw your mother holding."

"Unbelievable. Here we go again," I tossed the bag of chips into the middle of the table. "Knowing it belonged to a ruthless drug lord, wouldn't *your* mother have hidden this secret from *you*?" Washington nodded. "Exactly—of course. It's probably extraordinary, so a mother might *want* to reveal it or let others touch it, but if a devil owned it and would do anything to get it back, she'd hide it forever."

"So you believe Ms. MacDonald saw the cross? Walked into your mother's casita as she placed it back in its box, then in her closet?" I stayed silent. "You buy her story?"

"How many times can you guys ask me the same question in slightly different ways? Do I believe her? Yes, I'm inclined to. Should you? That's your call. All we know is what she told us, right? Also, the cross isn't my primary concern. Grabbing Delgado is."

"Of course. I realize my probing is difficult, Mr. Morales. But my job is to repeatedly ask questions—sometimes the same question—to gather and evaluate vital information."

"I'm a Green Beret. Spent years in combat. Yes, information gathering is critical. But I don't see anyone in the DEA or any other agency breaking new ground here." I scratched my temple, hoping my faith in the DEA wasn't misplaced. "It's been weeks since the murders. You and your team continue to pose the same questions as if I'm stupid or lying. I only care about what *you* are doing to capture Delgado."

"That's going to take time. We are doing everything possible to gather intel and track Delgado's movements. Our commitment to capturing him is unyielding."

My face probably appeared frozen in annoyance. "I trust your intentions, but that means little without results. I want results. As you would if the tables were turned."

Washington leaned back in his chair and fiddled with a silver pen. "We may not impress you, but my team is more capable of tracking down cartel heavies than any agency globally. We're effective. Give us time."

"I'm not wired to be a spectator. I probably wouldn't be sitting this out if I were healthy." He likely considered me belligerent. The unbearable truth that I'd never see Brooke again sometimes engulfed me without warning.

Realizing it was time to wrap up, we delivered curt goodbyes. I-405 southbound was a mess, giving me time to tell Brooke how much I missed her. Loved her. A couple of tears rolled down my cheek.

CHAPTER 16

Using passwords over an encrypted line, Marshal Austin connected with SAC Washington and me inside the Los Angeles DEA office. I heard him tell Ashley, "We are live." She audibly struggled for composure.

"Ms. MacDonald, start the conversation," Marshal Patton said. "The clock is ticking." She collected herself and leaned forward.

"Jamie?"

"Hello, Ashley. I hope you're holding up well."

"As well as can be expected. You understand what that means better than anyone."

"Yeah, I do."

"Jamie, it's difficult for me to accept the selfish and absurd decisions I made. I should have stayed focused on flying lessons. Not gambled away my inheritance. Not behaved like a privileged bitch." She sniffled. "Not tried to sell the Emerald Cross. I can't believe . . . It's just so painful to accept. But it's a burden I deserve. I'm a terrible person."

"No, you're not. And I'm going to force you to change gears, Ashley. I understand your remorse. But in our short time on these calls, let's stay upbeat with an eye to the future. Does that make sense?"

She stayed quiet for a long pause. "The future? Okay, that's fine. Have they closed in on Delgado?"

It wasn't a question but a directive: *They need to get that murdering bastard.* She'd always been able to change gears in a heartbeat. "Not yet." I glanced at Washington. "They tell me progress is being made." I wanted to tell everyone I doubted their claims of meaningful headway. "They'll get him, Ashley." My eye moved between SAC Washington and a woman shadowing him, Assistant Special Agent in Charge Renée Sheffield. "The DEA wants to take him down as badly as we do. We're all on the same page."

"Getting Delgado is all that matters. It's all I think about."

"Let the DEA do its job. Tell me about the place you're living."

Marshal Patton interrupted, "Don't be too specific."

Ashley acquiesced to the change of topics. "It's beautiful." She took a deep breath and gazed out her breakfast room window to an expanse of sloping grass where a deer was feeding at the edge of the property. "I can see rolling hills and nice homes built on large lots. It's getting cooler at night, and I watch billows of chimney smoke rise and float across the valley."

"Sounds like a scene out of a painting."

"I guess it could be. Of course, there isn't much to do here. I've been reading one or two books a week."

"Impressive. I'm a slow reader. If I get through five books in a year, I consider that success."

"You don't mean that," Ashley said.

"I do indeed. My memory is decent, but I've always been a slow reader. If I could have devoured books like you in high school, I would've had more time to spend with your sister." I could almost see her smile through the phone.

"I miss all the good times we had. You and Brooklyn always included me in outings and celebrations, and I cherish those memories." In the distance, a high school band could be heard practicing. "Football season has started. Do you pull for Army or USC nowadays?"

I was happy our discussion had moved to the mundane. "Army matters most when we play Navy and Air Force, two organizations filled with pussies who rely on Army grunts and the Marines to save their asses and the world." Laughter echoed through both phones. "West Point is in my blood in a way SC will never be. But if I ever start my own company in SoCal, I'll be playing up my SC cred, trust me. Trojan alums dominate the business landscape down here."

"Yeah, and they're hard-core. I dated a USC grad who thrived on belittling UCLA alumni. He told me a Trojan is a Trojan for life, but a Bruin is only a Bruin for four years. Although I'm pretty sure UCLA is a better school."

DEA Agent Washington interjected, "It most certainly is." He twisted his class ring.

"I'm sitting next to a Bruin, Ashley." I smiled, and it felt good. "I think your story exposed an insecurity." I orchestrated five more minutes of lighthearted banter before Agent Washington whispered it was time to wrap up.

Ashley said, "The marshals are telling me it's time to go. This went by much too quickly, Jamie. I want to say you've always been so good to me. I'm not sure I can ever fully reciprocate your kindness and support, but I'll try."

Her words were so sincere that I wish Brooke could have heard them. "You hang tough. Let's hope the DEA gets Delgado soon. Then we can lead more normal lives."

"I look forward to that. Miss you tons. Bye."

"Stay well, Ashley."

I hung up thinking I owed this woman nothing, yet here I was, nursing her back to a less guilt-ridden future. Sometimes, I deemed that irrational, but it's what Brooke would have wanted.

CHAPTER 17

The freeway traffic was lighter than expected. The easy drive allowed me to dissect information I devoured last night. I tapped into government websites, Wikipedia, journalism sources, blogs, and anything else I could find regarding the history and current events surrounding the drug trade in Mexico and its effects on the US. I considered all of it while driving to meet with SAC Kirby Washington inside the DEA Los Angeles Field Office. The research was enlightening.

Mexican and American authorities hardly eradicated the drug trade in Sinaloa State—the Golden Triangle—despite billions of dollars and extensive manpower. The region included Durango and Chihuahua, where every drug enforcement agency globally understood the majority of the heroin sold in the United States was produced. Much of Sinaloa was a mountainous agricultural area comprised of subsistence farmers supplementing income by growing opium and selling extracted gum to the cartels, who processed it into injectable heroin. These landowners grew poppies primarily because they had no option. Not bowing to the cartels' demands prompted misery or death.

For decades, Mexican drug empires were built on the backs of marijuana farmers. But with the legalization of pot in a growing number of US states, profits for cartel farmers plummeted. For the cartels, sinking marijuana profits inevitably led to a prosperous alternative.

Mexico recently displaced Colombia as the largest supplier of high-grade heroin in the US. Today, a "hit" of powdered snow-horse-smack could be acquired on city streets for four bucks, slightly higher in the suburbs.

Synthetic opiates also grew highly lucrative despite recent efforts by the US to crack down. So, as American resources got focused on limiting fentanyl and its knockoffs, La Buena Familia and other cartels ramped up harvests of poppies to stay diversified. Beautiful white, blue, and purple poppy flowers dominate the higher elevations of the Golden Triangle.

La Buena Familia went on a killing spree during its rising heroin production. The DEA estimates the cartel's mules and sicarios murdered dozens of "non-compliant" farmers and their families, plus hundreds of competing traffickers, in the past five years.

There were no college graduates besides Marco Delgado leading drug cartels in Mexico. A gifted student, he entered Duke University as a freshman the same year Mike Krzyzewski became head coach of the Blue Devils in 1980. He joined the debate team and sang with the Acapella Club before graduating with honors and a finance degree. None of his classmates considered him capable of leading a drug cartel or inflicting the horrors that have become his trademark.

Was Delgado a deranged psychotic? Most experts believed so. They also labeled him an unusually cool character within a frighteningly lethal industry. One of Delgado's favorite mantras never wavered: *I am not a killer!* Perhaps not with his own hands, but he'd undoubtedly ordered torture and executions to keep farmers and conscripts "focused."

Students at Mexican and American university psychology departments were often mesmerized by studying the drug lord's rule and infamy. No single word defined the man. Ruthless and enigmatic were standard labels.

Delgado owned several posh residences in his hometown, Culiacán, which served as Sinaloa's state capital. He cherished Culiacán, the surrounding mountains, and the beaches of Baja Mexico, where he spent his teenage years surfing. US agencies agreed he was a law-abiding citizen before graduating from Duke.

CIA and DEA intelligence experts claimed narcos disappeared overnight after triggering violence in Culiacan. Some of La Buena Familia's own mules were executed, owing to Delgado's contempt for anyone blighting his hometown. The man's devotion often baffled the authorities.

Perhaps all my drug trade research was now moot. Two days ago, Agent Washington suggested we meet. He sounded optimistic. Due to my Green Beret days, I felt I had decent skills in gathering and deciphering information, sometimes through voice intonations. My gut says the DEA may have grabbed Delgado.

After parking, I entered the building and relieved myself of a Starbucks grande latte and two bottles of water. I washed my hands, applied Chapstick, and centered the eyepatch over an empty socket.

Assistant Special Agent in Charge Renée Sheffield, Washington's protégé, greeted me in the foyer. We entered a room where her boss sat beside a DEA expert on electronic surveillance. Washington stopped speaking as we approached. He held out his hand with a glum expression and flexing jaw muscles.

We exchanged curt greetings as a male administrative assistant laid a file before his boss. The three DEA agents' collective gazes focused on my good eye. Washington exhaled loudly. "I hoped to deliver encouraging news today, Mr. Morales. That's not going to happen."

Not a good start. I shook my head dismissively. "You know Delgado killed my wife and mother, right?" I regretted the unnecessary, searing remark.

"It's a truth I remind myself of every day. I can only imagine your pain."

I pushed my chair from the table. "You sounded upbeat on the phone. What happened?"

"We had a fix on Delgado. Coordinated DEA and FBI resources with the Mexican Marines." He pointed to a flexible cast encasing his right foot. "I've got a hairline fracture, so I'm out of action." He shook his head and rubbed the lobe of his right ear. "Anyway, he slipped away."

"You've just made your job much harder. Once a target perceives a real threat, he can disappear for months. Even years. Same situation with the Taliban, ISIS, or Al Qaeda." I glared at the three agents. "This is more than disappointing."

"Agreed," Washington replied.

"Who tipped him off?" My knitted fingers rested atop laminated faux wood. Peering intensely at Washington, I said, "The DEA has its procedures. You know what you're doing, I'm assuming." I paused for a long stretch. "Did you miss him by seconds, minutes, or hours?"

Washington pursed his lips and glanced at Assistant SAC Renée Sheffield before clicking his gold pen three times, which resonated in the otherwise dead-quiet space. "We aren't sure. He may have departed as much as forty-eight hours earlier. I've told you more than I should have, of course. Certainly more than I need to. Know that we'll figure this out."

"You'll never get Delgado if you don't."

"I called you on Tuesday anticipating good news. Things have changed. I wanted to inform you in person. You deserve that. But we can stop meeting if the updates are too difficult for you."

Washington and I locked eyes, both pissed off. Agent Sheffield said, "We are committed to apprehending Delgado, Mr. Morales. Everyone in the DEA wants justice for your wife and mother. We'll do whatever it takes to bring him down."

I struggled to keep from losing it. The three agents stared at me. What did they expect me to say or do? I bowed my head, hunched over, and stopped talking.

Washington gave additional updates that felt forced and offered me nothing hopeful. He appeared distracted or disinterested. "I'll keep you further informed as it makes sense, Mr. Morales." He limped with his casted foot while guiding me toward the door.

Seconds after exiting, I abruptly turned to meet his gaze. "Years on the battlefield have worn me down. I only have one eye. My skills have diminished since I was discharged." Did he know where I was headed? "*Please* don't put me in a position where I need to make this a personal mission."

"Meaning what exactly, Mr. Morales?"

"Meaning, if you can't bring Delgado in, then maybe I'll be forced to do it myself. It's not what I want. And I'd probably fail."

"A personal vendetta? You would indeed fail if you took this on alone—badly. You know that. Let us do our job."

After studying a coffee stain on the carpet, I raised my head and said in a monotone voice, "Just capture Delgado." I pulled out my sunglasses and strode to the elevator.

CHAPTER 18

Staring at my reflection in the window, I chastised myself. After leaving the Army, I promised Brooke I'd never own or handle another weapon. Ever. The trauma of killing, of watching patriots die in horrific ways, including best friends and little kids getting obliterated by bombs, became too much to shoulder upon discharge. Yet here I was, about to purchase a Beretta M9 at a gun show.

Telling Brooke I would never pick up another sidearm or carbine soothed both of our anxieties for very different reasons. We both felt it signified hope. Thus, mixing with a crowd of gun enthusiasts wasn't a place I expected to find myself—ever. So much for honoring my unambiguous pledge.

Eight hundred dollars cash was handed to the seller of the Beretta, enough for the gun, a fifteen-round clip, and thirty 9mm bullets. After reaching for the ammo clip, the tattoo on the underside of my forearm grew visible. The vendor recognized the Green Beret motto: *DE OPPRESSO LIBER*, Latin for "To free from oppression." We shook hands before I disappeared into the crowd.

The people waiting to enter the Kentucky Trailer Mobile Shooting Range outside the Los Angeles Convention Center smiled and chatted. The blasts of spent rounds popped and whirred, echoing beyond the range's sound- and safety-reinforced walls. I breathed deeply and felt relaxed as if I somehow knew there'd be no PTSD flashback today.

Two armed and actively scanning guards were positioned inside and outside the range. Several shooters studied me through bullet-proof windows as if I might be someone worth observing. Was it my eye? My gait? The way I instinctively handled my weapon?

The target was one hundred feet away. A white paper target hung from a track spanning the length of the roof. The four-inch red bullseye was sharply in focus.

Step one was adjusting to single-eye variables. This would be the first time I'd shot a gun since Wes disappeared. Silence reigned when I fit the earmuffs over my head. Glancing behind me through the observation glass, I noticed the gentleman who sold me the gun. Next to him was a woman with a ponytail who flashed a quick smile.

Both appeared to have high expectations for my shooting. I was convinced they were about to be greatly disappointed. I raised the Beretta with my right hand, encased it with my left, and fired five rounds. I smiled at my performance—the bullets were bunched but about eight inches from the bullseye. The two spectators probably stopped paying attention.

Spending minutes staring at a new target, I internalized the variables of being a one-eyed shooter. I raised the gun and snapped off five rounds. There was only one bullseye, but three were on the circle's edge. Improvement. Knowing time was running out, I took mental notes and got back in line. On my second trip, I fired fifteen rounds, and six hit the bullseye or were within three inches. Before my third and final trip inside the range, I further analyzed all the variables affecting a shooter with one empty eye socket. I raised the Beretta and pulled the trigger ten times. Each bullet struck the bullseye, with six bunched up smack in the middle. While exiting, I recalled something Wes liked to say: Jamie Morales can shoot like a big-screen cowboy.

The late-day sun soothed me as I stepped through the parking lot. Before getting in the car, I cleaned the lenses of my sunglasses with the hem of my polo. Grabbing the bag holding my Beretta from atop the car, I opened the door and was about to sit when the young lady from the shooting range stepped forward.

"Hey there, that was some impressive shooting. I'm guessing ex-military?" she said while adjusting her visor.

This emotionally wounded warrior wasn't in the mood for small talk with a stranger. *Be polite, Jamie.* "Thanks. And yes, Army. Green Beret."

She straightened and confidently said, "You look like a nice guy. It's not beyond me to take the first step." She extended a folded piece of paper with a scribbled name and number: "I'm Melissa. If you'd like to chat over coffee or a beer, here's my number."

She must not have noticed my wedding ring. Glancing at my hand, I realized it wasn't on my finger. I hesitated but took the note. "I should get going. Nice meeting you, Melissa. Aim straight." The door shut, and I tossed her number onto the passenger seat. Halfway home, the skies grew stormy.

The air felt unseasonably cool as I walked from the mailbox to our front door. It wasn't raining, but I sensed downpours were certain. I enjoy the occasional Pacific storm and drought-stricken California desperately needed water.

"Alexa, turn on the TV. Alexa, channel eleven." With the dark brew bottle top popped, I settled onto Brooke's favorite TV-viewing sofa. There were still remnants of her fragrances on the furniture, in the house, and around the yard. Or maybe I imagined it.

"Alexa, volume level six." The words La Buena Familia snapped me to attention.

A street in what the reporter described as an affluent section of Culiacán appeared flooded with ambulances, military vehicles, and the police. The reporter said at least two officers had died. Three others lay critically wounded. Then I heard something I'd suspected as the update progressed. "Sources say drug lord Marco Delgado was the target of a sweep involving Mexican and American drug agencies and military personnel."

Delgado was the real deal—a dangerous man who was heavily protected, difficult to track, and unafraid to die. But when was the DEA going to gain the upper hand? I said to the TV, "That's strike two, Agent Washington." That thought was interrupted by a whiff of spent gunpowder lining the barrel of my Beretta.

CHAPTER 19

"Finally. It's been too long."

I sensed her loneliness. "It's good to hear your voice, Ashley. It's hard to believe it's been months. Are you staying optimistic? Finding things to occupy your time?"

"The marshals have driven me around town three times, and I checked out the license plates. I'm somewhere in Indiana. Getting out helps keep me sane, but it is a strange experience. I have no connection to this place or its people." She chuckled. "This ain't Laguna Beach."

The contradiction of my beachcomber sister-in-law living near quaint towns in my imagined rural, small-town Midwest forced a smile. "How have you been holding up?"

"Much better than the last time we spoke. Your advice helped. I'm trying not to let guilt and regret devour me."

"Great news. The less time you spend dwelling on things out of your control, like Delgado and what happened, the better."

"That's not exactly what I said, Jamie."

"Sorry, that's what I heard."

"I'll clarify. I'm not drowning myself in sorrow for the horrors I've inflicted on you and others. But that doesn't mean I spend less time thinking about Marco Delgado."

"Don't let him rule your psyche."

"I won't. But it's impossible not to fantasize about vengeance."

"That doesn't sound healthy. I'm not even sure what it means."

"He doesn't own my psyche. But I can't help it if he enters my dreams. I have a recurring vision of tracking him down, aiming a gun at his head, and ending his life. But when I pull the trigger, I wake up. I've dreamt it four or five times."

"I'm sorry, Ashley."

"Oh, please. You must have similar thoughts. You sounded skeptical about the DEA taking Delgado down the last time we spoke. Haven't you ever imagined doing it yourself? I know you wouldn't try—that's a total death wish—but haven't you ever envisioned it?"

She was more perceptive than I realized. "No, I don't think about exacting lethal revenge. To what end? Brooke, Maria, and Samuel are gone forever. We live in different realms than Delgado. Killing him would only further burden my life. But I share your demand for justice."

She stared blankly at the stainless-steel refrigerator across the room while collecting her thoughts. "This discussion is a good segue to something that might shock you. I've begun studying for the Law School Admissions Test. I want to become a lawyer."

I internalized the news. Somehow, it didn't surprise me.

"You're not speaking. You're shocked or think it's absurd."

"I'm taking it in. Tell me more, like what prompted the idea?"

"Delgado prompted it, of course. I've been researching more about his rule and the pure evil he inflicts. But there are too many Delgados. The tens of thousands whose lives the drug lords have taken or destroyed need justice. My passion could fade, but I doubt it will."

"Would you help those in Mexico?"

"Great question. I'm not sure yet. There are victims of cartel violence and crimes throughout the US—like you and me. My language skills would be valuable north or south of the border. While I'm not ready for the LSAT, I can tell by the sample tests I can do well."

"This is quite a conversation. You sound resolute." I questioned how long her zeal would remain. Becoming a lawyer takes years of commitment. But no dreams would be squelched today. "Ashley MacDonald, attorney-at-law. Brooke would be proud. She was always your biggest fan." I'd often told Brooke her sister would eventually grow up, get her act together, and be productive.

"One more thing. I promise to pay you back for my mother's funeral expenses."

"That's unnecessary. It's water under the bridge." *You were right, Brooke! She finally offered to pay.*

"I cringe thinking about the inheritance I squandered and never paying for any portion of my mother's burial or reception. It sickens and embarrasses me. The best way to get past it is to make things right. I'll do that as soon as I start earning money."

"Well, this has been quite a conversation. I'm impressed with how you're reconciling the past. You're a capable person, Ashley. Stay focused and work hard."

"Thanks. You've been supportive since Brooklyn introduced us." She exhaled loudly. "Is there anything you can share about Delgado?"

Seated between Washington and Agent Sheffield in Los Angeles, I decided to lay bare gnawing truths. "The DEA has blown a couple of opportunities. They'll deliver better news soon."

Washington grew visibly annoyed and tapped on the bezel of his watch. He leaned forward and muted the phone. "Maximize your time, Mr. Morales. She doesn't benefit if you trigger anxieties."

My faith in the DEA's efforts to capture Delgado waned further by the day. I couldn't tell Ashley that.

"Jamie, you still there?"

Washington unmuted the phone. "Sorry, I am. We took a moment to down some water. The Santa Ana winds have arrived in SoCal, so it's hot and dry."

"But do you honestly believe they'll get Delgado?"

Her tenacity impressed me. I hunched over and spoke inches from the phone's mic. "Absolutely. Zero doubt. It's just a matter of time."

"I hope you're right. Part of the reason I went into this witness protection program was because I expected the DEA to get him by now. It's been over seven months. If I'm wasting my time . . ."

"You are where you need to be, Ashley."

"You'd think it wouldn't be difficult to find Mexico's most notorious drug lord with today's technology. Then to apprehend him."

Was I the only one in the room who thought she was spot-on? "Relax and bide your time. Study for the LSAT."

Two minutes later, Washington stated it was time to end the call. Ashley and I bid adieu. My eye moved from face-to-face as I tried to read the agents' thoughts.

Washington cleared his throat. "There is something else I want to discuss, Mr. Morales. It's coincidentally related to your conversation with Ms. MacDonald."

"You have my attention."

"You purchased a Beretta M9."

I grew instantly irritated and ground my teeth. Seconds ticked by. "Please tell me you aren't following me." I swept my forearm like a windshield wiper over the table. "Look, that's not okay."

"We've monitored movements for your safety."

"Or you believe I'm not shooting straight with you. You might even think I'm part of the problem. That's more than insulting, sir."

"You're wrong. My instincts, like yours, have been honed through my work. I trust you, but I also know you're in constant danger—even if you disagree. It makes sense to have you tailed."

"Ex-Green Beret. Flawless record. Trained in all manner of guns. It's legal to buy one. What's the problem?"

"You previously divulged that you promised your wife you'd never again pick up another weapon. It seems fair to inquire. Agreed?"

"I disagree. Your job is to catch Delgado. To crumble his empire. Not to analyze me. I bought the Beretta for protection, as most people do."

Washington softened his tone. "Look, I'm concerned you might be seriously considering taking things into your own hands, Mr. Morales. As your sister-in-law just correctly expressed, going after Delgado would be a suicide mission."

I stood and stepped toward the large, tinted window, staring at the constant motion of LA traffic on the streets below. Sliding a hand over my forearm, I challenged myself to answer why I'd bought the Beretta. Of course it was a fair question.

"We haven't caught Delgado because he's a powerful man with undue influence in Mexico and the US. He's cunning and intelligent. Ruthless enough to make even our seasoned veterans uncomfortable. People like him are rarely apprehended quickly."

We faced each other. "All due respect, sir, those are excuses. I don't enjoy being contentious, but I thought you'd have made more progress by now."

"It's clear I can't appease you today," Washington replied. "You haven't answered my question about the gun purchase. Are you planning a misguided pursuit of Delgado?"

"I don't think so."

"That's not an answer."

"It'll have to suffice." I drew a deep breath while removing my eyepatch and grabbing my sunglasses. "Look, I see the effort. But it's as if Delgado's always a step ahead of you guys. It's hard to understand." I squinted and raised my shoulders. "Sometimes I wonder if he's getting tipped off." My eye darted between Washington and Assistant SAC Sheffield.

"I can assure you there's no chance of that," Washington said with a hard stare. "Give us time, Mr. Morales."

"I'm trying. I really am. Good day, sir." I nodded and found my way to the lobby.

CHAPTER 20

My job at RKD Aerospace was a great diversion from all things Delgado. The firm was a fast-growing defense contractor manufacturing state-of-the-art missile guidance systems. During the probation period review, management highlighted my work ethic, multitasking ability, and project management skills. The work was fulfilling, and I aspired to reach the executive ranks.

The first year of my USC MBA studies had just ended. My cohort consisted of four other ambitious Type A personalities in their thirties. People treated me like I was special. I told myself that if I were half as smart as them, my future would probably be all right.

Uncle Manny, Natalie, Manny Junior, and Daniel worked hard to distract me from anguish by committing me to family dinners and social events. We would sometimes shed tears, but I appreciated their efforts and support. Manny Junior once suggested I consider dating, a well-intended remark I wasn't prepared for. I wondered if his father put him up to it. "Maybe one day."

Unexpectedly, Manny Junior's comment triggered days of introspection. I was lonelier than I'd conceded, a penetrating solitude so overwhelming it felt wicked. I missed the intimate and ordinary moments with Brooke. Sometimes, I wondered if I'd taken her innate goodness and support for granted. A person's most beautiful essence can be underappreciated until they're gone.

Days later, I sipped from a warm mug of morning brew while reading an early edition of the *Orange County Register*. My eyes shifted to the casita, where I discovered Brooke and Maria's bound and lifeless bodies. Could I ever sell the property that separated me from the two people I held most dear? It was an impossible consideration for now.

A person never plans such things, but I awoke one day longing to find someone to share even a moment of life's ordinary pleasures. Someone who might smile at the beauty of a fragrant rose or a pelican gliding over crashing waves. That pang for companionship prompted my call to Melissa Taylor, the friendly woman from the gun show's parking lot.

Melissa assumed I'd never call based on my lukewarm response to her introduction. She was stunned to learn about my background and why I was no longer married. She said she'd closely followed the news reports of the murders and couldn't imagine my agony. Her reaction was consoling. She sounded deeply compassionate, and we agreed to meet at the Coffee and Bait shop on the Redondo Beach pier, splitting the distance between our homes in North Tustin and Santa Monica.

She approached, and I beamed. "Hello again, Melissa. You're right on time. I thought the traffic might delay you." I motioned toward a small round table.

"I planned for it, so no surprises." She muted her phone and placed it and her Native American embroidered purse.

"Thanks for meeting with me."

"Hey, it was originally *my* idea. But admittedly, after four weeks,

I'd given up. Then your phone call. And here we are." She removed her sunglasses. "Jamie, I want to reiterate I'm so sorry you lost your wife and mother." She shook her head with a pained expression. "And before that, your poor father." She'd done her homework.

"I appreciate that. We never really know what tomorrow will bring." The words instantly sounded stupid—in their worst nightmare, no one would ever consider the possibility that loved ones might get murdered at home by cartel assassins.

She sensed my self-judgment. "Guess what?" Her tone ensured surprise. "You've met my father. He presented you a medal for valor."

Recalling my most recent medal-pinning ceremonies—the Silver Star in 2016 and the Purple Heart at Fort Benning in 2018—the answer turned obvious. "Unbelievable. You're not just a Taylor, but *General* Taylor's daughter." I laughed. "What were the odds of that?"

"They were low! Yet here I am, sitting across from a true hero on a pier in Redondo Beach." She grinned and shook her head. "Dad says I have to do this." She stood and quickly saluted.

"I just did my job. They gave me a medal. Tell General Taylor thanks. I'm humbled." Her smile appeared permanently affixed. "You saluted precisely. The general taught you well."

"It was an inevitability in our family. Generations of officers. But this girl decided against a life in the military. Instead, I went to the University of Texas in Austin and partied."

"As an Army brat, you knew what the lifestyle entailed. I was clueless, though I'd settled on attending West Point and serving the country when I was thirteen. It was fulfilling—well, most of it."

She lowered her sweating glass of ice water. "You might not want to hear this, but thank you for your service. Tired of my hero worship?"

I laughed. "Just a little bit." A server dropped menus on our table, telling us she'd return momentarily. As she stepped away, my muted phone vibrated the table. I disregarded the highlighted screen for five seconds, but my gut said check the caller.

"I'm so sorry, Melissa. Do you mind?" I raised the phone, then rudely answered without waiting for her reply. "Agent Washington," I said while stepping to a wooden rail overlooking the ocean.

"Yes, Mr. Morales, I wanted to inform you of news hitting the airwaves and internet soon. There was a firefight at one of Delgado's haciendas this morning. Two Mexican Marines lost their lives. Delgado escaped again. Extremely disappointing. Keeping you in the loop. I need to go." The line went dead.

Any prospects for a nice afternoon with Melissa were ruined. Every agonizing emotion and memory from the day I lost Brooke and Mom invaded my psyche. Hopes for justice darkened, triggering light chest palpitations.

She touched my shoulder. "Jamie, you look troubled. Is there anything I can do?"

"I just received news that I need to process." My goodbye hug was stronger than intended. She appeared confused and hesitant. I pressed my palm to her cheek and tried to smile, but I couldn't. Then I grabbed my wallet and tossed a twenty onto the table. "I'm so sorry, Melissa."

"It's okay. Please take care of yourself, Jamie."

The traffic on I-405 moved at a snail's pace, but the gridlock was welcoming. Clarifying. Sometimes futures change in the blink of an eye, like after the execution of loved ones. Or after a call from the DEA.

Taking a short detour, I visited Brooke and Mom's mausoleum. Despite the agonizing event that delivered them here, it was a peaceful and soothing place to reflect. Very different thoughts eventually dominated my psyche. Feeling conflicted by having violated my promise, I whispered, "Forgive me, Brooke, I don't see any other way to get this done."

CHAPTER 21

I took a hiatus from my USC MBA studies. Any hesitations were pointless delays. The mission felt inevitable and imperative. Frustrated by the FBI and DEA's lack of progress, it was time to literally and metaphorically lock and load.

Most people would consider my plan flawed and impossible. Most of my Green Beret brothers would disagree with those naysayers; nothing derails a soldier and his mission when intentions are good and the enemy depraved.

A year removed from live battle, with surely diminished skills, I would need to retrain myself mentally and physically. The weapon I'd always been most comfortable with, the M4A1 carbine used by the Army, would play a crucial role in achieving my goal: capturing Marco Delgado and returning him to US authorities. I wanted the drug lord incarcerated for life but wouldn't hesitate to kill the despicable human if circumstances required it.

Arriving at a forty-acre avocado farm in Temecula, I embraced retired Major Jack Kershaw, a fellow Green Beret. We'd served together during my second tour in Afghanistan. He had a hole in his left ear and was missing half of his right pinky, injuries sustained during an intense battle with the Taliban.

Our eyes glistened, unspoken acknowledgment of battlefield

memories and the recent murders of a cherished wife and mother. We walked arms-over-shoulders toward the porch, comforted by a friendship forged through hellish events most citizens could never understand. Jack's wife, Erin, stepped through a screen door holding a tray of drinks and snacks. She set the pitcher and glasses on a table and embraced me, wordlessly expressing her condolences. All our eyes were teary.

Jack was his typically direct self when asking what prompted my request to spend a couple of days emptying M4 magazines inside Erin's shooting range. "You asked me not to question you. I'm not an idiot. You're going after Delgado."

"I just asked for time in the range, Jack. You obliged. But if you're uncomfortable with any of this, just say the word. I'll find another place to shoot. My challenge is the DEA is tailing me, and I need to keep things under wraps. Erin told me her range is soundproofed."

"It is. Our neighbors got annoyed with her nighttime training. And I've been known to spray a few bullets inside myself." He rubbed his nose with the remaining half of his pinky. "Buddy, this is *not* a good idea. Just let the DEA do its job. That asshole Delgado could have fifty lieutenants protecting him. It's a death trap." His weathered face stared at me. "I promised Erin I wouldn't get involved. She's memorized too many close calls from our tours. So it's a bad idea, *and* I can't participate."

"Erin's advice is always better than mine. I had zero intention of bringing you along, soldier." Jack had earned his second career as a farmer. It was easy to determine which ex-soldiers should never reenter battle zones. Jack was right where he needed to be—growing guacamole fruit in Temecula.

The plan was to defy the odds and operate solo, bringing a notorious drug lord to his knees. Something the DEA, FBI, and Mexican Marines apparently couldn't do. Only I would die if the mission failed—and those odds were good. If I got shot at, I guess some really bad people could also die. Either way, this had always been *my* mission, odds be damned.

Erin was a member of the International Shooting Sport Federation and had nearly shot her way into the 2020 Olympics, missing qualification for the 50-meter rifle three-position shooting team by one place. Honing her .22 caliber rifle skills in a range nestled among the couple's acres of avocado orchards, she hoped to realize her dream of representing the US and medaling at the 2024 Olympic Games in Paris.

After dinner, Erin and I entered her range. She fired ten rounds from each of three positions—standing, prone, and kneeling—and laid waste to red bullseyes. I mentioned I could never shoot that well. Pulling out my M4 carbine and staring down a new target with my only eye, I snapped off fifteen rounds. Erin stood frozen with her eyes wide. I reloaded.

"No way," she said with an expression of amazement. "*Are you kidding me?*" She bit her upper lip and shook her head. "With *one* eye? No strain? No flinching?"

"I've been practicing in the desert."

"I've never seen anyone shoot like that with a military rifle."

"I have. Your husband shot like that in Afghanistan. Including the day he lost part of an ear and finger." I regretted the graphic comment, but she didn't blink. "He saved lives during a hellish firefight, Erin. If he's never told you that, I'm glad I just did. I've fought with some real heroes in my life. Jack is one of them."

"Thank you. He never mentioned it." She walked over and put her hand on my arm. "If you can already shoot like that, why drive all this way to practice?"

I opened a duffel and tossed nine high-capacity magazines onto a table, ammunition for my Beretta M9 pistol and the M4A1 I'd just unleashed. "More is always better. I need practice swapping mags and weapons quickly." She watched me reach into a second duffel. "Including this." She stared uneasily at an M249 Squad Automatic Weapon, a bipod machine gun nicknamed the SAW, and ammo belts hinged with the same caliber rounds as my M4. "These belts can link together and fire 750 rounds per minute."

"Oh, Jamie." She paused to choose the right words. "Please don't do this. Please don't die."

Her face strained as she waited for me to change my mind. I said nothing and hugged her. "Time to play Army man again. It's probably best you head inside now. I'm sorry this is unsettling, but thanks for giving me a place off the beaten path to prep."

"I'm so concerned," she said. I squeezed her shoulder.

Minutes after Erin stepped away, hay bales were stacked at one end of the range. I holstered the Beretta, grabbed the M4, and turned off the lights. I adjusted the night vision goggles before firing dozens of rounds from both weapons at various targets. Lying in a prone position, I adjusted the SAW's bipod and unleashed a torrent of bullets.

When finished, I packed the duffel bags and set them in a garden shed. Stepping onto the home's front porch and scanning the brilliant sky, I relished the calm and quiet. On the ceiling near a recessed light, a large green praying mantis waited patiently for a moth to land within reach of its jagged claws. Moments later, I reached for a peeling section of green paint from a wood post and studied it, blocking out thoughts of what was to come.

Go time was imminent.

CHAPTER 22

The three of us shared early morning coffee. The soothing aroma reminded me of mornings with Brooke and Mom. Jack drank from a green mug with black lettering that read: *Smart, One-eared, Good-Looking—Sounds like a Green Beret.* "That's me." He pointed at the mug. "I'm one-eared. Plus those other things."

"And I'm a one-eyed man."

"True enough. But only one of us is that other special thing."

"You're dumb as a rock, so I'm guessing you mean handsome?"

Our collective half-smiles and mundane conversations slowly led to confronting the elephant in the room. I informed them I'd be driving to Twentynine Palms to meet with a Marine Corps Lieutenant Colonel I met in Iraq. "And tomorrow, I also hoped to leave my car here for at least several days."

"Come on, Jamie," Jack said with annoyance. "What you're planning is tantamount to suicide. And guess what? There's been a sedan parked across the street from our driveway since you arrived. You know that, right? DEA, I'm assuming?"

"Probably."

"If we quickly smoked out your intentions, so can the CIA, FBI, YMCA, or Boys & Girls Club. It's shockingly obvious what you're up to." We set our mugs down. "You get that, right?"

"I told the DEA I'd stay put and let US and Mexican authorities do their jobs. They failed three times. It's as if someone's tipping him off. Or it could be DEA incompetence. Whatever the reason, I'm forcing the issue. The DEA Special Agent in Charge questions whether I'll go after Delgado myself. But he also believes I'm too smart to actually try it. Surprise."

Jack appeared annoyed and baffled. "If maverick cowboy bullshit is your game plan, you're doomed." He glanced at his wife. "Erin told me about your cache of weapons. *You are just one man, damnit!* Against who knows how many. He killed your wife, mother, and father. I want him dead, too."

"I don't want him dead. I want revenge in the form of justice. Incarceration in the US."

"That's your plan?" He shot back with a louder, more anxious tone. "You think they'll let you take him out of Mexico? Please, you're smarter than that."

Erin calmly interrupted, "Jamie, it's this simple: As I said last night, we don't want you killed. Especially by the man who's destroyed your family. Who happens to be the most dangerous drug lord in Mexico. You aren't thinking this through." She moved forward and tenderly set her hand on my forearm. "Our intuitions are dark. This might not end well."

"Seriously, I appreciate your concern." Stepping through the dusty sliding glass door, I stared out at a property lined with avocado trees, a stable holding Appaloosas, and a flower garden bustling with mockingbirds and bees. Brooke would have appreciated the scene.

"Delgado is as overconfident as you two are lacking confidence. His compound is surrounded by cement and masonry walls topped by chain-link. Past the wall, his property is a make-believe safari land: giraffes, large cats, zebras, and such. It isn't protected by sophisticated technology—just meat eaters and narcos brandishing AK-47s. His arrogance will enable my breach."

"So you're going to scale the wall, cut the fencing, trek up to the hacienda, dodge the tigers, grab Delgado, and drive away? Please tell me that's not your plan."

"Come on, Jack. You know the routine." My hosts remained silent. "The element of surprise wins wars. These drug thugs shoot their enemies in the back. Or unarmed strangers for sport. They're cowards. Woefully unprepared for someone like me. I think you know what I mean."

"Of course I do. But it's also a numbers game. I repeat, you're just *one* man." He sighed and glanced at Erin in frustration. "Jamie, I can't keep lecturing you. I'm getting nowhere. You're clearly fully committed." He peered into my brown eye. "We tried to change your mind. It didn't work. There's no use standing in your way. Tell us what you need."

I grew skeptical of his sudden change of heart, but I had too much to do. "The Marine lieutenant colonel I mentioned will transfer munitions to my car. He's the same guy who got me the SAW and M4. I'll be back this afternoon to enjoy Erin's world-class chili. I'll sneak off your property tonight. Leave my car parked where it is until I return."

"Who's picking you up from here? And are you going straight to Delgado's compound?"

"That's only revealed on a need-to-know basis," I said. Jack appeared annoyed and didn't respond. "You've been generous. Thanks for the two days of cover. I'm bringing an untraceable burner. Commercial phones are too easy to trace. If you get a call from an unknown number, please pick it up. Will that work?"

"Of course."

"You're good people. Brooke always . . ." I inhaled deeply and grabbed my keys from the countertop. "There are bullets and such waiting for me. Ciao."

The ammo transfer happened in a secluded section of Twentynine Palms Marine Base. As he had one week earlier, Marine Lieutenant Colonel Brookings urged me to let him recommend two or three men for what he considered a justifiable but low-odds-of-success mission. The officer understood this could be the last time he'd see Captain Jamie Morales alive.

Arriving back at Jack and Erin's at five thirty, I parked near an obscured carport and transferred everything for my mission into duffels. Each bag weighed about one hundred twenty pounds, but shoulder straps made it easy to lug the weight.

Erin's chili was as good as Jack advertised. She shoved a copy of the recipe into my pocket, insisting it would bring me good luck. The spicy treat included copious amounts of spicy red, green, and yellow peppers. Mom would have approved.

As the time approached for my stealthy departure from US soil, Jack said, "We'll be waiting for you." Erin forced a smile.

I rubbed my neck and forearm before adjusting my eyepatch. "Seriously, don't worry about me. I have zero intention of getting whacked." Such words were ludicrous machismo from an outwardly upbeat soldier needing to assuage good friends' fears of plausible doom. But I had grown weary of discussing their concerns. Further debate was pointless. I knew Jack would probably tell Erin later that he had no idea whether I would survive my pursuit of Marco Delgado.

Forty minutes later, under eerily dark skies, I waited between two avocado trees in the grove's last row, sixteen feet from the quiet intersection of Landry Street and Dorinda Drive. Water trickled from irrigation lines, liquid gold to any farmer in the arid state. A mass of insects swarmed around a bright yellow porch light on a home down the street.

Two headlights swept around a street corner and headed toward me at about twenty miles an hour. A 1980 Jeep slowed to a stop. The driver rolled down a window and flicked her chin toward the back. I tossed three duffels into the compartment and hopped inside.

"It's great to see you, Jamie. I saw the DEA sedan on the other side of the block. No issues."

"Good work. Thanks for stepping up tonight." I squeezed her arm.

"Of course. And like I said on the phone, I'm heartbroken about Brooklyn. She always treated me like family. And your mom . . . I can't imagine the anguish."

"Thanks. It was nightmarish. Still is. A chill that'll never go away." We stared ahead in silent reflection.

Minutes later, southbound on I-15 toward San Diego, Sylvia said, "Hey, plans have changed a little. The plane and pilot I'd negotiated to fly you to Culiacán aren't available. Instead, you'll get shuttled aboard a twin-engine Piper Seneca that flies businessmen in and out twice a week. No flags will be raised."

"That's a problem. Surprises have a way of adding up, wreaking unexpected havoc. You know that from your time in the deserts."

"I do. But relax; I've vetted this crew well. It's my fiancé and his brother."

"*Damnit.* Are you serious? Unacceptable. And just as things are heating up."

"Settle down. My fiancé is not only a pilot but ex-Army special forces. Rick Bonham, from Oklahoma." She smiled and winked.

"The last time we spoke, you said you were engaged to a *sailor.*"

"That was Brian from Hawaii. He *was* my fiancé nine months ago."

"You messing with me? This a joke?"

"No joke. Rick's my *new* fiancé."

"Then this is your third engagement in three years?"

"Impressive, right?" She grinned.

"I don't know how to answer that." Thirty seconds passed. "This mission is fraught with crazy risks, Sylvia. I can trust these brothers to get me and my gear to Mexico undetected?"

"Absolutely. Rick's as solid as they come. Distinguished service. Two bronze stars. More than worthy. Direct and honest. Reminds me of you."

"And his brother?"

"Solid. Runs in the family."

"Fair enough," I replied. "Is the plane in a private hangar or public tiedown?"

"Private hanger."

"Operated by who? Or who owns it?"

"It doesn't matter. You needed a covert flight to Culiacán, and I delivered. Rick and his brother are qualified to fly—they have a combined seven thousand hours of flight time."

"Flying what and for who? That's a lot of hours."

"Please, Jamie. Relax."

"It just seems odd you coincidentally have a friend who can fly me undetected and spur of the moment into Culiacán Airport."

"I'm resourceful. You're fortunate."

"And Brian, I mean Rick—I can't keep track of your lovers—or his brother will fly me and hopefully a drug lord back to San Diego?" That's assuming I don't get shot, do somehow abduct Delgado, and then navigate a path back to the airport undetected.

"He will, or I will."

"Will what?" Swiveling quickly to the left, we locked gazes. "*Sylvia!* I sensed something wasn't quite right. That is *not* going to happen. You're *not* getting on this plane. This is bullshit."

She turned away and focused on the road. "Rick's my very accomplished fiancé. There's no reason for me not to join him. So we're officially a team. Neither of us is a risk to your mission. Quite the contrary. We're enabling success."

"This is a solitary mission. At least, it was supposed to be. I didn't ask for your help. Nor your fiancé's. Nor anyone else's. I just needed a ride to the airport. I can achieve my objective alone."

"That's tough-guy crap. No one I spoke with agrees with you."

"*Enough!*" I shook my head with furrowed brows. "So who else knows about this? Or is in on this?"

"Jack Kershaw, Erin, my guy Rick, his brother, Marine Lieutenant Colonel Brookings—"

"*Brookings?* You know him? What the hell? I'm *not* happy, Sylvia."

"Get real. We weren't going to let you die alone. You need support."

"I should have known. You're wired to engage, not to lay back.

But you *committed* to not inserting yourself. To stay on the sidelines." I sounded too hostile and dialed it back. All of us ex-soldiers were an annoying bunch. Stubbornly strong-willed and absurdly loyal.

"Settle down, please. We're here to help. We care about you."

This is why Band of Brothers is such a revered term. Because there's no tighter fraternity than those who battle together. Sylvia and I experienced some crazy shit in Afghanistan. Events that bound us together permanently.

We reached the Landmark Aviation hangar adjoining San Diego International Airport. Two jets and the twin-engine Piper Seneca they'd be flying were parked inside.

"Jack told me you were bringing burner phones, so Rick and I did the same. We left our traceable phones at home. I borrowed this Jeep for two weeks. The owner's in Europe."

A thick blanket of fog moved in, obscuring the shoreline and airport. We lugged our oversized duffel bags into the hangar, which now contained enough firepower to start a war. Sylvia set her bag next to the plane's cargo bay.

Rick and his brother stepped from the shadows and introduced themselves. Rick kissed Sylvia and offered to haul her supplies aboard. She stared him down as if he were delusional, emphasizing it weighed a mere seventy pounds. Then she hoisted it aboard.

The clock was ticking.

CHAPTER 23

Rick's brother, Ted, flew left seat in the cockpit. Rick copiloted. The Seneca lifted off Runway 27 and veered south. At its 300-knot cruising speed, the brothers expected to reach Culiacán Airport in about three hours.

Ten minutes into the flight, Sylvia approached me with an empty plastic tray. Her body movements resembled those of sexy women donning fashionable gloves in 1950s commercials. "Good evening, fine gentleman. Might I offer you cigars or cigarettes? Or an ounce or two of our finest?" I'd missed Sylvia's mischievousness, which often complemented my sense of humor.

Rick left the cockpit and approached us. "A drink sounds wonderful, classy madame." He sat facing me and reclined his tall frame.

"Why don't you and Jamie get to know each other," she said.

"Sylvia informed me about your wife and mother, Captain Morales. Horribly tragic. I don't know what else to say beyond I'm sorry."

"Thanks, Rick. I appreciate that. Please, call me Jamie." I suddenly liked both siblings a touch more. "Sylvia tells me you're a pilot like your brother. It runs in the family."

"It does indeed. Our father flew F-4 Phantoms in Nam. He taught us both to fly at an early age. My brother's flown a wider range of aircraft than me, but I guess I've . . ." He paused as if he didn't know what to say. "I've been involved in more crazy adventures."

"Do tell."

Sylvia stepped forward with drinks, handing us both whiskey sours. "I've told the siblings you don't like surprises. They know you weren't keen on learning we'd inserted ourselves into your mission. But they're honored to be here, Jamie. You need to appreciate that."

I leaned forward in my seat. "I don't even know you guys. Yet one of you is flying me to Mexico. And you're willing to risk your lives—according to Sylvia—on a mission you know nothing about. I'm sure you can appreciate my apprehensions." I stared at Sylvia. "Rick was telling me he's an adventurer. I'm all ears."

"Then listen up," Sylvia said. "He's collaborated with mercenaries on several continents. The CIA and US militaries on top-secret missions. Fought alongside rebels committed to democracy. Performed counterespionage. There you go."

A large swallow of whiskey sour channeled down my throat. After staring out a window for seconds, I turned to Rick. "Look, I'm still uncomfortable. Did Sylvia describe the dangers of what I intend to do? The risks are extreme. When you drop me off in Mexico, perhaps you should turn around and go home."

"That's ridiculous," Sylvia snapped back. "Rick and I aren't going anywhere. Don't be a dumbass."

"Sylvia, please. People are very likely to die. Delgado and his lieutenants have stolen everything important to me—with zero remorse. Delgado, his sicarios, or I could all die." I stared into both of their faces as earnestly as possible. "So could anyone tagging along."

"Well, too damn bad, Jamie."

"Sylvia, come on." Her obstinance lay somewhere between annoying and infuriating.

"We're going to help you get Delgado. And we're going to keep you alive. That's what I promised Brooklyn."

"What?"

"Two days ago, Jack and Erin Kershaw called me. Since then, I've tried to touch Brooklyn's spirit. To let her know you've got company. We couldn't prevent your stubborn ass from going to Mexico, but Rick, you, and I are completing this journey side-by-side. Get over any hang-ups. You've got company."

Rick sipped his whiskey and pressed back in his seat. Without being spoken to, he said, "We can help you, Jamie. You should acquiesce. Even if you don't, you won't be able to shake Sylvia. And if she goes, I go."

Sylvia said, "You need help to pull this off."

I put both hands on her shoulders. "Dealing with Brooke and Maria's deaths has been excruciating. I just want to capture my target and return him to the States. Losing you along the way would crush me."

"None of us are dying. We'll help you get Delgado. Just lead the way."

Glancing to the right, I watched cockpit instruments spin, tilt, and flash numbers while deliberating. "Okay, then, we're a squad. And thank you."

Sylvia beamed.

CHAPTER 24

THE UNMISTAKABLE SMELLS OF AN EARLIER DOWNPOUR complemented the still shimmering tarmac reflecting a brilliant moon. We stepped across the airport while Ted refueled the Piper Seneca. Minutes later, red and green wingtip lights blinked as the plane lifted off for its return to San Diego.

We loaded five duffels into a blue VW taxi van, heading straight for the Airbnb *casa de pueblo* I'd reserved using a fake identity. The cabbie was handed a thirty-dollar tip, to which the silver-haired gentleman with etched lines on his face remarked, "God bless you, Señor. And welcome home."

It wasn't my home anymore in the traditional sense, but I was proud of my heritage and appreciated the greeting. Despite the horrors inflicted by Delgado and his sicarios, it soothed me to be among the decent, hard-working people Maria described and raised me to respect.

La Buena Familia weighed heavily on the psyches and souls of millions nationwide. I fantasized about rallying citizens to deliver a threatening message to *el patrón* and his lieutenants: *Justice has ridden into town. Born in Mexico and raised on American soil, he's here to end your reign, Delgado. God will one day hold you accountable. Until then, Jamie Morales will.*

Upon arrival, I met with the property manager and overpaid in pesos for a three-night stay. We shared glances while presenting forged documents reflecting citizenship in three English-speaking countries. We all carried cash for unexpected necessities. I carried considerably more than Rick and Sylvia.

"That's a lot of money. Hoping to impress a beautiful señorita?" She immediately chastised herself and apologized profusely.

Gently squeezing her arm, I said, "It's fine."

After settling in our rooms, we gathered to assess weaponry. When Sylvia opened her duffel, I grew impressed and unsettled—she'd correctly anticipated fierce fighting, which meant she understood the strength of our enemy. *Please get them home safely*, I silently implored.

Sylvia pulled two SIG Sauer M11 pistols from her suitcase, weapons she carried as an Army Black Hawk pilot in the Middle East. She'd also packed a dozen fifteen-round magazines filled with 9mm ammo. "By the way, I'm now a better shot than Rick, and he's damn good."

"That true?" I asked Rick with a doubtful smile.

"If Sylvia can shoot better than me, then I'm the better whirlybird pilot."

"Cocky male insecurities," she replied. "It's okay for my fiancé to be a damn good shot, but not for me to be better? And I have no problem admitting he's a good fixed-wing pilot, but he'd kill himself trying to fly a Black Hawk. Copters take special skills to pilot. Airplanes are easy—pull back on the controls, and up you go." She lifted her brows. "Agreed?"

"Sorry, Rick, I think she might be right about that."

Rick put Sylvia in a headlock and kissed the top of her short bob.

"I'm a man of the times, baby. A big advocate for women's rights. Willing to acknowledge you can kick my ass at certain things—like flying the whirlybirds." He kissed her again. "Feel better now?"

"I do, very much so. Though you strategically failed to mention my shooting skills are superior."

"That's because that's a pipedream. Let's move on."

She pulled out an M320 grenade launcher, which prompted my nod. "And that little M320 mounts onto this beast." She also pulled an M4 carbine from the suitcase—thirty-three inches long and about nine pounds—with a 30-round box magazine of 5.56mm bullets inserted. She revealed eight additional magazines.

Reaching deeper into the shoulder-strapped cotton bag, she tossed more battle implements onto the bed. "Night vision goggles, knife, extra grenades, ropes—and more. Let's hope most of this stuff won't be needed." She scanned the men's faces.

Her comment struck a nerve, and expressions grew more serious. "Okay, Rick, show us what you brought."

Opening his duffel, Rick tossed two AK-47s onto the bed. It surprised me.

"My old man said American soldiers died unnecessarily in Nam because their M-16s jammed. These Russian things didn't. I've been shooting them for fifteen years—sport and covert ops." He tossed six hundred-round drum magazines for the AKs onto the comforter. Next, he pulled out a Beretta M9 sidearm. "Plus eight 15-round mags for the Beretta. And goggles, knife, rope, a suppressor."

"Communication will be key," Rick said while tossing two PNR 500 systems to Sylvia and me. The units would enable assigned channels for communications. We'd clip wireless mics to our vests.

"You assembled this in two days?" I said while inspecting the equipment. "We used PNR 500s in Syria three years ago. Huge fan."

Rick continued, "Time sync and GPS will be critical." He pulled watches from a side pouch and tossed them to us. "Garmin TACTIX GPS. We can program these using our intel or after we surveil Delgado's property."

"We can set the coordinates tonight," I said. Days earlier, I'd called in favors from Army contacts. They sent me infrared aerial photos of Delgado's jungle-themed compound. We studied maps showing our route through poppy-covered mountains. One chart I shared prompted the couple to glance at each other. "Those infrared images circled in red are Delgado's men. At the very least, assume they'll carry their signature AKs."

"Narcos don't know how to use AKs like I do," Rick said. He stared at my aerial photos and performed a quick count. "Eleven bodies. Were you able to get the same images taken on different nights?"

"Good question, and no, I wasn't. Therein lies the big unknown. Eleven men could've been a light night. There may have been twenty the next day. Let's assume more will be scattered throughout the hacienda—the place is massive."

We studied magnified printouts. "These images circled in blue are not human. Most are small. Others are clearly larger than people. Giraffes, rhinos, tigers, or lions. Of course, they present challenges. If we shoot on our approach, Delgado will know we're here. If we don't shoot them, we might get eaten." Rick didn't react. Sylvia chuckled.

"Calm down," Sylvia said after Rick commented he was tired of her dismissive jokes. "Lions? Tigers? Make-believe jungles? Rich people do the strangest things." She asked, "How do you know Delgado's there?"

"I've pulled in more favors. Based on that intel, I'm ninety percent sure Delgado arrived on the property two days ago. Nothing's certain—he moves around often. His average stay at this location has been six days, looking back twenty months." I peered into questioning eyes. "I think the magnitude of their response will tell us whether he's on-site. I wish I could say something more certain."

Rick glanced at his watch, Sylvia, then me. "And tomorrow we're driving to the mountains for a recon of Delgado's property and compound?"

"That's the plan," I said. "I'll buy or rent transportation."

"It all gets very real in two days," Sylvia said. "But right now, I'm famished. How about you guys?"

We agreed a good meal was in order. Friendly neighbors outside our condo recommended Cabanna, a seafood fusion restaurant they raved about. Locals always have the best suggestions. The atmosphere was upbeat, and the food was incredible. We paid the bill and traveled back to our Airbnb.

Upon our return, few words were spoken. My room stood at the end of a hall on the first floor, below a spiral staircase ascending to Sylvia and Rick's loft. Thirty minutes later, the sounds of lovemaking drifted downstairs. Inevitably, thoughts of Brooke filled my head.

CHAPTER 25

Shadows stretched across the landscape as the sun rose above cloudless skies. We shared coffee, nibbled on rolled tortilla snacks called Takis, and shared strategies for our siege on Delgado's compound scheduled for the next day. I presented my original blueprint: apprehend Delgado, escape in an acquired vehicle, and disappear into the countryside for an unspecified period. I suggested we stick to the initial plan and improvise based on cartel and government responses. Rick and Sylvia listened to me with increasingly strained expressions.

Sylvia rubbed the side of her head with dark violet fingernails that needed fresh paint. "Or we kill Delgado, escape to the airport, and fly north. Simple and effective if we do it right."

"You keep saying that, Sylvia. You know I want to take him alive."

"Yes, you and I disagree." She shook her head, appearing disgusted. "You're suggesting we grab him, hide until things cool down, and *then* beeline for the airport?"

"You should've said something earlier," Rick said. "My brother's expecting a call for a rendezvous time. He's planning to fly us home."

"You two showed up at the last moment. I don't know your brother. The more people aware of the mission, the bigger the risk of failure." Their faces told me they continued to question my judgment. "I'm saying we grab him and hunker down in a remote location between here and

Texas. Everyone will assume we set up air transportation to escape. La Buena Familia heavies will flood the airports. Instead, we lie low and choose a covert route home."

Rick remained skeptical. His brows formed into jagged intensity after drawing his head and shoulders back. "I'm not on board. Hanging around Mexico with a drug lord sounds half-baked. Let's get the sonofabitch, flee, and contact my brother to get us the hell out. He's got access to multiple battle-worthy private aircraft."

"You know better than that!" Sylvia snapped. "He's right. Whether we kill or kidnap Delgado—I still vote for kill because that prick doesn't deserve to live—every airport and road in Mexico will be policed. And it'll happen quickly."

"I get it," Rick glared. "But you also expected a quick exit—right? This isn't my first rodeo, and I'm not an idiot. But . . ."

"But what?" she snapped.

"Sylvia, he's worried about you."

A stretch of silence passed. "Look, babe, you and I are comfortable with quick strikes. We're best at *gun-and-run*. A protracted exit from Mexico is high risk. The cartels and militaries have access to big-time resources. Bad things can happen to . . ." he glanced at Sylvia and whispered, ". . . to any of us."

"Oh my God. Get real. You sound like you've never done this before. Or like I haven't. You know as well as anyone—missions have variables." She turned to me. "Do you have a town in mind for us to lay low in?"

"Creel. It's small, remote, and quiet—about five thousand residents. I'll blend in because I was Mexican before I was American." I turned to Rick. "You're concerned about Sylvia. I admire that. There's still time to disengage. No hard feelings."

Rick studied Sylvia. "She'd just continue on her own."

"Of course I would," she replied. "This man who's lost everything—his father, mother, and wife—will pursue Delgado with or without us. I love you, Rick, but I'm not backing out."

My eye darted between them, awaiting a thumbs-up or down.

"Let's keep her alive—we haven't gotten married yet. Trekking through Mexico with Delgado doesn't thrill me. But you're right; most people will assume we hightailed it for the border. Hiding out for a while makes some sense."

Did Rick know he was Sylvia's third fiancé in three years? Some intel wasn't meant to be shared. But also, why should I care who she's engaged to?

Moving casually to a sofa and reaching for my burner, which lay upside down and mostly covered by a cushion, I glanced at the screen. "*Crap.* Jack Kershaw called fifteen minutes ago. The volume was turned off."

"How did you graduate top of your class at West Point?" Sylvia shook her head. "So call him back."

"I stared at her as if to emphasize, *of course.*" As I dialed, I said, "By the way, I graduated fifth in my class."

"Hey. Is everything okay?" Jack asked. "Why didn't you answer?"

"Phone was silenced."

"Kind of defeats the purpose of me having your number if you don't answer, right?"

I replied annoyingly, "Maybe you should have tried *Sylvia's* phone. She's right beside me. Would you like to talk to her?"

"Well, that cat's out of the bag. When did she fill you in? Just before takeoff? Wait, don't tell me. And don't be pissed. You need their help."

"No worries. The three of us are aligned. But you should have told me what you were doing behind my back in Temecula."

"Fair comment. But you would have pushed back and considered putting a hole through my other ear."

"I'll do that later."

"There was no way in hell I'd let you go after Delgado alone. Sylvia was 'all in' before I even finished explaining the mission. And I checked out Rick's background through guys he served with—he's got a stellar reputation. Not sure she told you yet, but they're engaged."

"She did. Anyway, why did you call?"

"The DEA knows you're no longer here. Because you disappeared for a day, they put two and two together. Paid Erin and me a visit and didn't buy our claims of ignorance. Placed me in their sedan—I'm assuming he wanted to intimidate me." We both smiled into our phones. *Like that would work.* "I played stupid. 'Jamie and I are friends. He just stopped by for a visit. No idea where he is or how he left.'"

"Kudos to the men with black letters reading DEA for realizing I'd slipped them. Sorry you're left to deal with this, Jack. My plan is—"

"*Surprise! I bugged the agents' car!* With a tiny mic glued to the front passenger seat. They talked business nonstop on their way back to LA. They're storming Delgado's compound the day after tomorrow." I let the information settle. "Hang back so the DEA and whoever they're aligned with can have another crack at him."

Yes, I was impressed by Jack's wiretapping of a DEA car. But there'd be no halting this mission. Instead, my resolve strengthened, and I accelerated the timeline to invade Delgado's compound. I'd lost confidence in the DEA. Three warriors were already in Mexico. It was time to grab a cartel boss. "I need to go. Give my love to Erin. The three of us will see you soon."

"De Oppresso Liber. Please be safe, soldier."

"Not to worry. I'm looking forward to more of Erin's chili. Next time we speak, I hope to be returning to Los Estados Unidos with an infamous criminal." After hanging up, I hoped it wasn't my last conversation with Jack Kershaw.

Rick and Sylvia stared at me wide-eyed, needing an update. "We've got a bit of a problem, but I've got a solution." As usual, Sylvia looked excited. "The DEA's planning to go after Delgado tomorrow night."

Rick replied immediately, "Their resources far exceed ours. DEA won't take kindly to us interfering with a US government mission. We need to stand down. The fourth time might be the charm."

Sylvia exploded. "Come on, Rick! Stop acting like you don't want to do this. You're injecting bad karma. If you want to bail, then—"

"Stop," he said. "We have new information. *Game-changing* information."

"Rick's right, Sylvia. You two should reassess. I'm not about to let the DEA eff things up again. I'll subvert their timeline and go after Delgado tonight. He's escaped three times just hours before coordinated assaults. Not this time."

"*Damn straight!*" Sylvia said with a raised and clenched fist. "Let's succeed where our government keeps failing. Let's grab this underworld drug lord shithead."

Rick shook his head. "You're always so excited to put yourself in harm's way."

"And you're not?" she replied. "The one who's freed political prisoners from North Korean work camps. Been part of an expedition to cross the South Pole on foot. And smuggled weapons to rebels on the Crimean Peninsula? *I* put myself in harm's way?"

She was right, and Rick failed to suppress a snicker. "But I've never gotten *as excited* as you do." He growled as he grabbed Sylvia's arm and yanked her in for a bear hug. He turned to me. "Am I right? Doesn't she get a little *too* enthused?"

"You're asking me to take sides. I'll say this—there's an element of truth to your future husband's words. Your penchant for chaos borders on obsessive." My serious tone returned. "One last time. Jumping off this train is okay, guys. I meant what I said earlier."

"Enough with the silly MacArthur speeches. Please," Sylvia said. "And stop glancing at Rick when you discuss our options. I love my honey, but he has zero say in whether I stay. He knows that. He also knows what my decision is going to be. You two need to let this badass soldier chick do what she's damn good at doing. Deal?"

The debate was a waste of energy. "I don't think there's any way to talk her out of this, Rick."

Rick placed his palms on her cheeks and pressed his nose against hers. "Let's dethrone this narco king, babe." Then he turned to me. "I guess we're ready for battle."

With the issue settled, we reviewed the aerial images and maps of Delgado's animal kingdom. I shared my plan for infiltrating his lair.

After negotiating for a used Jeep Cherokee from a car lot on the edge of Culiacán, we loaded up our cache of weapons. Our battlefield senses grew sharp. Few words were spoken. Sylvia told me the opioid kingpin was a dead man walking if we ever captured him. I told her to relax.

CHAPTER 26

Driving from Culiacán to the mountains of southwestern Sinaloa State took less than three hours. Millions of swaying red poppies greeted us upon arrival. Beautiful flowers represent a trade that gets traffickers and addicts killed. According to the DEA, ninety-three percent of all heroin sold on American streets originates in Mexico, double the amount from 2010.

Field workers "tapped" the beautiful flora each harvest, slicing horizontally with machetes inches below the bulbs. Trucks moved the harvests to transitional structures camouflaged as residences and local businesses, where the opium solidified and oxidized for days. Next, workers scraped sticky white substances from their bulbs. La Buena Familia traffickers subsequently transported the opium paste to heavily guarded labs for processing into heroin powder.

But it wasn't all just about heroin. US authorities had aerial images of chemical labs dotting the Sinaloa poppy farms. It was sometimes more cost-effective to produce fentanyl in the vicinity of heroin production because security, transportation, and workers were in place. Despite US government crackdowns on Mexican imports of fentanyl from 2010 to 2020, six hundred thousand citizens of the United States died ingesting synthetic opioids manufactured south of the border and by America's infamous Sackler drug companies, the latter giving dark connotation to Made in America. Want to get high? Prefer heroin powder or fentanyl pills? Pick your poison.

"So I'm a fly-fishing guide taking you two American clients to uncrowded streams filled with trout."

Rick glanced at Sylvia and said, "Sounds like lame justification for two and a half gringos passing through heroin country, but you're in charge."

Sylvia hoisted two of the three forty-inch tubes containing fly rods I'd purchased. "Hey, rich Americans do nutty stuff—the entire world knows that. I agree with Jamie; it's a solid cover."

"You tend to agree with him on most things. Should I be jealous?"

Having gotten used to Rick's sense of humor over the previous two days, I smiled from the front seat. "Jealousy is a natural human emotion." I winked but quickly reminded myself a one-eyed wink from a one-eyed man must certainly lose its intended effect.

Two hours later, after the weather-beaten pavement transitioned to potholed dirt, our Jeep bottomed out in a large crevice. Then another. The supplies clanked heavily against the rear compartment—nearly two hundred pounds of munitions.

After the road leveled, no one spoke for ten minutes. We'd soon ditch the Jeep and begin hiking up a streambed toward our target, where ferocious animals and even deadlier traffickers roamed.

A white Toyota Land Cruiser appeared out of nowhere and sped in our direction over rough, dusty roads. It was an unfriendly approach. The M4s, SAW, and AK lay camouflaged below seats and under fishing gear. Rick and I concealed our Berettas inside our rear waistbands. Sylvia's Sig Sauer lay in the rear compartment. She slipped her serrated knife between her skin and jeans, its handle hidden by an untucked shirt. We understood firing shots was a last resort. It would announce our arrival and doom the mission. And possibly get us killed.

Three presumed Delgado disciples armed with La Buena Familia's signature Russian AK-47 machine guns sprung from the Toyota. They separated and approached us hurriedly from different angles. One gang member appeared jittery, his nose red and runny. "What the fuck do you think you're doing here?" the edgy man said to us in Spanish.

"I'm a fishing guide," I replied like a multigenerational local. "The trout fishing in these streams is excellent."

"Fuck you, hombre," the agitated man replied. "Nobody comes here to fish. I think you're here to steal poppies to make your own batch of smack."

Stay calm. "I've got an article in the car. It talks about the great fishing in these mountains. Uncrowded streams, native trout."

"Shut up, asshole. Show me your fishing gear."

Flicking my chin to the rear door, I carefully extended my hand. "May I?" After requesting permission to reach through the open door, the jumpy leader obliged. He aimed his AK-47 at my head and grinned. I slowly leaned into the SUV and pulled out the fly rods.

One of the armed men joked he was sure I'd be unable to produce any fishing gear. After the trio of traffickers sneered, one stared down Sylvia. A repulsive gaze. He moved beside her and pressed his gun barrel to her temple. After placing his phone in his back pocket, he reached down and violated her with his free hand.

"Get your damn hands off her," Rick said while rushing forward.

Scowling with crooked, discolored teeth, the anxious narco jabbed the barrel of his weapon into Rick's temple and said to his fellow traffickers. "I would have just killed him, but I want him to realize what's in store for this bitch. I need my fill of her. She's *fine*."

Because Rick knew very little Spanish, he turned to me. "What did he say?" I didn't answer.

The sicarios circled like vultures, screaming and aiming at our heads. Cursing and threatening, eager to empty twenty-round clips.

"*Calm down!*" I yelled, raising my arms. Glancing at Sylvia, I noticed a tear slide down the cheek of her impassive face. What tormented Rick and me was that one tear became many. But her expression remained stoic.

"Look at that; she's even more beautiful when she weeps. Don't worry, bitch, I'm going to take good care of you," said the ugly, infatuated, twitchy gunman. He disgustingly grabbed her a second time.

Meanwhile, one of the traffickers rummaged through the rear cargo space of the Jeep, tossing fishing supplies onto the dirt. He suddenly exploded. "I see the tip of a gun barrel underneath a tarp! *Let's waste them!*"

The man clutching Sylvia grabbed her arm to keep her close. He pointed his machine gun at Rick and me. "Kill them, but not this one. She wants me. I'm going to do her all night long," he said with grotesque anticipation, an eager nod, and the confidence of a serial rapist.

The fingers of Sylvia's shooting hand moved toward her waistband almost imperceptibly. Salty anguish continued to flow from vacant eyes. Quick as a rattlesnake, she pulled the ten-inch jagged knife from her jeans and thrust it into her assailant's chest, slicing into his heart. His fellow mules watched in a momentary stupor before raising their AK-47s. Bad decision. Rick and I had already reached for our tucked and obscured Berettas. We killed both with well-placed single shots to the head.

A phone rang from the back pocket of Sylvia's dead aggressor. "Delgado's men heard the gunfire," I said before picking up the phone and saying calmly in Spanish, "Just a couple of warning shots. Idiot Americans wanted to fly fish for trout."

The man on the other end laughed. "Well, now they can tell stories about their fishing holiday from hell in Mexico. Stay on the perimeter for two more hours, then check in with me. Kill the Americans if you get bored."

"Just might," I replied. "Adios."

Rick tried to console Sylvia as I hung up. "My God. That was terrifying." She maintained a confusingly unemotional stare.

I squeezed her arm as Rick embraced her. "What a nightmare."

She gazed into a strip of forest sloping upward toward Delgado's hacienda and animal compound. "I was just . . . caught off guard with how quickly it all went down. I should have anticipated. Should have responded when he first grabbed me."

"You're shaking. Hang back here while Jamie and I go after Delgado," Rick said.

She snapped, *"That isn't going to happen!"*

"Sylvia, please. Based on that first contact, these sick bastards would love to . . . hurt you." His voice grew strained. "We can do this without you."

She gently touched him. "I'm okay. Really. It just triggered a flashback." We could all hear light breezes whistling through tall pines. Comforting sounds totally disconnected from the moment. "I was held captive by Iraq's Republican Guard for three days on my first tour. Our

Black Hawk was shot down, and they threatened to rape me day and night. Their leader grabbed me just like that guy did. I cried because I felt transported. And paralyzed. I'm sorry."

"*Sorry for what?*" I said. "That's absurd. I can only imagine your fear and anxiety. Then and now." Her demeanor belied her tough-as-nails façade. "And yet you stayed in the Army. Kept flying Black Hawks. What a remarkable soldier. And amazing woman."

"Why didn't you ever tell me?" Rick said. "Or Jamie. Or your friends. This tears my heart out. And then this piece of shit . . ." He tipped his head toward her attacker while rubbing his hands up and down her arms. He used his thumbs to brush her thick, dark eyebrows. "You poor thing."

"It just felt better to lock it all away, to put it behind me. I guess it never goes away completely. Anyway, now you know the truth."

The words were so heartfelt that I felt I was breaching their intensely intimate moment. Then I reminded myself that the most challenging work still lay ahead. "Sorry, but it's time, guys. Difficult as it is, we need to march on."

Sylvia took a deep breath. "Hell yeah, we do. Justice for Brooklyn. Lead the way." She wiped crimson from her dagger onto the cream-colored shirt of the lifeless would-be rapist.

"Okay, then. Step one—let's hide these bodies and their Land Cruiser." The engaged couple appeared thankful for something else to focus on. "Check the gas level. If it's full, we've got a second getaway option."

We found the unnamed stream that would lead us to Delgado's hacienda and compound. Through darkening skies, a great horned owl drifted over our heads. We hadn't begun our primary assault, and three men were already dead. Missions like these never go according to plan.

But we were still alive.

CHAPTER 27

We stamped wet boot treads atop streambed boulders partially covered in moss. We each understood the quiet hike was only a fleeting pause bracketing two violent events. The first one resulted in the killings of three insidious men. The likelihood of more bloodshed inside Delgado's compound was impossible to expel from conscious thought.

I thought of loved ones lost. The burden of Brooklyn and Mom's unthinkable final moments often overwhelmed me. Nobody knew, no one could understand. The emotional pangs felt like physical pain. I wanted to rest amidst the babbling waters, ponder three decades of a life punctuated by extraordinary drama, and reflect on those I desperately missed. No time for that. Not today. If the stars aligned, I would soon confront my family's killer, overcome the urge to shoot him in the head, and ultimately topple his kingdom by delivering him for American justice.

Sylvia trudged behind me. What was she thinking? She'd never understand my reluctance to kill Delgado. She held no moral dilemma about ending his life and seemed eager to make that happen. He was a monster, not human.

Sylvia was independent and capable. Intelligent, curious, and fearless. A decorated soldier. Extraordinary in ways few men or women would ever be. But when she lowered her guard, she expressed compassion and gentleness that many who knew her would swear didn't exist. I found her addictively beguiling.

Rick was sympathetic to my cause. Hell, he'd committed to the mission before even meeting me. He said Sylvia described me as *uncommonly honorable and a prescient battlefield warrior*. Both points were exaggerated and could have more accurately described his future wife. Clearly, Rick had fallen so deeply in love with Sylvia that thoughts of their future consumed him. I hoped his feelings for her wouldn't diminish the fighting prowess he might need to help keep her alive. *Keep them safe*, I pleaded to God.

A portion of the hilltop compound suddenly appeared through trees and a clearing. We huddled in the quiet shadows of towering evergreens, preparing for what might lie ahead. The calm before an inevitable battle.

At a bend in a stream, we found our first glimpse of Delgado's stunning hacienda built atop a knoll. I turned to Rick and Sylvia. "Full disclosure, I'm going in alone. They won't expect someone to scale the wall and approach through the pretend jungle with all the big cats. I'll scout the compound for Delgado. Cover my retreat if he's not there. And if he's not, we'll abort the mission. I understand this isn't what I presented last night. But it's the plan. Tell me you're on board."

Neither replied. "I need to hear a *roger that* from both of you."

Sharing glances of resignation, they simultaneously nodded their reluctant compliance. "Roger that."

"My gut says the shithead's here," said Sylvia.

"In that case, I'll need your help, soldier girl," I said. "Together, we'll extract and sneak him across the border."

"I hope he dies during a firefight." She disregarded my expression of annoyance. "I know, I know, you want to take him alive. I just don't get it. You're a better person than I'll ever be."

That wasn't true. "You think Delgado should die for what he did to Brooke? Fair argument. But I honestly believe life in solitary confinement within an American high-security prison would be a fate worse than death for this devil."

Her body language showed she was wholly unconvinced.

"Rick, position yourself outside the northern perimeter of the wall. The satellite images showed two stands of trees providing access and cover. Sylvia, take the east. Stay separated until I command otherwise. If things go well, we'll sneak a famous drug lord out through the western boundary's gated entry. GPSs are programmed with coordinates. You might need to blow a hole through the gate. Is it all clear?"

"Copy that," Rick said.

"Don't keep us waiting," Sylvia added.

"Thanks for taking this on. See you on the other side."

After separating, I studied the sixteen-foot cement barrier surrounding much of the property. The wall narrowed to about twelve inches at the top, then continued higher with metal poles and gray industrial fencing stretched between them. Capping the chain-link was two feet of barbed wire to keep climbing animals from escaping. *Or batshit crazy ex-soldiers from entering*, I thought.

After scaling the cement, my wire cutters clipped through metal fencing. I studied the cavernous Mexican hacienda built on the crest of a hill with panoramic views of Delgado's jungle and distant poppy crops. After detecting no movements, I gathered the rope from one side of the wall and fed it down the other. It would be impossible to return the same way with a prisoner. With my feet on the ground of Delgado's inner sanctum, I gripped my Beretta with its ModX-9 7.75-inch suppressor.

"Sylvia, Rick, I've entered the abyss," I said in a low monotone voice through my mic.

"Copy that," Sylvia said into her headset, a static-free response heard clearly by both men.

"Copy that," Rick added.

Twenty paces from the wall and into the compound, I sensed a terrible stench of decaying animals wafting through dry, still air. I moved quickly and quietly. I saw no humans with AK-47s, and the only sounds were the occasional shrieks of birds and monkeys.

Thrashing noises approached from something very much alive and powerful. I crouched and aimed, ready but hesitant to lay waste to one of Delgado's henchmen or jungle beasts. Any gunfire, even muffled by my silencer, was a last resort. Suddenly, a zebra's striped head and chest sprung from the brush. It leaped forth and planted its hooves before darting toward an open field. I almost pulled the trigger.

"Jamie," Sylvia said through her mic. "I've got you in my sights. I was convinced you'd pull your trigger. Unbelievable control. Out."

"Roger that," I said. "Wondering where the meat-eaters are. Out."

"Rick here. I found the meat-eaters. North end of the compound. Just beyond the hacienda. The second wall intersects steel cages. I also see multiple sicarios, some armed. They're poking caged animals with gun barrels and sticks. Spraying high-powered water on them. I'd guess fifteen to twenty lions, tigers, and, I think, hyenas. Bad guys are whipping them into a frenzy. Out."

"Sylvia here. I'll move closer to Rick and the killer beasts, human and four-legged. Out."

"Copy that," I replied from the base of the second wall. "Hold fire until I locate Delgado. Assuming I get that lucky. Out."

"Roger that."

The rank odor of death grew more intense. I glanced to my left and halted. A partially consumed hand lay on the ground, a wedding band still attached to its finger. *These guys are sick, feeding humans to . . . to whatever devoured this guy.* Other revulsions probably riddled the property. The prospects of my own tortured demise prompted my appeal for God's protection. But would God shield a man who'd eagerly use vigilante justice as an excuse to fire at Delgado or his men if things got ugly? *Am I just another kind of killer?*

Taking one last glance at the arid trees and brush, I gripped the ropes I'd removed from a bag clipped to my belt. I flung it upward, latching it to metal fencing atop the second cement wall. There was always risk and trepidation when pulling oneself over a natural or artificial barrier with no line of sight to what might be lurking just beyond.

I descended after scaling the wall and cutting a path through the chain-link. No more cement barriers separated me from the hacienda, so I hid behind the flowing branches of a thick Japanese maple. Soft landscaping lights illuminated sections of a manicured yard dotted with plants and trees. Floodlights affixed to the veranda lowered the odds of advancing unseen. I moved behind a massive bronze statue of a conquistador saddled atop a stallion, the Spanish warrior's sword raised high toward the skies.

My M4 rested strapped across my back. The Army-issue Improved Outer Tactical Vest hugged my torso, deltoids, and groin. The layers of Kevlar felt somewhat reassuring. The lines separating life and death on the battlefield were always thin, but the IOTV vest painted them with slightly broader strokes.

A door on the side of the house swung open. I crept stealthily toward the rambling residence, using bushes as cover. I halted behind a tall green and yellow shrub with no lights shining upon it. The approaching man moved unhurriedly while smoking a cigarette. A pistol was holstered to his hip. He headed directly toward me. The grip on my Beretta tightened, a tense finger upon its trigger.

The man stopped and continued to draw on his Marlboro. He unzipped, and I could feel warm urine slapping against my legs and feet. The man's gaze remained centered on the leaves and branches separating us. Slowly reaching for another weapon, I stared into the oblivious eyes of a sicario. The man's focus sharpened. He realized he was standing inches from an intruder.

I pulled his body forward, my right arm targeting the man's neck. Letters across the knife spelled out Yarborough, honoring an Army legend considered the father of modern special forces. I'd never slit a throat before, but a Green Beret never forgets their training. I aggressively pulled the man's head forward as blood spewed from a severed esophagus. It was a sickening sensation. I told myself not to feel sorry for taking the life of a hardened criminal and likely murderer. Easier said than done.

Pulling part of his shirt toward me, I wiped the blood off my blade. His gold and silver pistol had been ornately engraved with the image of a crucifix. I shook my head in wonder and hid the man's body behind thick bushes before burying his gun in the topsoil of a huge planter.

Realizing criminals would soon search for their narco comrade, the only option was to trudge forward with added urgency. I was here for a reason, a necessary reason. A damn good reason. Remorse for the life I'd just taken faded as contrived moral justification eased my conscience.

Raucous chatter and celebration continued on the other side of the compound. La Buena Familia's killers and mules were in a festive mood. For the moment, it was good fortune having them preoccupied.

Unlike the wild sounds outside, the hacienda appeared quiet. Only two rooms were illuminated. I approached a corner chamber, careful not to make a sound with my back pressed against the windows' shutters. Looking closer, I realized the shutters were metal, not wood. *Of course they're metal, idiot—they built this place to defend against armed assaults.*

There were never any guarantees Delgado would be on the estate, but my intuition aligned with Sylvia's. All three of us possessed sixth senses honed over years of conflict. But then I remembered Wes Berkeley had also utilized instincts, and Wes was dead.

Delgado's home resembled Mission San Juan Capistrano. I scanned its walls, beams, and roof for cameras but saw none. I told myself they've got to have closed circuit television. Was I being recorded now? Likely. I envisioned cartel gangsters shooting my legs, then sawing off limbs for amusement, capturing the torture on a zip drive before FedExing it to family members for viewing.

Except I no longer had a family. My wife and mother were bound, gagged, and executed on orders from Delgado. The day everything beautiful and worthy in my life was taken. Recollections of their gruesome ends again inflicted punishing loss. My breathing grew labored. A single tear gathered in my eye. *God, I miss you, Brooke.*

Moments later, my strained face relaxed. My vision cleared. I doubted Delgado lived affected by dangers, real or imagined. But he should because the warrior approaching was fearless, had nothing else to lose, and was driven by unwavering justice and vengeance.

The son of murdered parents was in Mexico to end your wicked reign, you twisted sonofabitch.

I glanced skyward. *Please let him be here. And keep Rick and Sylvia alive.*

CHAPTER 28

Approaching the room with open shutters and soft light, the background sounds of excited men on the northern section of Delgado's property reached a crescendo. Whatever was happening, I hoped they'd remain distracted. Stealthily moving toward a grand patio, the wireless comm unit sprung to life.

"Sylvia here. They've brought a naked, terrified man to the animal cages. I think they might feed him to the beasts. Jamie, Rick, should I intervene?"

"Jamie here," I said in a hushed voice behind an outdoor fireplace. "We don't know anything about him. He could be a trafficker who's stolen fentanyl or heroin. How imminent is it? Out."

The screaming reached another decibel level, causing me to stiffen while scanning the property for gang members rushing to join their partying narcos. Something big had just happened.

"Sylvia here. Too late. Unbelievable. Rick, can you see this? Out."

"Rick here. Affirmative. Crazy. Out."

"The naked man was prodded forward from just beyond the cages. He ran for his life. They opened all the doors, and fierce animals made a beeline for him. Sickening. They're tearing him apart. Out."

Cheering like Roman citizens extolling gladiators who slaughtered each other in the Coliseum, gang members slapped fellow cartel members on the back, cheering and beaming while throwing back bottles of Modelo Negra. It was all too much fun. Pandemonium ensued after a limb got ripped from the victim's body.

"Sylvia here. They're mesmerized. No one's leaving. Out."

"Jamie here. Don't make a move. Sorry you had to watch that. Stay focused. I'm steps from the hacienda. Out."

They replied in unison, "Roger that."

I moved across the slate patio. Overhead, hand-scribed beams protruded beyond the tiled roof. The shutters and windows were open—a potential entrance.

Faint yellow shone from inside the room. I heard something. Was it television or radio? Moving closer, the edge of a flat-screen television was visible. I recognized the voice of Anderson Cooper. Would Delgado listen to news updates in English? Possibly, but unlikely. If the drug lord were on site, wouldn't he have joined his raucous men celebrating on the property behind his residence?

The echoes of cheering gang members lowered my concerns about sounds from weapons, gear, or boots announcing my approach. I guessed my pulse was about 110 bpm. *Stay calm, soldier.*

I approached the open window, which was part of a den. Could this be a wealthy, murdering bastard's private enclave? Seven endangered species mounts hung from two walls. An impressive collection of swords and rifles adorned one section of the room.

The fragrance of Macanudos drifted out the window. My research revealed that's what Delgado smoked. My commanding officer enjoyed the same classic brand in Afghanistan. It was immediate recognition.

There he is! Delgado leaned back in a red leather chair, smoked his stogie, and savored his tequila while watching news updates about more

Washington dysfunction. As I studied the relaxed drug lord, images of Brooke and Maria flashed through my consciousness.

Don't screw this up. I didn't think I could cleanly jump through the window with my M4 carbine—too unwieldy. I set it down carefully in the hall against an exterior ledge. Not a sound. I'll pick it up on the way out. If it doesn't get picked up, then I didn't make it out. If one of Delgado's posse grabs it while I'm inside, I'll soon be dead. There were many ways Jamie Morales could die tonight. I crouched below the stone sill.

After unholstering my Beretta, I visualized the next steps. Grab the windowsill with my left hand, elevate, crouch, and swing inside. Hit the tiled floor with my sidearm aimed. Blow Delgado's head off if he reaches for any weapon. *One, two, go!*

"*Not a fucking move, Delgado!*" We locked eyes. "Hands in the air. *Do it!*"

He dressed as I would have guessed—an exquisite belt, heavy gold watch, and chain around his left wrist. An intricate cross hung from his neck. Miniature flags of Mexico and America arose from a wooden base upon his desk. He was the personification of a walking dichotomy. Calm as a lake in the early morning, he slowly extended his arms with palms turned up, appearing neither surprised nor worried. Nor like a killer.

Stay focused. Be wary.

"Good evening, *Jaime* Morales. Or do you prefer the Americanized *Jamie?*" He spoke in English and a relaxed manner. "You must be skilled. A small army of loyal defenders and some unfriendly animals live on this property."

"You killed my wife. I despise you. Please give me a reason to pull this trigger."

"Not true. I did not kill your wife. Nor your mother."

Stepping closer, I pointed the barrel at his head. "You ordered their deaths. You told me that in a letter."

"I did indeed. But I did not pull the trigger, and their deaths remain warranted. Your mother knowingly left this country with something that belonged to me. Something I held dear." He added, "Something I am quite pleased to have regained possession of. Thanks to your sister-in-law, Ashley."

"You killed them over a piece of jewelry."

"Oh, it is much more than just a piece of jewelry. Your mother understood that."

"You also executed and beheaded my father. You're a disgusting human who I just dethroned. Say adios to your kingdom, bastard."

Delgado tilted his head slightly and smiled. "You are way ahead of yourself. And name-calling is a useless provocation. Your father's false exposé on my family's legitimate business dealings got two of my brothers slaughtered by Federales. Your mother's theft of the Emerald Cross doomed her and Brooklyn. You also would have been justifiably eliminated if you had been home when my men arrived to repossess my family's cross."

"I don't care about your precious cross. And I won't lose sleep if I send a 9mm slug through your forehead. You've got a decision to make. Leave silently with me or resist and die."

"Relax. You cannot get off this estate alive. Even if I am wrong, my people will track you down to kill you. *After* they torture you. You are in over your head."

I thrust the butt of my pistol against his skull. He fell hard into a wooden table with ivory tusk legs. His splattered blood was a stark contrast to the tabletop. I pressed the gun barrel against his ear and commanded him to rise.

"If it is revenge you want, kill me now. Whatever you do to me, you have no future. You have sealed your fate."

"You killed my family. Hundreds of innocent people. Maybe thousands. But you don't intimidate or frighten me." I reached down and thrust him to his feet. "The justice my father fought for will soon be served."

"Your father, of course." He stared at me almost respectfully. "A noble man by society's standards. But he made bad decisions. He is paying a fair price."

Speaking of Samuel in the present tense halted me. "*Paid*, you evil prick." I unclenched my jaw. "He *paid* the price. Or don't you remember ordering your men to cut off his head? You're a monster!" I was repulsed. There were no bounds to my hatred.

"I did not kill Samuel."

"Yeah, yeah—so you had one of your worthless sicarios do it. Either way, *you* killed my father, Delgado. And *you'll* pay the price. But it won't be in a dilapidated Mexican jail like the one El Chapo escaped from. Hell no. Your ass will rot in a virtual Fort Knox, courtesies of the US government."

He chuckled softly. "At the end of this night, you will be dead. It is not the end I seek, but you are too stubborn and principled to a fault—like your father. He is the same."

"*Damnit!*" Thrusting my elbow into his head, I opened a one-inch gash above his left temple. I gritted my teeth and raised my fist for another blow but exhaled and lowered my arm.

His expression confused me. After wiping blood from his face with a tanned forearm, he said, "Your father is alive."

Flinging him into the wall again, I opened a cut above his right eye. "You talk about him in the present tense once more, and I'll waste you right here. Right now."

"Even if it is true? Samuel is alive. Let me prove it to you." He flicked his chin toward a steel door encased within ornate dark wood. A rotary dial was on the left-hand side, halfway down the vault's door. Below that was a two-inch glass square I presumed was a fingerprint scanner.

It was impossible not to dissect Delgado's shocking claim. My father had been murdered and mutilated, a horrible truth confirmed after an investigation ordered by Mexican President Cornesa. The drug lord was trying to buy time.

"Inside the safe is a laptop with evidence Samuel is alive. Give me sixty seconds to prove it."

In the distance, the rowdy cheering of the men of La Buena Familia grew louder. My wireless sprang alive. "Sylvia here. Now there's a naked young woman the men are screaming at and mocking. A couple of them are prodding her with AKs toward a gate separating her from the animals. I'm not going to stand here and watch this happen. Have you found Delgado? Out."

"Dammit." I realized my thoughts were spoken aloud.

"A problem?" said Delgado.

While internalizing Sylvia's words, I pointed my Beretta at his chest. She would absolutely pull the trigger before letting this unknown woman get mauled to death. All hell was about to break loose. Sylvia's sense of duty and moral compass were admirable, but she picked one hell of a time to complicate an already precarious mission.

"Jamie here. I have Delgado. I need two minutes. Save the woman if you can. Shoot the narcos if you must. Whatever happens, follow the GPS coordinates when you escape. Out."

Rick replied, "Roger that." Sylvia said, "Shoot him."

Pushing Delgado toward the safe, I forced him to kneel, then pressed the Beretta's cold barrel to his temple. "Get the laptop. Any surprise, you're done."

He nodded and turned the dial left and right.

"Faster, or I'll shoot you."

The cartel boss picked up the pace. I heard a click. A whirring sound was made after Delgado held his thumb to the reader. The heavy door swung outward about an inch. Delgado opened it fully. I pressed the circular steel of the suppressor barrel more forcefully into his head.

"Turn it on," I snapped.

As the laptop booted up, the pitch and decibel of the screaming men near the animal cages rose again. I considered shooting Delgado and taking a position opposite Rick and Sylvia, thereby increasing the odds of their safe retreat when mayhem erupted. All our options were fraught with tremendous risks. I got refocused on the only reason I was here.

Delgado opened the computer's Pictures folder, selected an image, and rotated the screen. "Impossible," I thought. He showed me more photos. The man depicted had to be my father, a remarkable likeness with graying hair. "Where is he?"

"In Orange County. Less than two miles from where you grew up and now live. In a bunker beneath a home in American suburbia.

Your father has always been, for him, excruciatingly close to his wife and son. Surprising, yes?"

"*That's impossible!* You're lying!"

Sylvia's voice shot through his earpiece. "I can only give you seconds, Jamie. Out."

"Roger that," I replied while shaking my head.

"I speak the truth. Samuel is alive, agonizingly close to the wife and son he loves so much. But unable to embrace them. We have kept him abreast of your life and achievements. He is aware of his wife and daughter-in-law's deaths. My personal brand of artistic evil. And now you will die knowing the truth." His laughter sounded demented.

After I punched him in the chest, the air was forced from his lungs. He rolled and writhed on the ground, then rose from his hands and knees and measured my glare. He rubbed the bottom of his bloodied jaw before staring at the dark red streaked across his hand. "Careful not to kill the man you want imprisoned. You said my death is not the justice you seek." He sneered.

"Maybe I've changed my mind. Killing you would make me the envy of justice."

CHAPTER 29

Sylvia Sokolov abhorred her last name, which translated to "meek" in Russian. Her grandmother, Irina Sokolov, whom she'd met sporadically on the outskirts of St. Petersburg, had spent days with her daughter and granddaughter just before they emigrated to America. Babushka Smirnoff foresaw great strength and promise in her granddaughter. Because Sylvia's grandmother considered all the Sokolovs to be incorrigible drunks and failures, she made Sylvia promise to change her surname after becoming an American citizen. She had yet to act on her grandmother's plea.

Twenty-plus years later, on the grounds of the world's most dangerous drug lord, Sylvia was in a situation she thought would crumble the meek. Narcos shoved the naked woman she'd described to us into the pretend jungle, where tigers and hyenas continued devouring the remnants of a man thrust from the same cage minutes earlier. After running about one hundred feet, the distraught woman's silhouette remained still as she stared at the man's corpse with tears dousing her face, apparently too emotionally numb to move. But the animals who hadn't yet finished dining on an unlucky man began to walk, then trot, toward her trembling profile. She closed her eyes and silently mouthed her final words.

Only four of the La Buena Familia cartel members were clutching their machine guns, but the unarmed were just feet away from their carbines leaning against a nearby wall. The cacophony of rabid yelling and pounding of fists and gun barrels against the cages' metal bars was electric and deafening. Even the animals appeared affected, tentative about tearing into the second serving of their easy human prey. A hungry lion standing below a large oak, fifty yards from the petrified female, suddenly broke into a quick trot toward more fresh meat. The hardened criminals grew even more delirious with anticipation.

Sylvia chose what she felt was her best of several high-risk options. Standing twenty yards from a thick metal gate with hinges set twelve inches into the cement of the wall corralling the hungry beasts, she pulled the trigger of her M320 grenade launcher affixed to her M4 carbine. It was better to fire the weapon from a greater distance, but she and Rick realized they'd run out of time. The explosion was deafening. The gate blew away, leaving a gaping hole in the wall. The reverberation of the blast knocked animals to the ground. Fragments of steel and cement flew in all directions, followed by a billowing cloud of thick dust. The detonation triggered fierce sounds from frenzied animal species. The shrieks of dozens of olive baboons taken from African plains blared loudest.

Traffickers rushed for their weapons. Within the jagged opening created by the detonation, barely visible through thick clouds of dust and smoke, stepped a single figure dressed in black and moving with purpose. La Buena Familia members instantly recovered their killer instincts after realizing this enemy was not an intimidated farmer or unprotected political figure. This enemy would fight back.

Watching the initial La Buena Familia AK-47 get raised, Rick unleashed his first 100-round drum magazine of 5.56×45mm NATO cartridges in 5-shot bursts, eliminating six threats. He aimed at the floodlights atop poles within the fake game preserve, quickly turning areas of light to darkness. An intense firefight spread throughout the compound.

While he engaged the cartel, Sylvia scurried toward the exposed woman. Despite the commotion, the hungry lion refused to leave his easy meal. Sylvia watched the woman cower to the ground, collapsing into a fetal position. The lion lunged forward to rip the bare woman's flesh. Sylvia fired three rounds into the animal's massive skull. Having laid waste to one threat, she fired at hyenas that refused to scatter.

Reaching down to pull the human paralyzed by fear to her feet, Sylvia sensed the draft of bullets whizzing past her head. Then a barrage of gunfire exploded from her right flank. Rick had re-engaged two groups of shooters positioned behind the animal cages. She wasn't sure he'd be able to protect both women. But she'd been in plenty of battles where nothing was sure.

Captain Sokolov shoved the traumatized soul behind the dead lion's carcass, then she threw herself atop the now-screaming young woman. Sylvia reached for a second M320 grenade to affix to her carbine. She assumed Rick was reloading, as she now heard only silence over her right flank. That silence emboldened both groups of narcos to unload on stationary targets using the lion carcass for protection. Rick and Sylvia's wireless headsets were useless. Neither could have deciphered anything transmitted.

Rick's AK-47 sprung back to life as he unloaded another drum of bullets on the enemy. Screaming penetrated the sounds of battle as Rick laid waste to his targets. Sylvia continued to lie atop the terrified victim, but she nudged herself forward just enough to get precise aim at one of the tightly formed pods of traffickers. Seconds later, the cluster she targeted got wasted by her grenade. Two bodies now dangled between the cage bars that the impact thrust them into. She uttered "evil shits" while simultaneously acknowledging her odds of escaping with the traumatized woman remained low.

The sounds from the naked stranger's mouth grew hysterical, more agonized. Sylvia embraced her tightly and attempted to console her through ineffective Spanglish. The woman pointed to her wedding ring and the scene of the disemboweled man's unspeakable end, muttering "Roberto" repeatedly. Sylvia thought she understood. The victim fed to the beasts was the stranger's husband. All the while, bullets penetrated the massive dead lion shielding their bodies.

As Rick continued delivering casualties, Sylvia decided it was time. She stood and yanked the bicep of the person she was trying to keep alive. The woman seemed unwilling to comply. Sylvia reached down and slapped her hard across the left cheek: Decide whether to live or die. With her limited Spanish, she screamed, "¡Vamos! ¡Ahora!"

The woman haltingly stood and nodded, appearing intent on living.

CHAPTER 30

The sounds of M320s were very familiar to me, but Sylvia or La Buena Familia could have fired them. The cartel's arsenal far exceeded the capabilities of most law enforcement organizations in Mexico or the US. The odds of getting Delgado off his compound were low. But I'd faced bleak, even insurmountable odds before. Soldiers can't let odds affect their resolve.

Delgado lifted his eyebrows inside the hacienda's den as if to emphasize *I told you so*. I grabbed the laptop containing pictures of the man I believed could be Samuel and shoved it into my backpack. The Beretta remained aimed at Delgado's head.

Walking past the sturdy safe that housed the laptop, I noticed a silk turquoise bag on a shelf and grabbed it. Was this the Emerald Cross? I glanced at the man who destroyed my family and finally perceived a wisp of concern etched across his face. After placing what felt like a cross in my backpack, I yanked a length of rope from my vest and bound Delgado's wrists behind his back.

"Lead me safely to the shooting. One misstep, and I waste you." Delgado nodded in compliance. We stepped down a long, tiled hall, where the drug lord flicked his chin toward a yellow arched door. Pushing him forward aggressively, I kept my pistol barrel firmly pressed to the back of his head. When we passed a bedroom door that was slightly ajar, I saw two dirty socks resting atop a mattress. I grabbed one and shoved it into Delgado's mouth and ran a loop of tape around his head and mouth.

Once we stepped outside the hacienda, I picked up the M4 I'd leaned against the wall before jumping through the den window. "Jamie here," I said into my wireless mic. "Can you hear me?" The lack of response heightened my urgency to help get Rick and Sylvia out alive.

Delgado and I moved toward the thundering sounds of gunfire. Flashes of yellow, red, and white illuminated thick billows of smoke wafting over the property. I checked the GPS coordinates to gauge my distance from our agreed meeting point, then rushed Delgado over a dark expanse of the side yard. Thrusting him into bushes, I clipped him to metal fencing with a sturdy carabiner. After binding his ankles, it was time to join the firefight.

There was a group of La Buena Familia killers hunkered behind a wall who fired wildly at Rick and Sylvia. They yelled excitedly about taking the Americans out. Dashing around a large veranda pillar, two men retreating toward Delgado's study caught my shadow. They raised their Chinese-made machine guns. I neutralized them with a spurt from my M4. Because so much gunfire was echoing from various points on the property, no one recognized my advance or the elimination of their fellow gang members.

Two hundred feet ahead, nine men in prone and standing positions, well protected by portions of a wall and a long barbecue counter, were targeting specific zones. Their aim led me to Rick and Sylvia. I took position behind a wide stone pillar supporting an immense scribed timber beam.

"Hernandez, Gutierrez, Aguilar—you three follow the outer wall and approach them from the west. Juan and Pascal, you two from the east. Quickly!" screamed one of the shooters. The men split apart, but I dropped them before taking five steps. When the other shooters turned to engage me, their deaths came quickly. The two appeared to be teenagers, victims of the gangland lifestyle they freely joined or were conscripted into. Unnerved, I reminded myself teenagers can kill like seasoned assassins.

It appeared that around a dozen killers remained. I measured the sounds, smells, and sights of flashing gun barrels attempting to kill Rick and Sylvia. Then I spotted narcos huddled behind an enclosure housing a generator I assumed provided power to the house and animal kingdom compound.

I discovered how sicarios could unleash their constant barrage of bullets on Rick and Sylvia. One man served as a "runner" carrying 50-round drum cartridges for the AKs, replenishing the cartel shooters. Suddenly, the flurry of La Buena Familia's gunfire swept left and right, up and down. My comrades were still alive and on the run.

Every second was precious. The odds were great that the commotion triggered a call for reserve traffickers. A helicopter circled within the dark, smoke-filled skies as if on cue. I assumed it was part of Delgado's private air force. Getting down the mountain alive, let alone out of Mexico, had grown more challenging.

Stepping from behind a thick tree trunk, I fired two rounds into the chests of what I hoped were the final sicarios. When this mission was over, I'd once again regret taking lives. I also knew I'd rationalize it.

With the enemy silenced, I adjusted the stem of my mic. "Rick, Sylvia, hear me?"

Rick stepped from the shadows. "Loud and clear, Captain Morales."

Then his eyes intensified, and he pointed his carbine at my head. It was a surreal moment. Before dying, my last thought was that Rick had inexplicably decided to shoot me. And warriors like him don't miss.

Thap thap!

The bullets whizzed past my head. A body behind us sailed backward and lay motionless atop a worn path. Two rounds from Rick's *Kalashnikov* left holes within a four-inch circle in the middle of the man's sternum. The trafficker's expression appeared strangely serene, almost innocent. I watched Rick extract a cartridge from his AK before securing a new one without speaking. When finished, he stepped forward. "Sorry. There wasn't time to explain."

Sylvia appeared from behind a large bush on the exterior of the outer wall, thirty feet from where Rick and I stood. Clutching her M4 with one hand and the bicep of a naked woman with the other, she peered into the eyes of her rescued victim while speaking to me. "This woman's been through unimaginable hell. Tell her everything's going to be okay. That we'll keep her safe." I hesitated, hoping we could in fact do that.

I shot off a few sentences in Spanish, and though the woman's demeanor hardly changed, she slowly nodded and spoke. Listening to her story, I glanced at Rick and Sylvia. "Her name is Lucia. The man driven from the cages and eaten by the animals was her husband."

"That's what I figured," Sylvia said.

Though she couldn't understand what I was saying to the other Americans, Lucia correctly guessed I was talking about her late husband, and she wailed for Roberto. Sylvia consoled her while placing a hand over her mouth for quiet. None of us knew how many traffickers might still be on the property.

Compassionately squeezing her hand, I said, "I'm so sorry."

A sharp snap caused the group to turn around. Rick raised his AK-47 to confront a threat, but he instead took three rounds to the chest from a version of his same weapon. Sylvia reacted instantly, glimpsing the shooter as he sprang forth. She killed him with a spurt of bullets.

Lucia flailed her arms and screamed, no longer comforted by my promises of protection.

Sylvia and I rushed to Rick's side and were shocked but ecstatic. His Kevlar vest had stopped all three rounds, though he was in excruciating pain with empty lungs struggling to inflate. Pain was better than death. Sylvia strode over to the dead man and put another round from her Sig Sauer into his head.

"Dear God! *He's dead!*"

"Yes, Jamie, but now he's even deader."

"What are you doing?"

"He shot Rick and wouldn't have hesitated to kill all of us. He's a raping, torturing, murdering trafficker strutting around with impunity. That last shot was my calling card for the rest of these scumbag fuckers. My only regret is he didn't feel it." She faced me stiffly, defiantly.

I shook my head. This was not the Sylvia I'd served with for years. Sure, she was a warrior like me, but shooting a dead man to send a message wasn't who she was at her core. Years of horrors and killing took a toll on all of us.

Another moment on Delgado's property lowered our odds of survival. "Take clothes from these bodies to cover up Lucia." I flicked my chin toward the shivering woman. In Spanish, I apologized for dressing her in the garments and shoes of dead traffickers.

"It is fine. I am happy they are dead."

After following a dirt road to the compound's gates, I reached into the brush, unhitched a carabiner, sliced through the ropes binding two ankles, and yanked Delgado to his feet. Lucia shrieked and waved her arms, horrified to be in the presence of the most pernicious man on earth. Delgado set his eyes upon Lucia, and though he couldn't smile with a sock stuffed into his mouth, everyone believed he attempted to.

Lucia pleaded, "*Kill him!* Kill him now!"

Sylvia stood oozing contempt. "You know my feelings. We should take him out. He killed your father. Killed your mother. Killed your wife, Jamie!"

"Let's march," I ordered. "Blow a hole through the gate, Sylvia. It'll take too long to check all these bodies for keys to the trucks behind the hacienda. We need to get the hell out of here. We aren't far from our Jeep." I glanced at the GPS strapped to my wrist and noted the coordinates for the SAW we'd hidden on our approach. We'd need it.

Hiking aggressively, we noticed the peering eyes of escaped African beasts searching for an easy meal. Delgado's eyes darted about, scouring the landscape for signs of La Buena Familia rescuers.

After exiting the drug lord's compound, we followed the stream toward our concealed Jeep. We heard the roar of two pickups and watched their high beams bounce over a distant road toward the hacienda. Delgado tracked them, then stepped in front of me and nodded, conveying any number of messages—all of them dire.

CHAPTER 31

The hills and forest had blunted some reverberation and thumping, but the noises returned. The three of us glanced at each other. "Yep, we know that sound, don't we?" Sylvia said. "UH 60 Black Hawk." The copter soon banked in our direction, and MARINA grew visible across the lower section of the cabin. "That's a Mexican Navy bird. I would have guessed Federales in this region. Either way, this is really good or terrible news." The Black Hawk turned away and circled Delgado's hacienda.

I grabbed the cartel boss and yanked hard on the tape that helped secure the sock to his mouth and mustache. Thick strands of hair got ripped from his face. "Is the copter friend or foe to us? Don't waste my time. Tell the truth, or she'll kill you." I knew he'd believe that.

"It does not matter. You are alive but overconfident," he said. "You will all die before this is over. Including her." He flicked his chin toward Lucia and added derisively, "Your husband deserved to be eaten, woman. And you deserved to be passed around like the whore you are." He repeated his message in English for Rick and Sylvia.

Sylvia slammed the butt of her M4 into his head. A loud snap rang out as she dislocated the cartilage of his nose.

Delgado wiped the crimson from his flared nostrils onto his shirt sleeve, then stared into Sylvia's face for a long pause. "The uglier you make me, the more brutal my wrath. You have sealed your fate, you foolish American bitch."

Rick pressed the barrel of his AK-47 into Delgado's mouth with such force it snapped one of his front teeth in half. "If you ever touch her, I swear I'll kill you myself, shithole."

"As you can see, my friends aren't too keen on keeping you alive. And while I apparently hold flawed rationale for letting you breathe," I glanced at Sylvia, "watching you die wouldn't bother any of us. Answer my questions, or these two will act as judge, jury, and executioner."

Delgado scowled and ran the tip of his tongue across his upper front teeth, measuring the gap left by the broken tooth. He spat blood, and the tooth fragment lay visible in the dirt. "You could never break me, as I have broken others. There are reasons I am el patrón." He ran his eyes up and down Lucia's body. "I personally do not find her attractive. I would never fuck her."

Sylvia kicked him in the face with her boot. "Let me waste this devil. It'll make the world a better place."

"Yeah, he's psychotic. But let's keep him alive for now." I looked at Lucia, Sylvia, and Rick. "I understand why you two—you *three*—completely disagree." Our faces were separated by inches. "Here's what I need to—"

The intensity of a not-too-distant firefight grabbed all our attention. Eerie silence then replaced the clatter of gunfire. I pushed the group toward the SUVs, our transport to safety. When we approached the SAW machine gun Rick had hidden for support on our retreat, he picked up the gun and a canvas backpack holding six 200-round belts to feed the weapon. Flinging the carbine and ammo over his shoulder,

Rick was a force to be reckoned with, armed with his trusty AK-47 and the brutally efficient SAW.

We detected Black Hawk rotors penetrating the sounds of nature in the forest we trekked through. As the bird continued in our direction, a powerful searchlight switched on. Its beam penetrated the darkness and swept across roads, poppy fields, and timber.

"Are they guessing or know we're here?" Rick said aloud.

I had no idea. "The SUVs are hidden from the road but might be visible from the copter. Let's pick up the pace."

"The Marines protect my interests. Everyone has their price. They will find us and kill you unless you lay down your weapons. Do as I say, and I will keep you alive."

His mandate was a mix of comedic and unsettling. No one responded. The Black Hawk and its searchlight made additional passes directly overhead. Heavy cover from trees concealed our movements. Nearing the two SUVs, we watched the helicopter hover before landing within a quarter mile of the covered Jeep and Land Cruiser.

"We don't have many options," I told Rick and Sylvia. "We can stay and fight, split up and trek through the farms and villages, or caravan in the vehicles and hope to go undetected."

Sylvia said, "If he's telling the truth about buying off Marines, we're in deep caca, whatever we do. But I vote to stay together, fire up the SUVs, and hit the road. Splitting up doesn't improve our chances. Rick?"

"Splitting up is a better strategy," Rick said. "All options are dicey, but separating presents a bigger challenge for the cartel or Marines to corral our scattered group."

"This is your rodeo, Jamie. You make the call," Sylvia said. "You okay with that, Rick?"

"Yep."

"We'll stay together. Rick, attach the bipod to the SAW. That'll help steady your aim from the rear of the Land Cruiser. Delgado will travel with me in the Jeep, roped and laid out in the middle seat. Lucia will ride shotgun." I gave her a quick overview of the plan. She had no objections and appeared incapable of processing anything happening around us.

Hiking within fifty feet of the vehicles, we settled behind a massive rock next to the creek. Rick and I trudged up a ridge to scan for unfriendlies. We saw no one. The Mexican Marines could approach any moment based on where we thought the Black Hawk landed.

"Let's go." I led the way up an incline and down the backside to the vehicles. Swaying pines produced haunting sounds mixed with the trilling of insects. Noises from the rippling creek disappeared quickly. We stepped over the bodies of the three narcos we'd killed upon our arrival.

Lucia flew into a rage. *"He raped me!"* She pointed at the man who had also threatened and grabbed Sylvia.

Grabbing her rigid body, I said, "He'll never hurt you or anyone again, Lucia. I'm horrified by what you've endured, but we must keep moving."

Sylvia stepped forward and spat on her assailant as she neared the driver-side door of the Land Cruiser. Lucia broke free of my embrace to do the same.

After climbing inside the SUVs, Sylvia distributed the remaining ammunition. She and I turned the keys and fired up both vehicles. We were bouncing over rough and dusty roads toward Highway 196 on our retreat to safety. Suddenly bullets and tracers flashed in front of both SUVs. Live or die—we dared not stop.

After rounding several bends, the gunfire grew distant. Then it stopped. "Can you guys hear me?" I said through my wireless mic. I received their simultaneous acknowledgments. "Very strange. Those were military tracers. It felt like they missed on purpose. As if it were only a warning."

"Agreed," Sylvia replied as she tried to stay on my tail, no easy task. "I'm not sure what it means, but let's keep this pace and disappear."

"*Damnit!*" I screamed through my mic. "Marines in the road with weapons trained! Follow my lead—do not engage!" Opening my door and shielding myself behind it, I yelled out in Spanish, "We are American special ops on an important mission, with permission from the Mexican government. *Do not shoot!*"

The soldiers split into teams, one in front of the SUVs and the other behind. The group's leader screamed at me to raise my hands slowly, or we'd all be fired upon. He bellowed commandingly, "Is Marco Delgado in one of these vehicles?"

Delgado screamed from the middle seat of the Jeep, where he lay with his wrists and ankles bound. I cursed myself for not stuffing the damn sock back into his mouth and reapplying the duct tape. "*This is Marco Delgado! These people have murdered my men and killed innocent people. Great work tracking us down. Each of you will be richly compensated.*"

The group's leader again ordered us not to make sudden movements. He approached the Jeep and opened the rear door, where Delgado lay agitated. "Congratulations," the Mexican captain told me, "You have accomplished something we have been trying to do for years." He turned and presented the drug lord with a stern gaze. "Marco Delgado, you are under arrest for crimes of murder, money laundering, political corruption, and the manufacture and selling of heroin and synthetic opioids around the globe."

I watched with great satisfaction as Delgado's face twisted into a blend of hatred, incredulousness, and a dose of genuine concern.

"Yes, Señor Delgado, you failed to understand that almost all Mexican Marines are patriots who love their country. You cannot buy them off. You will never see the light of day as a free man again." We locked gazes. "You must be Jamie Morales. DEA Agent Kirby Washington advised us weeks ago a one-eyed warrior might someday enter our country. He will be surprised to learn you are not only in Mexico but have captured the world's most notorious drug lord." He flashed a weak smile. "Quite a feat."

I watched the officer's face disappear from his head. Then I saw a soldier standing in front of the Jeep crumple to the ground, unable to return a single volley at his enemy. Turning to look behind the Land Cruiser, I watched two other Marines succumb to a barrage of bullets. The soldiers had no chance.

Lucia screamed and floundered as I lifted my M4 while struggling to keep the distressed woman from darting out of the Jeep. Bullets exploded from the forest, shattering the windows and penetrating the metal of both vehicles. Lucia wet herself and continued trying to open the door to flee. I punched and knocked her out. She'd either wake up safe with a sore jaw or be found dead beside three Americans.

But we had no interest in dying. Rick unleashed the SAW in the direction of the shooters as I engaged other gang members with my carbine. Sylvia affixed an M320 grenade to her M4.

CHAPTER 32

We remained unsure that we were fighting La Buena Familia or another contingent of Mexican Marine forces, this one successfully corrupted by Delgado. Regardless, we needed a break to remain alive. I'd accept old-fashioned luck or divine intervention. Whether Delgado lived or died was an afterthought.

"Okay, grenade is loaded!" Sylvia screamed to Rick from her prone position below the blazing bullets, between the front and back seats.

Rick hammered away with the SAW, then yelled, "Aim 11 o'clock. Cluster of shooters. Fire away on the count of three!" He sprayed his bullets to reduce incoming fire and give Sylvia a clean shot. "1, 2, 3!"

She had popped up at the count of two and aimed her grenade from atop the Land Cruiser's rear seat at a tight window among the gun barrels flashing red and yellow about two hundred feet from the SUV. It was one of three remaining M320s. She adjusted her scope and held her aim. Rick's three-count had already passed.

"*Pull the damn trigger!*" he screamed.

Two more seconds passed before she slowly squeezed her right index finger. The grenade hissed its way toward a target. A flash of color preceded the sounds and images of decimation. All incoming gunfire from that section of the forest ceased. Sylvia and Rick sent additional rounds into thick trees and brush. Having eliminated one threat, they pivoted to engage the assailants trying to kill me.

The duo fired from different angles until their enemies' guns fell silent. Sylvia then burst out the door of the Land Cruiser and sprinted into the forest with her M4 blazing spurts of three rounds.

Damnit, Sylvia! Rick screamed as he chased after her. As he approached, she stepped from the shadows with intensity carved into her face.

"There were six in that group," she said. "All have La Buena Familia tattoos. They're super dead."

"Why do you do that?" Rick hollered as she faced him with her carbine dangling from her right arm. "Just wait for me next time."

She stepped away toward the shelled SUVs as if she were no longer listening.

I peered down the hill toward our escape route while Rick continued lecturing Sylvia on unnecessary risks and staying alive. "Hey guys, we've got a problem. See those lights down there? Vehicles have assembled in what was our best way out. It might be a moot point as I doubt either SUV is up to the task."

Rick said, "We need to try. We can't escape on foot. They'll be swarming these hills. Load up the guns and ammo, and let's go."

"You're not listening," I said. "It's a narrow dirt road. Our transportation's beat to crap. And if we could drive in that direction, they'd block the road, spread among the trees, and take us out."

"I've got a plan," Sylvia said. "Let's march back and steal the Black Hawk."

"Holy hell. I'm losing my edge. Of course," Rick replied. "But it's a gamble. If there are any Mexican Marine survivors, they'll fire on us to remove unknown risks. Could we blame them?"

Marching toward the copter's landing site could trap us on ground closer to Delgado's residence. We'd be pinned between the gang members assembling down the road and any sicarios who survived the hacienda firefight. And if the Black Hawk was damaged and now unflyable, our fates would be sealed. "Trekking backward is fraught with crazy risks. Give me input."

"Any Marines would've left the copter to assist their comrades. My gut says those were loyal Marines, and now they're all dead," Sylvia said as she began filling a large duffel bag with unspent magazines and extra weapons. "I think we should take the Black Hawk. We'll likely get tracked by radar once we rise between one to four thousand feet."

"That's quite a wide range," Rick said.

"Few countries have the technology to track low-altitude flight, but I don't know the Mexican military's capabilities," Sylvia said. "Depending on the location and terrain, it's even difficult for the US to track at two thousand feet."

"So stay low, and we'll cross our fingers. Odds are good they'll try to blast us out of the sky in retaliation before we reach the border," Rick said. "They'll do a body count here, determine all the good guys are dead, and blame whoever stole their Black Hawk. I know I'm stating the obvious."

"Yes, you are, and Sylvia's gut is our best option. Agreed?" I stared hard for quick answers.

They nodded.

"What about Delgado," Sylvia barked as she continued to load weapons. "He's a burden and risk we don't need."

I opened the back door of the Jeep, yanked Delgado into an upright position, and advised the prisoner yet again that we'd shoot him if he fought or ran.

"I hope you fight or run, scumbag. A dead Delgado is a good Delgado," Sylvia told him with emphasized contempt.

The drug lord stared her down with a hateful sneer.

Sylvia panicked, realizing she hadn't seen the stranger she'd saved since coming under fire. "Where the hell's Lucia? Oh God, don't tell me—"

"She's alive," I interrupted. "Front seat." When Sylvia flung open the Jeep door, Lucia appeared to be sleeping.

"Why is she—"

"I had to knock her out. Let's see if one of these will fire up," I said, jumping into the Jeep's driver seat and turning the key. Nothing.

Sylvia walked to the front of the SUV and yelled, "Engine got shot to hell. It's going nowhere."

Behind us, Rick entered the Land Cruiser, and despite being perforated bumper-to-bumper, it shockingly turned over and started. They tossed their gear into the rear compartment and kept the lights off to minimize detection. I bent Lucia into a seated position between Rick and me. We drove back toward Delgado's residence, estimating the Black Hawk had landed in a poppy field.

The steel-gray helicopter blended into a dark horizon in one of the fields. Painted in white below the rotor casing was MARINA, with the flag of Mexico emblazoned on its tail. The main blade, nearly forty feet in diameter, spun slowly. Twenty feet from the craft, we found the pilot dead, lying face down with three bullet holes in his back. Silhouettes of unidentified African animals darted from below the cabin as we approached. They scattered among the waving poppy stems.

Rick took a ready-prone position in the field with the SAW while Sylvia and I lugged her fiancé's *Kalashnikov* and other weapons into the copter. Few words were spoken. We all understood that escaping with the war bird demanded extraordinary luck.

After dropping her weapons cache in the main cabin, Sylvia adjusted the seat and controls. There were English and Spanish versions of the manuals but flying Black Hawks had been hardwired into her brain years ago—manuals were a nuisance. The fuel tanks were 80% full, providing a range of about five hundred miles. Maybe enough to get us to the US border.

Lucia awakened after being carried inside. She touched her sore jaw with her right hand as I strapped her into her seat. I took a moment to explain what had transpired and what to expect. She said she understood and appeared calm until she discovered Delgado roped up and lying on the floor. She begged me to leave the powerful man behind, emphasizing he was evil and dangerous. Better yet, she pleaded, just kill him. Sylvia turned from the cockpit and nodded. I explained the wicked man will be spending the rest of his life in an American prison cell when this is all over. She considered that a dubious claim.

Two red flares rose into the darkness, illuminating a broad swath of land Rick estimated to be just beyond their abandoned Jeep. The incendiaries slowly parachuted back to earth. The bad guys were approaching. Rick looked for vehicles filled with sicarios.

Rick yelled to Sylvia, "How much more time do you need?" He kneeled just beyond the Black Hawk's landing skids, scanning the forest and poppy fields.

"I'm ready to fly. Just validating munitions," she replied.

"*What?*" Rick shrieked with exasperation. "We've got enough weapons to start a small war. We need to get the hell out of here!"

I agreed. "Let's go, Sylvia."

"Roger that," she said as she busily flipped switches in front and above her, turned knobs, and pushed controls. The main rotor whirred, and the poppies blew wildly with each rotation of the massive blade.

I yelled out the open main cabin door, "Okay, Rick, jump aboard!"

Rick continued scanning the field's perimeter for any signs of the enemy. Suddenly, the SAW and its 300-round belt unleashed a stream of bullets toward the road. I aimed my M4 at the light-colored pickup Rick had detected. The truck's passengers jumped out to engage us, hammering away with La Buena Familia's AK-47s.

To my right, Lucia cupped her ears and pushed her head to her lap, muffling her screams by pressing her face into her thigh. It had all become too much. Distinct sounds of bullets striking metal filled the cabin as shooters hoped to disable the helicopter or kill us with ricocheted bullets inside the cabin.

The craft rattled as it rose, and Sylvia screamed at Rick to hop aboard for takeoff. The pickup suddenly exploded, and Rick turned toward the Black Hawk's open sliding door. I kept firing in tight arcs around the detonated truck. Rick jumped aboard a landing skid that hovered two feet off the ground. He extended an arm to clasp my wrist. Just as he sprung toward the open door, a 39 mm bullet found the lower portion of his right femur. Splattered blood colored the helicopter's gray paint, and Rick fell backward into the poppy field.

Stunned and disoriented, I watched him roll over dense flowers before pushing his back to the soil. He waved at me to take off, to leave him behind.

Sylvia initiated autopilot and put the bird into hover mode—a perilous move when just feet off the ground. She grabbed her carbine and fired at the narcos from a standing position through the open door. I leaped out and knelt beside my incensed comrade, who blurted every curse word known to mankind.

Glancing at Rick's wound, I instantly grew more concerned. I flung him over my shoulders and worked my way onto the hovering landing skids. Leaning forward, I rolled him through the door before leaping out again to grab the SAW. I barely made it back into the copter. Sylvia thought it was reckless to risk my life for the SAW, but if a sicario had grabbed it, he could have shot us down. Glancing outside, we saw more vehicle lights at the edge of the field.

"Don't you die, Rick! *You hear me?*" Sylvia screamed. She dashed back to her pilot seat, and our Black Hawk rose from the field while turning toward the enemy. Because of the terrain's slope and the pine trees' height, Sylvia decided to escape directly over the flaming pickup and its assemblage of Delgado's men. She engaged the 20mm rotary guns, rotated the craft left and right, fired precisely, and decimated the threat. *That's why I took time to gauge weaponry, Rick!* At least, that's what she would have yelled if he weren't bleeding profusely. But she'd tell him later. After he'd survived.

As we descended the mountain's steep downslope, Sylvia said she saw another troop of African olive baboons scampering down a dirt road. We headed northwest. I tightened a tourniquet around Rick's gruesome injury, and my brain assessed the best strategies for getting us home safely.

CHAPTER 33

Sylvia internalized my questions and analyzed the copter's flight instruments. Interpreting the radar was rudimentary: Green was good. Yellow and orange could be bad. Green dominated the screen—no weather issues. Everything else checked off as hoped. We were currently airborne at one thousand feet with moderate outside air temperatures.

We flew northward after moving past Culiacán. We hoped to reach Fort Bliss Army Base, just beyond the US border in El Paso, Texas. But Sylvia recalculated key variables and concluded it was impossible to get there without a fuel stop. We'd run about one hundred miles short of the base, stranding us in the northern state of Chihuahua.

Fueling up at any private or military airbase wasn't an option. Our copter would likely get surrounded and fired upon. The government would assume we were criminals who hijacked a Mexican Marines Black Hawk and murdered its loyal soldiers. La Buena Familia would kill us for kidnapping their famous drug lord.

I asked to take control of the flight controls, allowing her to visit Rick.

"You're comfortable flying this bird?"

"I think so. I've never found it too complicated."

"God, you Green Berets are cocky as hell. Take the controls and prove you know what you're doing." She wasn't kidding.

"Sorry. That sounded condescending. I know it's not simple. Here's what I remember." I'd flown copters at Fort Benning and in the Middle East. Many Green Berets were trained to fly in the event of injury or death of the primary pilot. I removed the light backpack still strapped to my body. I re-familiarized myself with the placement and touch of the collective, a rod running horizontally along the left side of each cockpit seat that controlled the up and down of the copter. Then I gripped the cyclic stick in front of the seat and guided the chopper left and right. Finally, I placed my feet atop two anti-torque pedals that managed direction at a hover. She stared at me but didn't speak.

"Please, go check on Rick," I said while adjusting the collective and cyclic. She was nervous to see his condition. She'd seen it all on the battlefield, transported soldiers with missing arms and legs, but this was her future husband. "Sylvia, he'll make it." The comment was as much hope as conviction.

"I saw what it looked like when you brought him aboard." She squeezed my shoulder. "He's such a good . . ." Her voice cracked.

She took a deep breath and left. I considered the dangers Sylvia and Rick had volunteered for on my behalf. *This wouldn't have happened without you two heroes. I know that. You guys know that. I'm indebted.* I'd deliver my heartfelt words when our journey was over. *After* I knew Rick had survived, which was looking less likely every hour.

Sylvia stepped into the main cabin. Her fiancé's blood was splashed across the floor—more crimson than she'd expected. Had the bullet obliterated his femoral artery? No, she knew. Otherwise, he'd be dead.

She tested the tourniquet, the entry and exit holes in his leg, and the splintered bone fragments protruding from the wound. She silently mouthed a Russian Orthodox prayer her babushka had taught her as a child.

The altimeter in the cockpit: 980 feet above gently sloping topography. Meaning we were likely undetectable by Mexican radar. Airspeed: 160 mph ground speed equivalent. Direction: Almost due north, a straight line to El Paso. There was no radio chatter about criminals absconding with a Mexican Marines helicopter. Pilots' bad humor and typical aircraft or base communications were the only sounds heard.

After feathering the controls for stable flight, I reached for my backpack containing the laptop computer and what I assumed was the Emerald Cross. The bag containing the antiquity was lifted onto my lap. Even in the dim light of the cockpit, it mesmerized me. The rush of emotions was unexpected. Had my father been similarly affected when he first held the beguiling relic? I suddenly grew overwhelmed. *Samuel could be alive!*

A long period of reflecting on separate events that destroyed my family in horrific stages over thirty years passed. Then I tried to reconcile Delgado's extraordinary claims about Samuel. Sylvia interrupted my reflections and sat down.

"How's Rick holding up?"

"He's going to make it, Jamie. He must." Fresh tears started to fall. "We have a lifetime to spend together." She wiped her eyes. "And he wanted us to leave him bleeding to death in a field surrounded by cartel killers. Who does that?"

We stared at each other in admiration of her fiancé. After two days, I felt as close to Rick as some Green Berets and other soldiers I'd served with for years. "Rick adores you, and I can't wait for the wedding." I needed to move the conversation along, balancing sensitivity with urgency.

"You chose well. Rick's as solid as they come." I let that settle for a three-count. "Excuse my timing, Sylvia. I'm sorry. But I've been handed a stunning revelation that, if true, might have urgent life-or-death consequences. It came from Delgado."

She was prepared for anything after a day filled with the absurd and unexpected. "Of course. What is it?" She kept her left hand on my arm as she shifted to the edge of the right-side pilot's seat, leaning forward to capture every word spoken in the noisy cockpit.

Lifting the Emerald Cross from my lap, I handed it to her. "Brooke and Maria were killed because of this thing. An *LA Times* journalist had mentioned it in an interview about my mom. My sister-in-law tried to sell it back to Delgado. Apparently, his family had owned it for decades, maybe longer. Her attempt to broker a deal triggered madness. And here we are."

"*What? Wait.* Ashley got your family killed? Are you kidding me? And I thought she was just a pretty, self-absorbed, entitled nuisance. What an evil bitch!"

Predicting Sylvia would respond as she did, I said, "Ashley didn't know the dominoes would fall as they did. She isn't evil. She can be self-absorbed. And ignorant."

"You think? I've only met her once, at a bar with your softball team in Tustin, and I picked her out as trouble. People like her annoy the hell out of me."

I knew she wanted to say much more, but I must have expressed dread or real pain. She halted her diatribe. Her opinion would change nothing. Events had already played out. I was burdened forever. Lectures about Ashley weren't helping me.

"I shouldn't have said that. I'm sorry. You know her better than I do, and I don't know any details. It's just . . ." *That pretty witch got your wife and mother killed!* She finally clenched her jaw. "You were headed somewhere with the story?"

My chest expanded slowly, and my shoulders rose. She sensed other surprises were in store. "Finding out the Emerald Cross actually exists and now possessing it is the lesser of two discoveries. If I'm to believe his second claim." I rehearsed my words while staring at dark skies reflecting a seemingly infinite number of stars. I met her gaze. "Delgado says my father is alive. Held captive in a bunker near my home. That he's been there for thirty years."

"*Yeah, right!* What a load of BS. He's just looking for an angle. A bargaining chip. He didn't want you to put a 9mm slug through his head, which I'm still hoping one of us does before this is all over. It's a total fabrication from a desperate, wicked, disgusting human." She stared at me hard, but I didn't know what she wanted me to say. "Come on, you must agree."

"He showed me photos from his laptop as proof. The man looked just like me. Maybe twenty or thirty years older. I mean, as if I were staring at a twin. He would've been my age when he was killed. Or kidnapped. Or . . ." I shook my head, trying to extricate the burden of unknowns. "Would you look at the images and draw your own conclusions?"

"Of course, Jamie." She reached forward and patted my knee. "I just hate to see what Delgado's doing to you. At least, what I *think* he's doing. Filling your head with lies and doubts and impossibilities. I read the *Times* article, too. The journalist verified your father had been murdered. Even the president of Mexico confirmed it. It hurts to see you conflicted like this."

"I get it. But if you don't mind," I said, lifting my backpack. She reached inside, pulled the laptop out, and powered it up.

"You know the password?" she said with a tone of certainty.

"I don't. But I think—"

"Keep flying." She marched from the cockpit, pulled her Sig Sauer 9mm from its holster, and approached Delgado wielding a gun and the laptop. "What's the password?" she demanded while pressing her pistol into one of his ribs. "I'm not screwing around, Delgado, you piece of shit. Give me the password, or I'll throw your ass out of this helicopter."

He twisted a scowl through his battered face, appearing somewhat cartoonish with cuts and welts and half a front tooth missing. "Who do you think you are?" Nodding through squinted eyes, he clenched his teeth so hard Sylvia watched his jaw muscles quiver.

"You're a douchebag with delusions of being mighty and feared. You're neither to me. Password—*now!*"

He studied her face. "Stupid bitch."

She screamed at me to slow the helicopter to about 50 mph. I gripped the throttle at the end of the collective and slowed our warship. She set the laptop on a metal shelf and calmly opened the main cabin sliding door. I twisted around to watch her with a wary eye. Thrashing cool air invaded the interior. She grabbed Delgado's body by his shirt and slid his bound frame across the floor so that his head protruded into the turbulent draft of the slowed helicopter.

Delgado tilted his head from his prone position, appearing less confident than he had seconds earlier. She yanked him back into the cabin and shrieked into his ear amidst the sounds of a churning motor and vibrating cabin. "I hope you can hear me! Give me the password, or out you go. Nod, yes or no."

After seconds of no response, she pushed his head and shoulders further into the cool night air. With the drug lord appearing committed to machismo, she grabbed him by the shirt with one hand and waved goodbye with the other. Clutching his upper and lower body to throw him from the helicopter, I glanced behind me, assuming—hoping—she'd show restraint. But then she flashed *that look*. Just before I commanded her to release him, Delgado nodded in the affirmative. She pulled him back in and screamed, "Password! Or you're skydiving without a parachute."

His response was swift. "Duke Blue Devils 61. No spaces, no capitals."

"You think I'm an idiot? You're messing with the wrong woman." She reached for the laptop, which remained powered up, and lifted the screen before typing *dukebluedevils61*. She was in. *Unbelievable*, she silently muttered, what laughable security. She slid Delgado back against the fuselage, closed the cabin door, squeezed Lucia's arm to offer compassion—*you poor woman, you must be horrorstruck*—and rushed back to the cockpit.

"I got the password." She didn't need to look for the images Delgado insisted were of Samuel. The Pictures folder, still open from my confrontation with Delgado in his den, held multiple date-stamped photos from the past fifteen years. It also included older, weaker-resolution likenesses appearing to have been scanned from pre-digital era photographs. "Astonishing. This has got to be your dad—you're the spitting image of him. Sorry for doubting."

"Doubting is healthy. My mind's spinning. But if you and I are convinced, then, as mind-numbingly remarkable as it all seems, I need to act quickly. Grab the controls."

She took over as I stood to chat with Delgado. I was acutely hopeful of reuniting with my father but realized such aspirations could be replaced by crushing heartache. The pressing concern was timing: When Ashley first contacted Delgado about the Emerald Cross, it took only hours for the drug lord to deploy killers to our home. I kneeled beside Delgado. "Is my father alive?"

He didn't respond. "If he is, save him. You said yourself he was, or is, a good man."

"Are you going to threaten to throw me from this helicopter, as your *accomplice* did? And why would I concern myself with helping Samuel? He was responsible for the deaths of my two brothers."

"You're fortunate to be breathing, Delgado. You told me keeping Samuel in a bunker was your idea of artistic evil." I rubbed my forehead with the top of my dirty wrist, revealing the Green Beret tattoo to the drug lord. "Is my father really alive?" The possibility remained at once exhilarating and excruciating.

We measured each other while processing variables related to our and other people's futures. While I hoped for an unlikely reunion, he schemed about escape and legal options. "And if he is?"

"Then I'll appeal for your sentence to be reduced." *Sell it, Jamie—sell it! Make him believe.*

"That assumes you'll get me to the United States. In front of a jury. Found guilty. None of that is a given."

"True. But if my father is alive and remains so, you're in a much better position than if your men execute him."

He appeared pensive and did not respond.

"You murdered my wife and mother hours after learning Maria possessed the Emerald Cross. Is it also too late to save my father?"

After running his swollen tongue over a broken tooth, in a voice distinct from any he'd used since we'd first met, he said, "Again, I did not kill your wife and mother. My men exacted revenge as they deemed appropriate."

My body froze. What makes people this wicked?

"There are standing orders to kill Samuel in the event of my capture or death." He tasted the blood at the edge of his mouth, staring away. Another long pause. "Has my cartel deemed me captured or killed? I can only guess. Yes, Samuel is in grave danger."

A rush of emotions triggered by his cavalier manner enraged me. I ached for the chance to embrace Samuel, but what if La Buena Familia had already killed him tonight? Or if they'd done it thirty years earlier, as then-President Cornesa had insisted? Agonizing uncertainty engulfed me. Glaring at the face of the drug boss stretched out before me, I reminded myself that, one way or another, his reign of terror was over. Why didn't that truth console me?

Delgado motioned with his chin and eyes. I leaned in, and in a monotone voice, he said, "Ashley will also die."

That's impossible. It's an idle threat. US Marshals are guarding her in a secret location. But wait . . . this bastard's full of surprises. He could be spouting the truth. Then again, should that matter? Am I obliged to care about the welfare of a sister-in-law who triggered Brooke and Maria's executions?

Of course I am.

CHAPTER 34

"You doubt me?" Delgado asked.

"Shouldn't I? You're a desperate man facing a lifetime of incarceration."

"You are correct. As you Americans say, I am in a bit of a pickle." He pressed his tongue against the inside of his cheek. "I have a proposition."

I scowled and said nothing.

A high-pitched screeching sound swept through the cabin, not entirely drowned out by the engine and a rattling fuselage. It seemed remotely familiar, but I stood amidst the five copter occupants, and no one else reacted.

Delgado said, "I propose we align to save Samuel and Ashley. If successful, you convince authorities to drop any charges of my being an accomplice to your wife and mother's murders."

"You just told me your men have standing orders to kill Samuel. And that Ashley will soon die."

"I spoke the truth. Understand that we are running out of time. Commit to my request, and let's try to save your father and Ashley."

"If I'm foolish or desperate enough to accept your terms, how do I know you won't order their deaths from prison?"

"I have the best legal team in America. Harvard and Stanford trained. Notable stalwarts of the law community. I have a much better chance of being convicted for the deaths of Brooke and Maria than I ever do of running the largest cartel in the world. Drug charges against me have never stuck and never will. I simply pay people off. But the government could pressure weak or frightened lieutenants to squeal about the killings of your wife and mother." He gazed long and hard. "But if I were ever to face jail time, you have my word I will never issue orders to kill Ashley and Samuel."

Your word ain't worth shit, I wanted to yell out. "I despise you and everything you stand for. If Samuel and Ashley are alive and stay that way, we can discuss your terms. *After* they're proven safe."

"Do not take me for a fool, Jamie. I have all the leverage. Commit now or live with the truth: You may have been able to save them, only to learn they were eliminated tonight." He spoke casually. Like he was asking a stranger for the time.

My instincts suggested his words might be truthful, but I felt like I was playing poker with a psychotic master of the bluff.

The screeching sound pierced the cabin again, lasting just a fraction of a second. I glanced upward, wondering if it originated in the main rotor's gear housing. Sylvia turned from the pilot's seat to glance at me, though she seemed minimally curious. All aircraft produce random noises.

After considering all the moving parts, I turned to Delgado. "It's a deal. Now you better hope we can save them both." The prospect of freeing Samuel was mind-numbing. I also knew I had a responsibility to attempt to save Ashley. It's what Brooke would have wanted. And it's what my conscience dictated. "Give me the location of the property where my father's held. I'll pass it on to the DEA, plus the threat to Ashley."

"You will call Special Agent in Charge Washington at the DEA. Am I correct?"

Another surprise. "How do you know him?"

"I know many in authority, especially within the DEA, FBI, and CIA. Agent Washington's assistant has acted as an early warning system regarding DEA and Mexican military or police raids on my compounds." He gazed hard at me, surprised I hadn't yet asked a follow-up question. "Because she did not warn me of your assault tonight, she is now expendable."

"That's bullshit. This is all a wild goose chase, isn't it?" I felt simultaneously betrayed and stupid for having taken the bait he offered. There's no way a drug lord good be *this* connected. "Tell me the name of Agent Washington's assistant?"

"Agent Renée Sheffield." He spoke with confidence and a slight grin.

Sheffield and I met at the DEA field office in Los Angeles. Fixing my gaze on a rattling metal shelf, I internalized surprising bits of information while forcing myself to prioritize the next steps. "Give me Samuel's bunker location."

"I cannot remember the address, but the street is Monarch Drive in North Tustin. There are two massive palms on each side of the property's entry gates—much taller than other trees in the area."

Incredible. I know that street and the ivy-covered home well, having passed it countless times in my youth. It's a stunning Italian villa with a maze of manicured gardens. Hearing the narco boss describe its unmistakable towering palms provided credibility to his claims. But imagining Samuel being held captive for three decades within minutes of my childhood home prompted dark thoughts of retribution. *Don't go there, Jamie. Don't go there.*

Reaching down, I clutched the fabric of Delgado's shirt in my right hand and pulled his upper torso two feet off the floor, pushing our faces within inches. "You're an evil piece of shit." I struggled not to hurt him, to slam the butt of my Beretta into his temple, but such an act would accomplish nothing and waste precious minutes. "If you've lied to me, I'll let Sylvia shoot you."

Delgado nodded and replied in Spanish, "And I know she would enjoy doing that."

"You said Agent Sheffield is acting as your mole in the DEA. Prove it. Then tell me why you didn't buy off Agent Washington, as you have half of Mexico."

"Pennsylvania, Arapahoe, and Triton. Those are the codenames of three unsuccessful attempts to apprehend me over the past nine months. Confirm that with the DEA."

Rushing to the cockpit, I grabbed a red pen to write the codenames on my forearm.

"I did not buy off Agent Washington because he would not let me," Delgado said. "I have met few wholly incorruptible men in my life—most of us have our price—but he is one. Your father is another. And I suspect the apple did not fall far from the tree."

I squinted while tapping the keys of my burner.

Washington felt the vibration of his phone in the pocket of his DEA vest. He was in Mexico staring yet another mission defeat in the eyes, and his stateside phone was buzzing. Most of the people who'd typically dial it were milling about nearby. The caller was marked private, so he answered in a sharp tone of annoyance. "Who is this?"

"Jamie Morales."

His mind processed reams of data in seconds. He snapped his

fingers before putting one to his lips, commanding silence from three DEA agents and two Mexican Marine officers. Intrigue immediately permeated the room.

"I'm swamped, Mr. Morales. But the timing of your call seems beyond chance."

"I am in Mexico."

Washington turned away from the others in the room and stared impassively for seconds. "Please tell me you had nothing to do with the raid on Delgado's compound."

"Is Assistant Special Agent Sheffield with you?" I asked in a firm, crisp tone.

"Damnit, Mr. Morales, this isn't a time for irrelevant riddles. And I can barely hear you through the background noises—where are you?"

"That doesn't matter yet. Listen closely to everything I say and then act accordingly." I spoke loudly, straining to overcome the rattling cabin and engine sounds.

"I don't report to you. And if you were even remotely involved in tonight's events, you've just bought yourself jail time. Answer my question: Were you on Delgado's property?"

"I most definitely was. I want you to call me back on this number in five minutes. Ensure Agent Sheffield and my friend Jack Kershaw, whose property in Temecula you've had staked out for four days, get conferenced in on a single line." I precisely enunciated the ten digits of Jack's cell phone. "Make it happen, Agent Washington. Sir."

"I told you we'd eventually grab Delgado. Raiding his compound was an unnecessary risk and a huge mistake. It'll now be much harder to apprehend him. I've always respected you, Mr. Morales, but this blunder proves I was a fool."

"Give me a break! You had three chances to capture Delgado. What do you think of this: *Pennsylvania. Arapahoe. Triton.* You failed, so I was forced to act."

Both phones grew silent, and I imagined Washington's surprise. "Where'd you get that information?"

"I'll assume that's confirmation those were the codenames of each mission. I have bigger surprises in store when you call me back. Remember, I need Agent Sheffield and Jack Kershaw on the line. Time is of the essence." I hung up.

After lowering the phone, Washington internalized my startling truths and unsettling ambiguities. As he excused himself and bolted out the door, all eyes were upon him, including those of the DEA and Mexican Marines. Aggressively approaching his highly decorated subordinate, Assistant SAC Sheffield, Washington thought she appeared slightly apprehensive.

After putting my phone in my pants pocket, I heard the elusive high-pitched sound inside the Black Hawk for the third time. It seemed more human than before and appeared to come from the rear interior of the fuselage. Walking behind the cabin to a cargo bin, I nudged a large container to peek behind it and grew shocked when a terrified olive baboon screamed, flailed, and rushed past me toward the cockpit. Lucia cried aloud as it passed her, throwing herself sideways while the animal scurried toward Sylvia.

Hysterical and acting threatened, the baboon unleashed a flurry of claws at Sylvia. Its fangs punctured holes in her right forearm and hand. It attempted to lodge itself beneath the instrument panel extending the length of the cockpit, knocking into the critical cyclic and collective controls. The craft twisted wildly, at one point entering a 45° dive.

Sylvia had no option but to battle the baboon while maintaining her grip on the controls to stabilize the copter.

Finally gaining leverage, Sylvia reached for the Sig Sauer strapped to her thigh. But the wild creature attacked her even more violently, hitting the cyclic and pushing us into another dangerous descent. Lucia, Delgado, and Rick flew against one of the sliding cabin exit doors, eliciting screams and grunts. Sylvia bellowed from the cockpit, "Need help, Jamie!"

Pop!

My shot missed its target and hit the metal framing of the cockpit window with a resounding thud. Grabbing a parachutist's bar near one of the sliding exit doors, I steadied my boots, which were sliding across Rick's still-moist blood on the floor. Gaining leverage, I extended my Beretta and delivered a second round into the animal's chest, but it barely reacted.

The frightened animal continued relentlessly, its piercing screams adding terror to the struggle. Sylvia battled for control. As the Black Hawk twisted violently, I maintained my grip on the metal bar next to the main cabin door. I gained stability and aimed just as the baboon coiled itself for another spring at Sylvia.

Pop pop!

Blood and brain sprayed across the cockpit. Stolen from Africa, placed within a drug lord's pretend Serengeti, stowed aboard a flying machine it stumbled upon, and finally killed by an instrument he could never understand.

Sylvia appeared calm amidst the grisly scene and quickly secured the collective and cyclic to regain control and stabilize the Black Hawk. I pushed Delgado back against the fuselage. Lucia stared blankly and adjusted her harness. Rick awoke with groans and in obvious pain. Just as I inspected Rick's still-bleeding limb, my phone vibrated.

Agent Washington was calling back.

CHAPTER 35

Pressing the green button, I answered, "Morales."

"Agent Washington here. Jack Kershaw and Assistant Special Agent Sheffield are conferenced in. Now explain yourself."

"I've been informed Agent Sheffield is a mole for Delgado and La Buena Familia. If that's true, she's the reason Delgado's been able to disappear just before your forces arrived."

"You've wasted my time, Mr. Morales. I'm in the middle of an international disaster—*one you created!*—and you're making ridiculous claims."

"So, Agent Sheffield, you're on the line?"

"I am."

"Agent Washington, we both know it's difficult for guilty people not to divulge a degree of complicity. Examine her eyes, body movements, and tone of her voice."

"Your allegations are absurd. Agent Sheffield is among the highest-rated experts within the DEA. Her skills and reputation are impeccable. We debrief daily." As Washington spoke, his gaze locked onto Agent Sheffield's. Careful not to appear accusatory, he dissected every twitch, expression, and body nuance of the woman he'd promoted and worked alongside for years.

"It's also possible you are corrupt, Agent Washington." It needed to be said. "Jack, that's one of the reasons you're on this line. I want my ass covered. You're a witness."

"Roger that," the retired Army Major replied.

"Pennsylvania. Arapahoe. Triton," I repeated. "My gut says Agent Sheffield supplied those codenames to Delgado. But if it wasn't her, it could've been you, Agent Washington."

Washington continued to study Sheffield, careful to remain expressionless. He said nothing for a long pause, likely internalizing my contention and cycling through his memory banks while analyzing the previous failed missions. "Who made these unsubstantiated claims, Mr. Morales?" Washington noticed Agent Sheffield's lips were now pressed tightly together. Her eyes eventually broke free from Washington's and darted left and right before settling back on her boss. She took a cautious quarter step backward but regained full composure.

"Jack, when we're done here, call our guys to join you and Erin on your property. I don't know who to trust yet. You need to take precautions. Perhaps even move to another location."

"Roger that," Jack replied. "But we're going nowhere. We've got an impressive arsenal on the property, and Erin just discovered she made the USA Shooting Team. This isn't a property for unwanted guests. But I'll call our favorite grunts, just in case."

"I'm going to hang up now, Mr. Morales. I don't like the way this is playing out. Falsehoods and accusations," Agent Washington said.

"Marco Delgado gave me the mission codenames and the intel on Agent Sheffield."

"Really. And when did he do that?" Washington snapped back.

"Minutes ago."

Washington quickly solved a puzzle while watching a DEA SUV

drive toward Agent Sheffield. He shook his head. "Unbelievable. So then I'll assume the background noises are from a Mexican Marines Black Hawk helicopter."

"They are."

"And you're telling me you have Delgado?"

"I am."

"Then congratulations. You've just guaranteed an international incident, Mr. Morales. This isn't going to turn out well for you."

Jack Kershaw yelled, "Shut the hell up, Mr. DEA man. Jamie Morales is straight up. He's got Delgado—something your team couldn't do. Stand down and do what he says. Understand, you bureaucratic—"

"I've got this, Jack!"

"He could be another mole!" my friend screamed.

During the verbal exchange, Agent Sheffield gradually retreated another quarter step. Washington noticed.

"I said I've got this, Jack—stop." The ex-soldier finally fell silent. "Agent Washington and Agent Sheffield, one of you is dirty. Perhaps both." As I spoke, Delgado grew animated from his bound position on the floor, twisting and speaking words muted by engines and a rattling fuselage.

"What is it?" I barked at the drug lord.

"I can help you. Agent Sheffield and I have slept together. She has a two-inch white rose tattooed onto her left breast."

I knew it would elicit heated responses, whether truthful or not. "Delgado claims he's slept with Agent Sheffield. He says a white rose is tattooed onto her left breast."

Washington lowered his eyes to Agent Sheffield's uniform-covered left breast. He didn't need further proof. The two had been romantically involved for years before reaching higher ranks. Washington reset his gaze just as Agent Sheffield reached for her Glock 17 sidearm and steadily aimed the black weapon's barrel at his head.

"I trusted you, Renée. Promoted you. And I loved you fifteen years ago. Put the gun down. It's over." Washington slowly moved his right hand toward his own holstered Glock.

"Don't try it, Kirby. You have no idea what I'm capable of."

"Clearly, I do now."

Having overheard the escalating confrontation, several DEA agents descended upon Sheffield and Washington, screaming at their respected comrade to lower her weapon. Instead, she rushed at her boss and applied a chokehold while pushing the Glock's barrel into his hairline, demanding everyone drop their guns. "Any sudden moves, he's dead."

"Renée, please, it's over," Washington implored.

She refused to surrender. Two simultaneous discharges erupted from her left flank, directly behind her superior.

Sheffield was flung backward at an angle, spewing blood from her left arm and a hole in her chest bored by a 9mm round. Critically wounded, she was the latest casualty of a brutal evening. Agent Washington knelt and gently placed an open palm upon her writhing body with a countenance only an ex-lover could project. Sheffield controlled her breathing while fighting through the agony. "I'm sorry, Kirby."

Washington nodded to one of the other agents while pointing at his disloyal assistant moaning on asphalt. Stepping away from the chaos, he glanced at his phone to confirm the line remained connected. "You were right about the mole, Mr. Morales. Agent Sheffield has deceived me."

"That doesn't mean Washington isn't dirty, Jamie!" Jack interjected.

"*Jack, please.*" While I sensed Washington's genuine emotions due to Sheffield's betrayal, I also knew that further delays could get Samuel and Ashley killed. "I need your help, Agent Washington."

"Indeed you do, Mr. Morales. Thirty feet from me, two Mexican Marine officers wonder where their missing helicopter is. It turns out a Mexican military drone captured your battle on Delgado's property, prompting a group of US Navy Seal-trained Mexican Special Forces to attempt to grab Delgado without final authority from their commanding officers."

"None of those Marines are alive," I said. "La Buena Familia combatants flooded the zone."

Washington said, "Do you expect me just to stroll on over and inform them an entire team of Special Ops are dead? Because of the selfish and vengeful whims of a rogue American ex-soldier?"

"I don't care what you tell them, sir. The truth is typically a good place to start."

"That's rich, Mr. Morales. And you're a beacon of truth? You lied when you said you'd stay out of Mexico."

"That's not true. I implied I'd stand down while sending a clear message that if you couldn't do the job, if you couldn't get Delgado, then I would. You failed. I'm here." I heard a deep, frustration-induced exhale over the phone. "I appreciate your efforts, Agent Washington, but put yourself in my shoes." *Have people forgotten? My wife and mother were slain on orders from this man!*

"Let's move on. You mentioned needing my help."

"Yes," I told him. "Two urgent matters. First, my father may be alive and isolated in a bunker below a home in North Tustin."

An evening of surprises grew ever more captivating. "I've read about your father's case. It'd be remarkable if he were still alive. Who made the claim?"

"Delgado."

"Delgado . . . of course," Washington muttered. "And he offered an address?"

"I have the street, and I can describe the house. It's not too far from where I grew up."

"Tame your expectations. I hope your father's alive for your sake, but you realize Delgado is likely playing you."

"Understood. The second request is to send an extra detail to protect my sister-in-law, Ashley MacDonald. Delgado's informed me La Buena Familia is likely on its way to kill her."

"He's feeding you lies. The US Marshal Service has an impeccable record protecting witnesses enrolled in its program. And there's no way he knows where she is." Washington glanced at Agent Sheffield, squinted, and gritted his teeth. "Hold on. Give me a moment." He walked briskly toward his dirty agent, barked at a DEA medic to give him space, and crouched down. "Agent Sheffield," he said aggressively, no longer interested in speaking as her respectful superior and ex-lover, "Delgado claims he knows where US Marshals are keeping Ashley MacDonald. Did you somehow discover her—"

"*Yes, yes.* She's in danger. When this is over, please tell authorities I tried to help." Her speech was slow and slurred, and Washington wondered if she'd truly intended to assist or if the drugs numbing her pain had facilitated further admissions of complicity she'd soon regret.

"Wow, you're a piece of work. You've put untold lives at risk," Washington replied with a face contorted by dismay. He drew his head back, stiffened upright, and stepped away. He placed the cell phone back to his ear. "Unfortunately, Agent Sheffield confirmed Delgado knows where marshals are protecting your sister-in-law."

"Please do whatever's necessary to save her. And my father. If he's, you know, alive."

As he watched Agent Sheffield's gurney get rolled into an ambulance, Washington said, "Give me the details on where Delgado claims your father's held. I'll hop off the line to coordinate with various agencies. We'll do what we can."

"I'm indebted. Here's the information—"

"Stop! Wait for Mr. Kershaw to hang up. Your father's possible whereabouts are too sensitive to divulge to a man I know nothing about."

"Give me a break. Who the hell do you think you are, DEA man? Jamie, you requested I be on this call for a reason."

"Jack stays on the line. I trust him completely. I trust him more than I trust you, Agent Washington. In times like this, we all need to make concessions." After Washington acceded, I passed on the details of Samuel's location. "Have I given you what you need?"

"Yes," said Washington. "Give me time to set things in motion, then I'll close the loop. Let's hope this works." A beep told me he'd dropped off the line.

"Damnit," I said.

From his California avocado farm, Jack said, "What is it?"

"The phone's blinking. I can recharge it in the cockpit. But first, I need you to get ahold of General Taylor. Tell him about everything you just heard on the call."

"Roger that. But to what end? What do you need from him?"

"We don't have enough fuel to get to Fort Bliss. I think we'll come up about eighty miles short."

"That'll put you smack in the middle of the Chihuahua desert."

"Exactly. Washington's plan probably won't include the Army. I'd feel better if it did. We'll need ground or air support to extract us after we put down. Five people are on board: Delgado, a young Mexican woman, Rick, and Sylvia."

"I was about to ask, are Rick and Sylvia okay?"

"Not really, but they're alive. Rick's in bad shape. No time to debrief."

"Stop. You owe me more than that."

"An AK-47 round obliterated his femur," I said as quietly as possible. "I told Sylvia he'd make it, but it's 50-50 at best." I gazed at Rick's limp frame lying still twelve feet away. "Pray for him."

"Done. Godspeed, buddy."

The burner's battery light flashed more quickly. "Get a hold of General Taylor. I'll call back when—" The line went dead.

Lucia and I stared at each other. I tried to convey compassion and hope amid what had to be a mind-numbingly insane evening for her. Understanding the large, bloodshot brown eyes I peered into were likely windows into a mind devoid of optimism, I tenderly squeezed her arm before stepping toward the cockpit to recharge the phone.

The extent of Sylvia's injuries stunned me—the baboon had clawed deep abrasions down her right arm. "That's a lot of blood loss. Are you faint?"

"I'm fine," she said. "Can you get rid of this ugly monkey carcass? I'm sure it's freaking Lucia out, laying there like a horror movie prop. I'll slow down so you can toss it out."

"Done."

After dragging the blood-drenched baboon to the main cabin, I waited for the copter to slow, then slid the door open and hurled the carcass out. After closing the exit, I marched to the rear of the cabin to grab a medkit I'd seen earlier. Returning to the second pilot's seat, I swiveled sideways to Sylvia. After rubbing her arm with a sterile cloth doused with alcohol, I wound tight bands of two-inch gauze around her hand, forearm, and bicep. I was concerned about rabies but didn't voice those fears. What good would it do while fleeing Mexico in a hijacked helicopter?

"That ugly thing better not have had rabies," she said right on cue while staring at her bloodied arm. "He got it worse than me, but I hate big-ass needles, and I've been told rabies shots require big-ass needles."

After offering an assuring rub to the back of her neck, I gazed out the cockpit window into darkness dotted by faint lights spread across the desert floor one thousand feet below. I strained to conceal my apprehensions.

CHAPTER 36

"Do we still have the rattlesnakes?" asked the La Buena Familia lieutenant they called Gumby, a moniker he'd earned through his propensity for twisting cartel enemies' bodies into unnatural positions just before killing them. He was dressed smartly in dark custom slacks and a Tommy Hilfiger pinpoint Oxford with sleeves rolled up to mid-forearm. Tall with a chiseled face and lean body, he appeared more Hollywood than executioner. His English was impeccable, as it was for his two associates, a talent enabling them to settle into the neighborhood as "those handsome, successful Latinos from Chile or Argentina or somewhere south."

"Yes, we have two snakes left. But our orders from Delgado have always been to kill Morales and then disappear when circumstances require. Boss Man may be dead. If he is, all hell is about to break loose. Let's not waste time getting this done." The man speaking earned his nickname Picasso through his penchant for penciling detailed abstract portraits of dead cartel victims.

Gumby put his arm around Picasso's shoulder and kissed his cheek. "I'm in charge. This sonofabitch got two of el patrón's brothers killed thirty years ago. Samuel Morales must now die, and I'd like his death to be memorable. Something we can celebrate with shots of tequila as octogenarians." He smiled and mildly pushed the barrel of his pistol into Samuel's forehead. After a good laugh, they agreed that devising a creative, extended execution would indeed be time well spent.

"Grab a plastic tube out of the garage," Gumby said to the third and most junior gang member, also dressed as if he were ready to stroll through the upscale stores lining South Coast Plaza. "It must be wide enough for a snake to crawl through." The youngest gang member nodded before striding down a long hall toward the garage.

Meanwhile, Picasso reentered the room carrying a two-foot-wide glass terrarium. "These are basic-looking Western Diamondbacks. I watched a nature show on Discovery where they filmed rattlesnakes of all different colors and sizes. A red one was the exact color of the clay at the bottom of the Grand Canyon. And there were white ones in Mexico and Arizona."

"Wild," commented Gumby. "God created one amazing planet, didn't he? I get blown away by how complicated, interconnected, and beautiful the earth is." He pressed his nose against a pane of the terrarium's glass and jumped backward after one of the snakes coiled and struck at him. "She's the one! Grab the aggressive little bitch. I've got a job for her."

"Grab it with what?"

Gumby said, "Go to the kitchen and get salad tongs."

The third man returned with a section of rubber hose used for car radiator repairs. He held it up. "What do you think?"

"Perfect," Gumby replied. "Now shove it down Morales's throat."

"I get it! The hose isn't for a snake. We're going to pour hydrofluoric acid down his throat and watch him melt."

"No, you idiot," Gumby said while staring at Picasso, who was similarly annoyed by the man's cluelessness. "Then I wouldn't have asked for the rattlesnakes."

"I guess you're right," said the third man. "It's just that we've done the snake bit before, but I've never seen someone melt from the inside out. It would've been interesting."

Gumby laughed hysterically. "*Interesting?* Shit, homey, you're one sick bastard. Remind me to never get on your bad side." He slapped Picasso on the back, and they roared. "Am I right?"

Picasso controlled his fit and replied, "Damn straight. Dude's got a little Hannibal Lecter in him."

During the gang members' exchange, Samuel Morales, whose ankles were bound and wrists duct-taped to the arms of a wooden chair, stared placidly straight ahead. The mustache of his twenties had grayed like his head of hair. He'd been threatened with death many times during his years of captivity, but this moment felt different. Nonetheless, he remained calm, deeply mired in thoughts of his wife, son, and the daughter-in-law he never met.

Gumby measured Samuel's surprisingly tranquil demeanor, stepped to his side, and slapped him hard. "Fuck you, Morales. I know you're scared shitless." Dissatisfied by the lack of any response, Gumby lied and told him, "Your son—*Jamie, the war hero*—was killed three hours ago. We sliced his head off with a machete, ISIS-style. Marco Delgado sends his condolences." He grinned and stared for a long pause at the pensive prisoner. "Before you die, I want you to know we enjoyed killing your wife and daughter-in-law. You'll become the fourth dead Morales."

The three men grew mesmerized by what they witnessed next. Tears streamed down Samuel's face and splashed onto the cement floor. As if the years of torment had finally become too burdensome, his body appeared to twitch in pain, mucus draining from his nose and over the gray duct tape strapped across his mouth. The smiles dissipated from Picasso and the third man's face. Gumby's expression of scorn and hatred evaporated.

"Let's get this done," Gumby said to his accomplices. "Shove the tube down his throat. Make it hurt." Gumby ripped the tape from Samuel's mouth. "Your death will be painful."

Samuel gazed stoically as a man standing before the gallows, his head tilted toward the skies, tears slowing to a trickle. Just before they forced one end of the tube into his mouth, he lowered his eyes. "God may never forgive you."

"Perhaps not, but your fate remains sealed." Gumby nodded to the other men, who struggled to steady Samuel's head and insert the tube. "Not very accommodating, is he?" Gumby clenched his fist and thrust it hard into Samuel's temple, then a second time. Samuel's eyes fluttered as his head swayed in a circle. "Get it done. Shove it deep down his throat."

Startling the trio, Samuel recovered enough to mumble, "Love you, Maria, Jaime, and Brooklyn. I am coming."

※ ※ ※

MONARCH DRIVE WAS A narrow private drive intersecting Foothill and Skyline roads. Three hundred feet down the secluded cobblestone street, on the left, stood an ornate electric metal gate, ten feet tall and twenty feet wide. On each side of the grand entrance stood towering fan palm trees, ninety feet tall and over one hundred fifty years old, reportedly the oldest in Orange County. The Italian villa and three acres of manicured gardens had been chronicled through magazine spreads.

Foothill and Skyline roads were blocked to traffic one mile north of the magnificent estate. The four occupants arrived in a dark, unmarked SUV with heavily tinted windows. They navigated the last two S-curves to their present location with lights off. Two occupants had never seen the house before. They'd honed their skills through dangerous assignments in Los Angeles and Mexico, not in the affluent suburbs of Orange County. Like the others, the third man and sole woman were assigned to the mission twenty-five minutes earlier. The estate was within her police precinct's jurisdiction and less than ten miles from the homes of two SUV occupants. When the local police officers received instructions from TUPD Chief Younkin, they texted their spouses to say they loved them. Cops and agents possessed a sixth sense regarding which missions might be fraught with real peril.

Both seasoned agents of the secretive DEA Special Response Teams sat in the front of the SUV. SRT squads were scattered around the country and world, organized to act immediately, and feared by criminal enterprises globally. Only two members of the SRT team, staged just north of Camp Pendleton in South Orange County, were available to respond this evening. The rest of the squad had gotten deployed for a covert mission in Mexico. Additional TPD officers volunteered, but agency heads agreed an initial team of four might better surprise the enemy.

Paired into mixed DEA-TPD teams, they planned to approach the villa from the front and rear. A security system protected the property, but calls to the monitoring center revealed it wasn't engaged. Their orders were to locate and free Samuel Morales. None of the four recognized the name of the man whose freedom endangered their own lives, but when they were informed their adversaries were members of La Buena Familia, anxieties stirred.

Parking near the villa, SRT Agent Morris measured how much Officer Dixon's appearance mirrored his wife's. That coincidence inadvertently triggered his total devotion to keeping her alive. He assumed she'd be annoyed or offended by his thoughts, but he told himself one can't always control such contemplations.

Officer Dixon recognized trepidation from the middle seat while meeting DEA SRT Agent Morris's gaze in the rearview mirror. After exiting the SUV, Agent Morris said, "Well, Officer Dixon, we picked one hell of an evening to get introduced." He adjusted his Kevlar vest and grabbed his LAR-15, a version of the military-issue AR, while Officer Dixon inspected the 22-round magazine of her Glock 17.

"We can chat more when it's over. This is a major operation—our chief was uncertain and concerned when I left the precinct," she said, grabbing her carbine. "Whoever this Morales guy is, he must have one hell of a backstory."

"Let's do this," DEA Agent Morris told the three other team members. He pointed at a wooden side gate to the estate abutting Skyline Drive, just beyond a strand of towering eucalyptus trees. "Dixon and I will enter from there. You two approach from east of the entry gates. Do not engage too quickly, but don't hesitate to fire at will to keep yourselves safe. I've battled cartel heavies three times. They're undisciplined but ferocious. Unyielding."

Team Two moved stealthily down Monarch Drive and managed

their way up and over a stone-covered retaining wall capped with eighteen inches of ornate green wrought iron spikes. DEA SRT Agent Orlowski suddenly thrust his left arm perpendicular to his body, halting the advance of his TPD SWAT partner. Recognizing a slight yellow glow through a decorative four-paned rectangular window standing two feet above ground level, just above what could be a basement or bunker, DEA Agent Orlowski stepped cautiously behind a bed of roses to check inside.

Automatic gunfire from Picasso's tightly clutched AK-47 erupted through the window. One of the rounds exploded DEA Agent Orlowski's ankle, but he quickly got prone at the base of the house, shielding himself from additional rounds. His TPD SWAT partner caught the silhouette of a man bound to a chair—their target. The officer fired his Glock in four bursts of three with limited line-of-sight, careful not to hit the hostage.

Nearing the back patio, DEA SRT Agent Morris realized there were only seconds to save Morales. He signaled Officer Dixon for cover as he rushed toward an impressive ten-foot door. Blasting eight rounds through the double-paned beveled glass, Agent Morris thrust his body past shards lining the decorative entry. He slammed himself into the base of a stuccoed wall and covered Officer Dixon as she similarly flung herself into the residence.

"Cut the power!" Agent Morris screamed into his mic. Moments later, a rattling of LAR-15 gunfire echoed from the opposite side of the house. Then darkness filled the property.

"Team Two lead is down but alive," said the TPD officer who shut off the power from garage circuit panels. Sirens blared from multiple twisting hillside roads. A stealth approach was now moot. Through the mic fastened to his headgear, the officer in the garage added, "I think our target is in the basement."

"Headed that way," replied DEA Agent Morris. He and Officer Dixon secured and activated their night vision goggles from a corner of the kitchen, near a set of stairs leading into the pitch dark of the home's lower level. This could all be for naught. Morales might have just perished—they'd heard enough gunfire to wipe out a large crowd.

"Kill Morales! Shoot him!" screamed Gumby, leaning against the thick trim of the basement door. Gumby and the third gang member had grabbed their AK-47s just after Picasso recognized the armed DEA SRT agent outside the basement window and fired indiscriminately.

"Where is he? I can't see a damn thing!" bellowed Picasso. "We need to get the hell out of here. *Now!* Or we'll all die."

"We need to waste Morales!" Gumby again yelled out. "If we don't, Delgado or his replacement will kill our families."

"I see him!" said the third gang member. There was a crashing sound, including broken glass, followed by the warnings of a rattlesnake. Darkness and confusion reigned.

Thap thap thap!

"I got him! I fucking killed him!" said the third man triumphantly.

"You positive?" Gumby yelled. "I can't see shit through this smoke—how can you?"

"I got him. I know it! Now let's get the hell out of here. ¡Vamos!"

"Wait. My eyes are adjusting. Can you see me, Picasso?" said Gumby. "Picasso?"

A groaning arose from the floor. Gumby's eyes followed the faint sound, almost a gurgling, until he could make out a yellow dress shirt.

As Gumby took two steps toward his comrade of over ten years, the snake's rattling grew louder, more high-pitched. Reality struck. *"You shot Picasso!"*

Just beyond his dying friend, Gumby made out the shape of Samuel's chair and body bent sideways across the floor, the black tube still protruding from his mouth. "You just took your last breath, Morales." He pressed his AK-47's barrel into Samuel's eye socket, and his brain commanded his finger to pull the trigger.

A split second earlier, DEA SRT Agent Morris's brain had ordered his finger to squeeze the trigger of his LAR-15 carbine, whose bullets obliterated the basement's doorknob. The agent crashed inside and put three bullets into the third gang member's torso. Gumby fired on Agent Morris, who crumpled to the ground after taking a 122-gram projectile, which blasted a hole through his shoulder.

TPD SWAT Officer Janice Dixon rushed into the room with her night-vision goggles and aimed her Glock into a six-inch circle in the middle of Gumby's chest. She didn't miss. With no more dead or dying gangsters in the room, she ordered the Team Two TPD officer to switch the light circuits back on. Seconds later, Dixon stood awash in a transfigured world. She examined DEA Agent Morris's wound and told him, "You're going to make it."

Ambulance and police sirens remained blaring from every direction. A crescendo of voices cascaded onto the Italian estate from officers and agents who had sealed the property's perimeter and surrounding areas while both lead teams engaged La Buena Familia.

No one had yet answered the most crucial question. Officer Dixon pulled the tube from a disbelieving man's mouth and righted his chair just as TPD Chief Younkin and two other officers rushed forward.

Gazing compassionately into the eyes of a middle-aged man strapped to the chair, Officer Dixon asked, "Are you Samuel Morales?"

The whites of his eyes were veined and moist. He steadied his head and replied, "I am."

"Mr. Morales, I am Chief Younkin of the Tustin Police Department. You're as much a hero as your son."

"No." Samuel shook his head slowly. "These men," he pointed at the dead gang members, "said my dear son was executed tonight."

"Not true, sir," Chief Younkin flatly stated. "We've learned Captain Jamie Morales is very much alive."

CHAPTER 37

US Marshal Austin ended the call and clutched the phone as he approached Marshal Patton. "Major breach. Imminent danger. Our location's compromised—a mole in the DEA. La Buena Familia is potentially on its way. Delgado's been captured, making Ashley an urgent target." Marshal Austin had stopped calling her "Ms. MacDonald" months earlier in defiance of regulations. "We've been ordered to hunker down, defend, protect. Additional marshals are getting helicoptered nearby within ten minutes. Local police, DEA, and FBI resources are en route. I'll get her up."

Marshal Austin darted to Ashley's bedroom and approached her bed without turning on the lights, then he carefully ordered her to get up immediately. She appeared to be internalizing his words while moving confusedly, as people awoken from deep slumber typically do. Then he ripped off her comforter and sheet, exposing her body dressed only in a tee and panties.

"*Please!* I'm not even dressed. What are you doing?"

"Do exactly as I say, Ashley. We have a situation." He guided her aggressively toward the door.

"*Stop!* At least let me get dressed, then please tell me what's happening." Over the previous months, she'd developed feelings for her protector and been soothed by his presence. Not this time. Real fears flooded her mind.

"No time for that." He placed a hand on her lower back and guided her down the hall.

"You're scaring me. Are we going to be okay?" She quickly acknowledged it was a stupid, unanswerable question.

Pushing Ashley into his bedroom, Marshal Austin dimmed the lights before rushing to his closet to pull out a dark plastic case holding his second of two Glock 17s, a Colt 9mm submachine gun, and ammo clips. Protective vests and body armor filled a second, larger container. One set of gear had been sized for a smaller person.

Marshal Austin stepped forward, put large hands around her bony shoulders, and gazed intensely into her typically striking blue eyes, now obscured by darkness. "Marshal Patton and I have been expertly trained for any situation. But we need to take cautionary steps. Stay in this room. Understand? Under *no* circumstances do you walk out that door," he said with a flick of his chin. He disclosed nothing else, having learned she possessed an active imagination. Talk of bullet-proofed rooms aiming to protect her from drug traffickers' AK-47 bullets might be too much to digest.

Concussive blasts rattled the house. A rocket-propelled grenade exploded into the protective windowpane inside Ashley's now empty bedroom. Marshal Austin shoved her to the floor. She curled into a fetal position next to a nightstand holding a short stack of books. There was no time to strap body armor to either of their bodies.

Cascading sounds of assault reverberated relentlessly. Smoke and dust filled the house. Marshal Austin motioned for Ashley to stay put, then crawled down the hall toward his partner.

Without speaking, the two marshals took positions that provided a line of sight through several of the now missing windows—there were limits to the pounding even bullet-proof glass could take. The three home-dwellers were doomed if their enemies were equipped with multiple RPGs. But the only certainty in battle was uncertainty. In quick bursts of five rounds from their Colt submachine guns, they returned fire from as many windows as their barrels could aim through. Because of the amplified sounds of gunfire, Ashley assumed backups had arrived and entered the home. No such luck.

The second RPG discharge decimated the kitchen, not far from where Marshal Patton had been exchanging fire with La Buena Familia. The blast and concussion seemed to yank the home from its foundation. After Marshal Austin called out to his partner, he discerned a faint reply. "I'm hit."

Slowly, the dark, damp sky beyond every window turned fully illuminated by the projection of multiple helicopter searchlights. The penetrating vibrations caused by the copters shook the books off the nightstand Ashley lay beside. A painting of Lake Michigan fell from a wall onto her legs. She ignored it.

Mixed sounds of battle—screaming, scrambling, handguns, machine guns—turned deafening. Concussions from exploded grenades resounded one or two hundred feet beyond the home. The distinctive *thap thap thap* of machine guns remained constant. Smells of spent rounds and fighting permeated the air.

Sirens blaring from dozens of police and inter-agency vehicles flooded the area. Tires screeched to a halt on damp pavement, followed by the heightened eruption of even more gunfire. Marshal Austin made his way toward the kitchen. Awash in the glow of beams from searchlights, he found his partner staring upward, his expression peaceful. He was dead. Pain distorted his face as he whispered private words to a fallen comrade.

Gunfire throughout the neighborhood sounded like the climax of an Independence Day celebration. That was followed by dispersed weapons discharges before, finally, the battle with La Buena Familia ended. There were no more Delgado narcos to kill.

US Marshals, DEA Special Response Team agents, local police, and other authorities approached in droves, battering locked doors and climbing through windows blasted away by gunfire and RPGs. One of the first US Marshals helicoptered in approached with an expression of disbelief that anyone had survived inside the home. Marshal Austin said, "You saved Ms. MacDonald. And me. Marshal Patton didn't make it."

His comrade squeezed his bicep. "I'm so sorry."

Marshal Austin turned away and stepped to his bedroom, where he twisted a handle to guide the door open. Ashley turned her head from her curled position and looked justifiably bewildered but not the emotional wreck he'd expected.

She measured his distressed gaze and wet eyes. "Oh, Thomas, please tell me Dylan survived." It was a moment for more intimate first names.

"I'm sorry, Ashley. Dylan's gone."

"*No!*" she screamed, tightly draping herself around his rigid body, needing to transfer her grief . . . and guilt. Her fateful decision to speak to Marco Delgado about the Emerald Cross had once again triggered the death of an innocent human being.

CHAPTER 38

Sylvia studied the map, handed it to me, and pointed to Ciudad Cuauhtémoc, a small city in Chihuahua state, about halfway to El Paso. "At our current burn rate, we'll fall about eighty miles short of the border. Finding a safe place to land should be easy—the area is farming country."

"Got it. Pick a spot you believe we can reach. I'll relay the GPS coordinates to Jack."

Sylvia told me she hoped soldiers, agents, or police had rescued Samuel, but she conceded her mind was filled with doubts. As for Ashley, she said she despised the self-absorbed woman who triggered Brooke's murder and didn't think she could forgive her. Sylvia was an incredible woman in so many ways. But why share reservations with me while critical events played out? Perhaps I held exaggerated hopes, but why squelch them? It appeared stress from the mission was affecting her. And yet, in the middle of a battle with La Buena Familia sicarios, she risked everything to save the life of a woman she'd never met.

"I'm calling Jack," I told her before grabbing the sufficiently recharged burner phone from a cockpit outlet. Walking through the main cabin, I noticed Delgado's rictus half-smile had barely faded. *Evil bastard.* Walking behind a metal partition, I dialed Jack's number.

"It's me. Any luck with General Taylor?"

"Buddy, lots of news. Yes, General Taylor is spun up and on board. A technician is messing with the phones. Give us a second."

On board? Messing with the phones? What? I waited for Jack to fill in the blanks. My imagination grew unbounded while the line emitted strange noises. *Samuel had indeed been held captive? But was saved? No, wait. Shot but alive? Didn't survive but said he loved me? Ashley got moved to a new location? La Buena Familia never arrived, and they're both safe? Or maybe they're afraid to give me the bitter truth—neither survived.* The unknowns turned agonizing. *But . . . the way Jack spoke, the tone of his voice, the words.* Then I asked myself: *A technician in Jack's home?*

White noise, scrambled sounds, and muddled voices mixed in the background. *"Damnit, Jack!"* I ordered. "What the hell's going on?" Perhaps his phone was getting passed around or covertly monitored? *"Please, Jack!* Are you and Erin safe?" I hoped they hadn't been captured, that their words and actions weren't being orchestrated by cartel heavies who'd invaded their property and home. Then I heard someone in the background say, "Okay, we're all connected."

"General Taylor speaking. Can you hear me, Captain Morales?"

My first reaction was surprise, then doubt, and finally, wonder. Had Major Jack Kershaw been more successful than expected in obtaining the Army general's support? I chastised myself for questioning. Of course he'd delivered—yet again. "Yes, sir," I replied from inside the back of the cabin.

"Excuse the delay," the general continued. "Things are moving fast, and we needed to conference in multiple encoded lines. I'm on base at Fort Benning."

"Roger that."

"Special Agent in Charge Washington briefed me on your situation. We've quietly supported DEA missions in Latin America before."

Thanks for that intel. Now I can blame the DEA *and* the Army for failing to capture the guy lying at my feet.

The static over the phones suddenly grew louder, prompting General Taylor to exasperatedly bark at someone in his room, "Tell me we didn't lose Agent Washington."

"I'm still on the line, General."

"Okay then, it's your show now."

"Mr. Morales," Washington began, "I want to start by giving you life-changing news. Your father was indeed held captive for three decades near your home. Special Forces and local cops invaded the property less than an hour ago. There was a shoot-out. I've learned he is in surprisingly good physical and mental condition, given his hellish experience."

Growing lightheaded, I clutched the parachutist grip welded to the fuselage near one of the sliding exit doors. I needed to steady myself. "So, so, *my father is alive?* Are you positive? Have one of you talked to him?" I saw Sylvia pump her fist.

"I haven't spoken with him yet, Mr. Morales. But I assure you he's been rescued and is in DEA and FBI protection. I'm told he demands a single message be delivered: *He loves you.*"

"Dear God, he's alive. *Alive!* I love him, too. *Tell him!*" Dizzied by the startling news, I worked to settle myself. "But you haven't mentioned Ashley. Is she, did she—"

"US Marshals are safeguarding Ashley MacDonald. One of the men assigned to protect her was lost during an intense firefight twenty minutes ago."

Her recklessness triggered the killings of Brooke and Maria, but all I could think to inaudibly mouth was *She doesn't deserve the burden of this much anguish and guilt.* "I'm sorry about the marshal, sir. Please tell Ashley I'm thrilled she's safe and look forward to speaking with her soon."

"Done," Washington replied. "We need to move on. Our goal is to get you all home alive—even Delgado. Major Kershaw supplied General Taylor with your Black Hawk landing coordinates. Resources are amassing as we speak."

After Washington paused, I yelled the information to Sylvia, who suddenly grew preoccupied. "Agent Washington, please standby." She gave me the alarming news. "Our pilot, retired Army Captain Sylvia Sokolov, just informed me she's been tracking an incoming aircraft on the transponder. The bogey's approaching from the west, perpendicular to our route, about twice our speed. She's guessing it's a prop plane."

Several voices chattered in the background. I couldn't determine who was saying what. "Mr. Morales, Washington here. Your situation is even more complicated than you realize."

"Negative, sir. Our situation's been pretty damn complicated all day."

"Of course," he replied. "We have solid intel—an audio file—implicating President Valdes of Mexico in a bribe from La Buena Familia, orchestrated by Delgado in exchange for protection of him and the cartel. Twenty million in cash."

"Which means?"

"That Valdes might insert himself into this evening's developments. The people standing next to me would not be surprised if Mexican military aircraft or a contracted private plane attempted to engage before your Black Hawk reached the US border. If Valdes believes you've got Delgado on board, he may order you shot down. He's unaware we possess the implicating audio file. We'll inform him in minutes and hope he stands down. But he could grow desperate. More dangerous. Adding to the drama, because you've absconded with a Mexican Marines aircraft, an uninformed public might consider shooting you down justifiable."

Seconds of silence ticked by. "Understood. Here's what we need."

CHAPTER 39

After summarizing the required critical support, I disconnected from the burner. Glancing around the cockpit and cabin, the faces peering back looked haggard and concerned. Knowing that Sylvia and I were responsible for the lives of everyone on board was a weighty truth.

Rick hadn't spoken for thirty minutes. He appeared nearly catatonic and was noticeably shivering. Incredibly, I watched Lucia grab one of the thick green folded blankets from a shelf to cover his body. Then she stroked his greasy hair covered in dirt, sweat, and blood. A stark departure from the inhumanity I see on social media. Rick didn't move as Lucia tucked the blanket's edges around his body. Kneeling beside him, I checked his pulse and temperature. He would die soon without proper care.

Lucia sat upright like a disciplined student. Clutching her hands, I said in Spanish, "We'll make it through this. You'll be safe in America."

Tears spilled from her eyes again, dropping from her chin and blotting my shirt sleeve. "But I love Mexico. My relatives are here." She glanced at Delgado with scorn. "La Buena Familia killed half my family and cousins." A fit of sobbing turned to rage. "Did you see what his men did to my husband? *They let animals eat him!*"

I regretted prompting horrific recollections of a loved one being torn apart by African beasts. How do you console a witness to such perversion? "I did not see what your husband endured, Lucia. And he died before Sylvia and Rick could intervene. Knowing you were about to suffer the same fate, Sylvia took charge. She told Rick and me she wouldn't let you get killed that way. She is your hero." I grabbed gauze from a medkit on the floor beside me and removed the drainage from her nose before drying her eyes and gently wiping dirt from her face. An exhausted woman dealing with unspeakable terrors. "Are you religious, Lucia?"

"*Creo en Dios.*"

"Then, as horrific as this day has been, try to find comfort knowing your husband is without pain and in a glorious place." Maria or Brooke would have offered her similar words. She closed her eyes and said nothing more. After moments of remaining mute, I squeezed her knee and stepped away.

Delgado gazed into my eye. "I heard your conversation. Your father and Ashley are alive. I supplied the information that saved them. Now keep your word."

"How do you sleep at night? You've inflicted unimaginable evil on my family, Lucia's family, and countless others. You deserve a fate worse than death."

"People need to be held accountable. Lucia's family refused to grow poppies, as neighboring farmers had agreed. There is no room for arrogance or sanctimony when compliance is prudent and mutually beneficial. Most people understand that."

"So you kill those who simply want to grow their own crops? To distance themselves from the shackles of cartels? To live free?"

"It is about accountability. In return for growing poppies, Lucia's family would have profited handsomely. Her father erred, believing he could negotiate. Very few farmers in that valley made the same decision."

"Are those families still breathing?"

"Cartels are like the military. We require obedience for the greater good."

"Greater good? Comply or die? You're an insecure, murdering thug. That's your legacy."

"Not true. I've personally killed just four men. They threatened my family."

"My wife and mother never threatened you, but they're dead."

"Did I pull the trigger? Maria stole the Emerald Cross from me. She put her and your wife in harm's way. I justifiably ordered their deaths. My lieutenants chose the punishment they considered fitting. I let them choose the manner of retribution."

I shook my head in disgust. "Only insecure and despicable pricks do such things."

"That is a self-righteous delusion. How many men have you killed, Captain Morales? Ten? Fifty?"

"Death is a common denominator in war. But our cause was just."

He laughed condescendingly. "As a teenager, I was taught that justification is more important than sex."

I dissected the strange comment.

"Think about it. When was the last time you went a day without justification? Sex is infrequent. Justification is a constant." He appeared proud of his riddle. "Don't be a hypocrite. Stop justifying your killing."

"Cleverness born of desperation," I replied with dripping contempt. "Save your witticisms for prison. My court testimony will deliver you a lifetime of incarceration. It will go something like this: Mr. Delgado described ordering the murders of my wife and mother. He threatened to execute my father and sister-in-law. He recounted the slayings of scores of innocent Mexican citizens."

"Falsehoods and exaggerations. I see you are willing to lie. Bad decision. *We had a deal.* I help you save Samuel and Ashley, and you tell the courts I was not complicit in Brooklyn and Maria's demise."

"*Demise?* They were bound and shot in the head, you heartless piece of shit! I grow sick imagining the fear and agony they endured. Newsflash, el patrón—there's no deal. Never was. I played you. Rot in prison. Burn in hell."

"I urge you to reconsider. Otherwise, every person on this helicopter will experience torture and death in a manner beyond human comprehension. But only *after* every living relative they have is similarly killed."

Do everyone a favor—blow the head off this murdering lunatic. I relaxed the grip on my pistol and placed my palm on his cheek, then clutched his tanned skin and dark stubble. "Imagine solitary confinement. Every day until you die. Your empire will rattle after I speak untruths about you squealing on your La Buena Familia lieutenants and henchmen."

"Before this week is over, you will cry over the spilled blood of loved ones. Your aunt and uncle in Orange County and their children mercilessly slaughtered. Every Morales you know in Mexico—eliminated. You could have prevented it."

We locked gazes and peered deeply into each other's souls. Who was bluffing? Which of us would spend a lifetime looking over our shoulders?

※ ※ ※

WITHIN MINUTES OF WASHINGTON, Taylor, and I ending our call,

Army radar specialists located the plane beelining for our Black Hawk. Attempts to communicate with the intercepting plane were unsuccessful. The approaching pilots had likely been ordered to ignore contact with other aircraft.

The incoming bogey flew eastbound about one hundred miles northwest of our current position. The Mexican military no longer operated jet aircraft. In 2016, the country retired its dwindling number of Northrup F-5 fighters, so the threat of being shot down by one was almost nil. But militaries and cartels possessed modified single- and twin-engine planes equipped with 50mm guns and tactical missile systems. Such planes were serious threats to our Black Hawk.

Washington and Taylor grew convinced President Valdes was orchestrating events, perhaps compensating a corrupted Mexican officer to do the president's dirty work. Or lying about the Black Hawk occupants being a group of rogue criminals who'd murdered patriotic Marines before hijacking the helicopter. If Valdes ordered the stolen copter to be shot down, the only witness to his tainted presidency would disappear. A risk removed. A problem solved.

Sylvia and I desperately hoped General Taylor would respond to my request for Army support. But I understood chains of command often run through politicians and bureaucrats too often unwilling to do the right thing. We need to assume we're on our own. If help arrives, then great. If it doesn't, Sylvia and I will need to get creative.

The GPS coordinates Sylvia and I relayed were now pointless. US military radar tracking abilities exceeded those of even the most advanced ally or foe militaries. Washington and Taylor received live updates on our location. The general speculated the unidentified plane intercepting us departed from Ensenada airport south of San Diego, which also serves Mexican Military Airbase Number 3. Whether the twin-engine plane was military or private remained a mystery. I'm sure Taylor and I were aligned—the plane was clearly a hostile threat.

A flashing red light appeared on a panel of switches and gauges in the cockpit. *"Problem!* Jamie, get up here!"

Darting from the helicopter's aft section, I jumped into the second pilot's seat. "What's wrong?" Then I read the fuel-level warning.

"Ten minutes ago, we had thirty percent more fuel," she said. "I'm guessing a bullet weakened a fuel line or penetrated the tank. Either way, we'll need to fly low and slow."

"Roger that." I reached for my burner and dialed Washington. "This is Morales."

"You chose a good time to call. Give me a quick update."

"Not yet. We're losing fuel quickly. We need to drop altitude and reduce speed. Worst case, we'll need to put this bird down."

"Roger that. Any guess on—"

Sylvia screamed, "We're going down, Jamie! *Now!* Fuel tanks abruptly show empty. Get Lucia and Rick prepared for a rough one!"

"I heard that. Good—"

The line went dead.

CHAPTER 40

Fearing the fuel tanks would empty before she could land our Black Hawk, Sylvia maintained a dangerously steep decline. She expertly controlled the cyclic to level out before slamming to earth amidst apple and peach orchards. People and supplies pounded against the walls and flew about the cabin. Peering out cockpit windows, she focused on a faintly illuminated house roughly two hundred feet away. Flashbacks of the Middle East filled her mind: unfamiliar terrain, enemy territory, and possible weapons trained on her and the crew. Breaking free of the images, she rushed back to check on two people needing care.

Rick was barely alive. She knew he wouldn't last much longer. I remained awed by her ability to function expertly despite the extreme emotional burden of watching her fiancé slowly fade away. Lucia was physically uninjured, but she'd need years of therapy to grapple with the continuing day of horrors.

I assessed the situation, pointed, and barked orders. Sylvia and I were prepared for anything—a hard landing in unfamiliar terrain while being tracked by an unfriendly bogey sure as hell wouldn't shake us. Glowering at Delgado, she wished he would have knocked himself dead during their crash onto the parched ground.

Lucia scrambled to free herself from her harness. We moved toward the closed main cabin exit. Remaining aboard made us easy targets if

La Buena Familia sicarios had sniffed out our location. I unlocked one of the two main cabin doors and slid it open.

"Do not move! We will shoot you!" The strong voice bellowed in Spanish from the shadows.

Sylvia and I could have raised our pistols, but the blended sounds of multiple weapons firing warning shots skyward halted us. A man presumed to be the leader approached. He wore a leather cowboy hat and pointed his Winchester 101 double-barrel shotgun at my chest. "You have landed in my orchards. We just listened to a national broadcast about five Americans who stole a Marines helicopter after killing Mexican soldiers. Now, unbelievably, here you are." The rest of the group nudged forward, each of their guns aimed menacingly at the Americans.

My instincts said these were not cartel traffickers. They looked more like confused, frightened citizens startled by the surreal image of a military copter landing just feet beyond their front door. "Señor, we did not kill the crew of this helicopter. They are sadly dead, but you have been misinformed about their deaths," I replied in Spanish. "La Buena Familia murdered the crew of Marines. We stole this helicopter out of necessity to stay alive. We are three Army soldiers, plus one frightened Mexican woman . . . and . . . Marco Delgado."

Squeals and yelling burst forth from the armed group, the sounds of absolute terror. Two men about my age wearing brown baseball caps reading Miranda Orchards rushed forward. They peered into a cabin holding Delgado's squirming body and extended the barrels of their guns within inches of the drug lord's face. *"You brought this filth to our home!* Are you part of the cartel? You lawless La Buena Familia rats have killed twenty-seven people in this valley. *Including our brother!"*

Arturo Miranda stiffened his arm and placed his palm in front of the enraged younger man's gaze. I thought they looked like father and son. "Let me speak, Eduardo," Arturo said to the younger man. He turned to me. "Our president says you are killers. But he also said you are five Americans and did not mention Delgado. Something is amiss. But why should I believe you?"

"These are honest and good people!" pleaded the previously diffident Lucia, surprising the Mexicans and Americans. "They saved me after Delgado's men fed my husband to wild beasts!" She spit on the cartel kingpin, who remained bound and lying on the floor. "This monster will be taken to the US to spend his life in jail—a *real* jail. Not like the Mexican ones El Chapo escapes from."

"*Heed my warning!* Assist these criminals, and you will die!" screamed an agitated Delgado from his prone position. "Do not make foolish decisions. I am a powerful man with a powerful army. Help me, and your reward will be grand. Get in my way, and you will die. Remember, I am Marco Delgado!"

"*And I am Arturo Miranda!*" yelled the farmer. "My wife and I grieve for our beautiful boy your cartel tortured and executed. And for neighbors whose family disappeared after standing up to La Buena Familia." Collecting his runaway emotions, he added with a sneer, "Many of us have lost too much because of you, Señor Delgado." He kept his shotgun aimed at the drug lord's head.

"*No!* If you kill him, all our children will die in retaliation. Is that what you want? Haven't we lost enough?" Señora Miranda pushed the barrel of her husband's weapon downward, defiance etched across her face.

Her husband's scrunched-up face didn't relax. He pointed at his wife and three other women who appeared about thirty years younger and demanded they drive to safety inside a king-cab pickup parked nearby.

"I will stay," said the bold matriarch. "But Juanita, Rosa, Noemi, you drive to Mundo's ranch."

"*No, Mamá!*" Noemi shrieked. "If you stay, we all stay!" Her expression froze as her jaw clenched in disobedience. "No way I am leaving." Juanita and Rosa voiced solidarity, and their mother gazed exasperatedly at her husband.

"I see. Okay, then." Arturo nodded to Lucia, dirtied and tattered from her nightmarish evening. She still wore the clothes of gang members killed in the shoot-out on Delgado's property. He turned to one of the younger women. "Get her cleaned up and properly dressed." A daughter or daughter-in-law clutched Lucia's wrist and compassionately led her to the front door.

Arturo pulled me aside as his armed relatives fanned out around us. I relayed his comments to Sylvia: "He says if our account of the past two days is convincing, his family will do everything it can to help us, especially Lucia and Rick."

A dreadful curse emanated from Delgado. Eduardo Miranda pressed his gun barrel into the cartel leader's chest, an anxious finger caressing the trigger. Based on Delgado's expression, I guessed he'd grown slightly unnerved. His fate now lay in the hands of honest people not paralyzed by his threats.

Arturo guided us to a fountain centered in a tiled courtyard. I explained our impossible evening. While describing lingering risks, the throaty sounds of highly revved engines powering large pickup trucks redirected everyone's attention. The vehicles' headlights bounced wildly as drivers navigated potholes on an unpaved country road. It was still too dark to make out details. The approaching caravan's intentions grew instantly ominous for the Americans and Mirandas.

Inside the bed of the middle of three pickups was a metal tripod welded to the bed's floor. An imposing machine gun rested atop the support. A man with his legs spread for balance crouched behind the weapon, his hands tightly clutching each of two vertical gun handles. He opened fire, scattering rounds in front of the Black Hawk and house.

Dhak dhak dhak dhak!

Sylvia and I, and perhaps even Rick in his half-dead state, detected the sounds of a weapon we knew all too well. A .50 caliber machine gun, possibly identical to those we'd been supported by in the Middle East. It was a lethal threat to everyone.

Señor Miranda and I instinctively locked eyes. The man in the worn cowboy hat had only seconds to decide if I was a good or evil man. "You must act, Señor Miranda. Your family needs our help. Please trust me." I glanced at Sylvia and back at the farmer. "Move your family inside. Let us return to the helicopter. We have weapons aboard that can hold them at bay."

Eduardo Miranda implored in Spanish, "I believe him, father. Set him free. Move the women and let the Americans help us fight back. It is our only option." Just as he finished speaking, the .50 caliber machine gun fired a barrage of rounds in their direction.

"*27 Miranda!* Text it!" one of the sons screamed at the family. Three relatives pulled phones from their pockets while scurrying for cover. None of that made sense to us.

Arturo Miranda nodded at Eduardo and pushed Sylvia and me toward the copter. He yelled for his wife and the other women to stay in the house. As I scanned their property, I noticed three twenty-foot-long, six-foot-high rows of thick, un-split firewood. I ordered half of the armed Mirandas to take positions there. The rest found cover behind what looked like a large farming equipment outbuilding about thirty yards away.

Delgado sneered when I entered the Black Hawk, "My cavalry has arrived. I have too many loyalists in this valley. You will soon die, betrayer." There wasn't time to castigate, so I thrust my fist into his balls before popping fresh magazines into my M4 and Beretta.

"Hey," Sylvia yelled as she arranged her arsenal, "We've got the SAW, and I've still got these." She presented two of her original M67 grenades. Just as she slid one of the steel doors shut to prep for battle, jarring sounds of engagement exploded from La Buena Familia's machine guns. I hoped they'd overshoot and dwindle their ammunition.

Sylvia opened the sliding door slightly, and I fired on the enemy. She unleashed her volley of 5.56mm SAW rounds just inches away from Rick's body, which hadn't moved since we'd landed. I saw the heartbreak in her eyes. We both knew he could already be dead. The distinctly weaker firings of the Mirandas .22 caliber rifles, unlikely to kill anyone unless expertly aimed, were drowned out as the firefight ensued.

"Sylvia, after I exit, I'll take a position below or next to the skids." I felt my burner vibrate, but this wasn't the time to answer. Besides, my ears were ringing. I wouldn't be able to hear a word from the caller—be it Washington, Taylor, or Jack Kershaw.

The Miranda sons and presumed sons-in-law inspired me while firing on La Buena Familia, but it was also gut-wrenching. They were committed but incapable of winning this battle unaided. It crushed me knowing that heavy losses were inevitable.

Cheers arose from the enemy combatants as six other pickups

arrived, with gun-toting killers filling the cabins and beds. Parking in a half-moon, a steep hill now protected their unguarded rear. Dawn was about to break. Tracing the red and orange barrel flames from the AK-47s and .50 caliber machine gun helped Sylvia and I find targets.

We discharged our weapons in bursts of three, and the list of cartel casualties mounted quickly. Our success appeared to embolden the Mirandas, whose guns fired in faster succession. The screams of injured and dying La Buena Familia henchmen filled the air.

Suddenly, the agonized shrieks of Miranda relatives bore into my consciousness. Eduardo had been injured or killed. Dear God, I thought, we brought these killers here. Two women darted from the family's home toward a cluster of their male relatives. One carried a shotgun, the other a pistol in each hand. The woman clutching the handguns passed them on to the men before pulling rags from her waistband to compress Eduardo's gaping wound. Another woman blasted away with her shotgun. One of the women near the front porch again screamed, "27 Miranda!"

Sylvia and I kept squeezing our triggers, pinning narcos behind the convoy of pickups. The body count of bad guys grew, but we remained heavily outmanned. Then the cartel's guns inexplicably fell quiet, replaced by eerie wind-swept fragments of their muted conversations. I rose and prepared to dash toward the wood stacks to assess Eduardo's injuries. My phone sounded again, and I dove behind a cart in the orchards used during harvests.

"Morales," I said into the phone's mic. Simultaneously peering into the Black Hawk cabin, I saw Sylvia slapping a new magazine into her M4 carbine. Beside her lay the SAW machine gun. Only static and garbled voices could be heard through the phone. "Be quick! We've been under attack, and my battery's almost dead again."

"We've intercepted communications from the cockpit of the plane tracking you. We've also received intel from a source within the Mexican government that President Valdes intends to eliminate his Delgado problem, putting your crew at heightened risk. We've advised Valdes we possess an audio and video file proving the twenty million pay-off from Delgado. We've argued there's nothing to gain by killing you or Delgado. He hasn't responded."

"*Too much information, Agent Washington!* That beep means my battery's almost dead. I don't care about Valdes. I care about the innocent people fighting a battle we dropped on their doorstep. We need help! Were you able to get us support?"

Gunfire erupted again, forcing me to take cover. "Are we getting Black Hawk support?" I screamed at Washington. The sounds of battle were too intense. I couldn't hear a damn thing. And if I couldn't, neither could Agent Washington. I yelled again, "Did you hear me? Are you there?"

Garbled noises filled my ear. I thought I heard, "I'm sorry. Yes." But *yes* to which question? The battery light went dark, and the phone died.

Sylvia covered me as I rushed toward the group of Mirandas huddled and firing from behind the three columns of stacked apple hardwood trunks cut in three-foot lengths. It was a worthy barrier. Eduardo had taken an AK-47 round to his shoulder, exploding it. One of the women had slowed the bleeding with a compress, but it wasn't enough. I cut a length of rope and tightened a tourniquet just above the shattered bone and horrid gashes. Though the arm might be unsalvageable, life without an arm was still a life.

Sylvia employed rusty softball skills to keep a trio of advancing sicarios from gaining position behind a four-foot-tall cement irrigation platform, tossing two M67 grenades in their direction. The first missed by an embarrassing margin, but the second took one shooter out and prompted the others to flee for cover. A moment later, with her M4 needing another reload, she grabbed her Sig Sauer from her vest and put two rounds into a man rushing her with a machine gun.

At first, it sounded like another pickup delivering yet more traffickers, but burgeoning daylight revealed a twin-engine airplane flying straight at us. The flurry of weapons fire from the cartel reached another crescendo. They believed the plane was there to support them, unaware its likely objective was to explode the Black Hawk and kill Delgado. Two more Miranda women and a man burst out the home's front door in the direction of their injured loved one, carrying medical supplies. I screamed for them to turn around, to no avail. Glancing again at the horizon, Sylvia and I realized the airplane would be upon us in seconds. It was too late to get Rick out of the copter. She might die with her fiancé.

Bullets flew from .50 caliber guns mounted on each wing of the twin-engine airplane, but that was just the warm-up. Two missiles screamed toward our Black Hawk. The first hit the copter's tail, triggering a dramatic explosion, its concussion overpowering. The second projectile hit the center of the steel door Rick, Sylvia, and Delgado remained exposed behind—but no violent flash of red and orange ensued. I found another vantage point and was stunned to see the tail of the helicopter was gone but that the missile intended to kill Delgado was protruding out the sliding metal door, unexploded, like a giant gray dart. *Made in China*, I thought.

The smells of detonated missiles and bullets wafted everywhere amidst choking smoke and debris. It prompted recollections of skirmishes in Afghanistan and Syria while fighting beside Wes Berkeley and my band of warriors. The carnage played in slow motion and triggered dramatic, emotional chords from a powerful score filling my head: Bach's Orchestral Suite No. 3 in D major.

Peering to my left, I halted. Images of Sylvia played frame-by-frame as the beloved kick-ass Russian-American Army pilot repositioned herself inside the pelted and smoldering helicopter. She pulled the triggers of her M4, Rick's AK-47, the SAW, and two Sig Sauers, trying to neutralize the rest of the cold-blooded killers. Her short bob bounced to the cadence of her gunfire amidst dancing shadows formed by flashes from her weapons. I'll never forget what I saw. *"You go, soldier girl, you fucking go!"* I screamed in admiration. No one heard me.

The plane continued directly over the Miranda household, then skimmed the ground in a wide loop. Valdes realized his presidency would collapse if American justice got Delgado to squeal about the payoff. Eliminating the cartel king today would allow the Mexican president to discredit the American's purported video tomorrow.

Excruciating irony engulfed me. Valdes's reign was doomed whether Delgado lived or died. But desperate, powerful heads of state aren't wired to wave the white flag of surrender. So here we are, victims and pawns in Delgado and Valdes's theater, struggling to stay alive against impossible odds. A tragic and twisted truth.

La Buena Familia remained committed to freeing Delgado. The Americans were trying to deliver him to US authorities. The President of Mexico needed him dead, an objective not yet achieved. More missiles, more heavy gunfire, and more casualties were inescapable.

The Miranda family members continued shooting from inside their casa, from behind stacked firewood serving as cover, and from the outbuilding. Our Black Hawk took a further beating from AK and .50 caliber rounds. Watching it all unfold, I knew I'd be forever impressed by the collective bravery of beleaguered strangers.

Amid the mayhem, three more trucks joined the procession of drug runners. There were now eleven vehicles. The recent arrivals positioned themselves in a cluster with line-of-sight of the copter and Arturo Miranda's ranch home. The incessant gunfire through the walls of a bedroom triggered a blaze. Dancing flames reached out the window, licking the roof and front deck posts. Stifling smoke billowed around the home, which was never designed to withstand barrages of large-caliber projectiles penetrating its walls.

Glancing into the faint light of the Black Hawk cabin, Sylvia twisted around, and our eyes met. Yes, we both understood. Experience and instincts suggested it was unlikely the Mirandas, three Americans, and Lucia would survive the next hour.

CHAPTER 41

The firefight remained too intense to remove Rick from the helicopter. We battled from three positions on the property. Arturo's son, Eduardo, lay gruesomely wounded. Sylvia and I would fight to the end for Lucia and the Mirandas, whatever that meant. *Please, God, make it somehow matter.*

Breaking dawn spread across the valley, a stunningly beautiful horizon of streaking rose and violet skies. That was probably a misplaced thought as I relentlessly fired. Half my M4 magazine remained, and I'd guess eight shots rested unspent in my last Beretta cartridge. Dozens of bullets whizzed past my head over the previous twenty-five minutes. How much longer would such fortunes endure? I heard cartel gunmen scream for their assault weapons not to errantly strike the unexploded missile jammed into the side of the Black Hawk's door. Their drug lord and my comrades would surely die if the protruding dart detonated.

With daylight forming, I recognized the returning twin-engine airplane, a Beechcraft King Air. I once toured a company hangar at Long Beach Airport that customized King Airs to serve as weaponized spy planes for foreign governments. Could one of their aircraft be about to decimate a Black Hawk and ranch home protecting ex-GIs and innocent civilians?

The airplane advanced. The targets were impossible to miss: a smoking Mexican Marines helicopter and a home partially engulfed in a raging fire. Heat-seeking missiles would soon be on their way. I glanced toward the heavens. *If you intend to help, now would be a really good time.*

No more guns were fired by anyone named Miranda—they'd just run out of ammunition. I gazed numbly at family members huddled behind tall stacks of wood and the outbuilding. They couldn't shoot at their enemies and would likely die running for safer cover. Staring through gun sights, my aim to protect them grew more precise. My tired eye struggled to cope with variables demanding keen vision.

That sound . . . Wait . . . Focusing intensely, I struggled to separate a distinct noise from gunfire. *Chuff chuff chuff chuff.* A deeply embedded memory of war? Or subconscious hopes cruelly misplaced, intended to counter the hellish inevitability of defeat? *Chuff chuff chuff chuff.*

Shadows stretched across the Miranda home and property. Inevitable demise met the vividly real sight of a U.S. Army Black Hawk helicopter skimming the burning home one hundred feet above arid earth. It flew directly into the path of the oncoming twin-engine King Air. I envisioned both pilots readying their trigger fingers. But the machine gun and missile triggers inside the King Air cockpit were pulled too late. Four laser-guided Hellfire anti-armor missiles struck and fully disintegrated the airplane milliseconds later. A stream of debris and incendiary colors spread widely and floated to earth, illuminated artistry contrasting death and destruction.

La Buena Familia unleashed everything in its arsenal as one contingent advanced on the Black Hawk that shielded Rick and Sylvia. They intended to pull their captive leader from the smoking copter before the U.S. Army Black Hawk could loop back and attack. The cartel killers never split their forces to attack from multiple angles in disciplined columns. If they had, we and every member of the Miranda family would already be dead.

Every neck on the property twisted back and upward. A second Black Hawk exploded onto the scene, rising menacingly from behind the ridge shielding the cartel pickups and traffickers. I hoped the copter crew hadn't underestimated the enemy's firepower. Sounds of the gang members' bullets reverberated while hitting and ricocheting off the Army copter.

Instincts took over, and I rushed the enemy with my Beretta blasting. I had witnessed copters getting taken down from close range with a luckily placed round. After emptying my last clip, I flung my body behind the cement irrigation platform. Simultaneously, Sylvia unleashed hell, tossing her last M67 to brutal effect.

The hovering Black Hawk swiveled and let loose four missiles and its .50 calibers, annihilating one band of criminals and three trucks they'd hoped would protect them. About a dozen determined triggermen remained committed to freeing Delgado. Two pickups with traffickers, spooked by the might of the Army helicopters, retreated over dirt roads at high speeds.

A cluster of narcos approached me and the cement platform I was pinned behind, looking excited to eliminate a prime target. Sylvia jumped from the copter and ran toward me, hurling her body onto mine, pressing an elbow into my back to steady her aim. She pulled the trigger five times. Only three rounds fired—she was out of ammo.

The first Black Hawk that destroyed the King Air looped around the farm and was ready to join the firestorm. The two desert-colored U.S. Army copters bore down. Frenzied drug lieutenants hell-bent on freeing their leader unleashed a furious attack. The innocent and wicked were pressed together, separated by less than fifty feet. Dense smoke from the burning home and smoldering Mexican Black Hawk made it nearly impossible to distinguish who was who from the sky. A Special Ops leader ordered the birds to land between the house and orchards.

Dust and smoke blew in every direction as the copters' skids settled upon arid earth and weeds. Soldiers wearing goggles, looking like something out of a space-age battle epic, sprung from the imposing helicopters. The soldiers' senses grew acute: Assess, engage, protect. Just after the Army Rangers dispersed, the La Buena Familia trucks that fled minutes earlier returned. Puzzlingly, the returning pickups fanned out in opposing directions, one facing the Miranda residence, the other aiming toward their escape route, apparently intent on keeping it clear.

I sensed a flash of movement to my left, then screamed a warning at two Rangers battling shooters shielded by slowly approaching Ford and Chevy pickups. I got their attention, but one of the Army soldiers was hit by an AK-47 round a moment later. The soldier's partner rolled in the dirt to his right, finding cover behind the bed of a farming ATV. He rose and unleashed a torrent of bullets, removing several threats.

The Mirandas were sitting ducks. Arturo prayed he wasn't witnessing his family's annihilation. The cartel smelled blood, like frenzied sharks in the water. And they weren't intimidated by the just-arrived Army Rangers.

Another Ranger was taken down, this time by a round from the .50 caliber machine gun mounted in the pickup bed. I grew relieved watching the soldier quickly reengage. The bullet must have only grazed him.

Fierce battling continued as half of Delgado's men swapped out 100-round drums on their AKs. The Special Ops arrivals were thinning the herd of ruthless killers, but not quickly enough. The bad guys had moved within thirty feet of the imperiled Miranda family.

Strangers came out of nowhere. The sounds of their engines had gotten muffled by ear-piercing, relentless gunfire. The leading motorcyclists wore folded red bandannas fastened around their heads, hunting rifles strapped across their backs, and boxes of bullets duct-taped to the gas tanks they straddled over. La Buena Familia aimed and fired, yet the bikers continued their frenetic advance, finally splitting apart hundreds of feet from the Mirandas' casa.

Behind them, a ragtag army of pickup trucks, SUVs, and family sedans flooded the landscape. The battalion of dozens of vehicles trailed dust clouds over dirt roads and open fields while approaching their neighbors' home. Leaders of the band of allies signaled their "troops" to halt while assessing the battle before them. Seconds later, commands were bellowed, and citizen warriors moved forward in separate columns. Soon, every manner of country-living weapon imaginable engaged La Buena Familia from multiple vantages. Peasant vigilantes poured from the orchards and grasslands.

"They came! They came!" I heard from members of the Miranda family. People had come, yes. But I questioned whether they were all good guys. That answer grew clear in seconds. Hope overcame me. The reinforcements plus Army soldiers would surely remove every cartel threat.

The Rangers quickly deciphered what was happening after initially assuming their enemy ranks had grown tenfold. It was fascinating but disturbing to observe what happened next. Instead of accepting their odds of success had evaporated, the sicarios fought deliriously, whooping and hollering as they shot and ran toward the Mirandas, Sylvia, me, and our Black Hawk. They had no chance. Soldiers and the Miranda neighbors brutally decimated them. The killers tattooed with La Buena Familia on their forearms devilishly grinned while pulling triggers until every one of them was killed. For sane witnesses, it was a climax that might haunt consciences for decades, even if those who died were despicable, pernicious humans deserving of their brutal deaths.

The sudden quiet was as remarkable as the sounds of combat had been. People ran forward, shocked by the number of bloodied corpses dotting the property but elated to find the farming family had survived.

As Arturo's children led their parents from a home partially engulfed in crackling fire, they celebrated in disbelief. Army medics attended to Eduardo Miranda's injury. Arturo swept his hand across beads of sweat covering his son's forehead, mouthing words I could only guess. He begged the medics to keep his oldest child alive. Then he snapped himself, loved ones, and others from delay. He ordered young men to fire up the portable generator to redirect irrigation water needed to douse the house fire. I screamed for soldiers to help the Mirandas battle flames stretching from the family's home.

Lucia wandered alone in a clearing near the outbuilding. She appeared numb and shell-shocked, moving in circles while talking to herself. I watched Sylvia approach the stranger she'd saved from African beasts. Their embrace was intense. Sylvia nodded with hopefulness. She kissed Lucia's cheek before rushing to check on Rick.

Sylvia and I entered the Mexican Marines Black Hawk with two medics. Rick lay still and unconscious. Or dead. She didn't have it in her to ask the obvious question, but the medics gave her good news. He was breathing.

Because the missile embedded in the copter's door could explode any moment, Rick was placed on a stretcher and hurried to one of the US Black Hawks. After clearing the area, I ordered a soldier to discharge a single round into the unexploded, protruding missile. Though witnesses expected the detonation, it was a stunning finale to the day of chaos and bloodshed.

Medics dressed Rick's leg wound and prepped morphine for injection. He'd need pain relief as he gained consciousness. Keeping him alive was going to be a challenge. A second medic inserted a needle into a forearm vein for a blood infusion. General Taylor had accessed Rick's Army records and ensured four bags of his rarer AB-positive blood made the trip inside a green cooler.

The first Ranger who'd gotten shot was lucky. While his fatigues were drenched in crimson, the bullet had passed through one inch of skin above his left hip, causing no organ or catastrophic damage. After getting transported to one of the Army copters, Delgado complained about not having pissed for eight hours. I unbound his arms and let him do his business next to an apple tree.

"We had a deal, Jamie," Delgado lamented. "You provide testimony absolving me of ordering your wife and mother's murders. I save your father and sister-in-law. They are both alive, *thanks to me!* You will pay for breaking your pledge. So will your relatives. And soon. As God is my witness."

Sylvia passed by and overheard Delgado's threats. She rushed him and raked fingernails across his weathered cheek, which immediately bled profusely. The drug lord clenched his fist and swung at Sylvia. I grabbed his arm midflight, forced it behind his back, and thrust him into the tree trunk. Two Rangers approached with their Glock 19s aimed at Delgado's head. One pressed his pistol barrel into the drug boss's ear and said, surprisingly in Spanish, "I know all about you, *Marco fucking Delgado*. If I blew your head off, I'd be a popular man on base. Watch your shit, asshole." The Miranda men tipped their heads and spoke in solidarity, but their wives scorned them for threatening the devil, fearing future retribution.

The portable generator hummed in the background, helping draw water to drench weakened embers hissing amidst plumes of gray smoke. With the fire and mayhem under control, Arturo Miranda, family patriarch, inconspicuously separated himself and ascended the ridge Delgado's men had used to protect their rear flank. He slipped and dirtied himself climbing the steep, dusty slope, and his hat fell. As he turned to pick it up, I handed it to him.

"Señor Miranda, I'm so sorry I brought this misery to your home. And that another of your sons has paid a price at the hands of La Buena Familia."

Arturo stared with a weary face and leathery skin, his eyes misting. He said nothing for a long pause. "Your apology appears sincere, yet of course, it feels hollow. We asked for none of this. I am tired. Señora Miranda is tired. We just want to live simple, honorable lives and to be left alone."

"I hope you can forgive me one day."

"I have already forgiven you."

"Well then, thank you for that. We'll get Eduardo excellent care in El Paso. You are right to let us transport him to the US. He would not survive treatment in your local hospitals."

Señor Miranda said, "I too seek forgiveness. I thought we would all die. I thought our friends and neighbors had abandoned us to be slaughtered by the cartel. I thought they would not come." Inured to lives of occupation and forced to pay homage to La Buena Familia, the motley army of mostly subsistence farmers had instead helped deliver a day of reckoning. "I hope they forgive me for doubting."

"I would also have doubted, señor. What your community did here was heroic against an enemy who personified evil."

"Delgado's sicarios had killed 27 innocent locals over the past three years. The ranchers and farmers in this valley gathered months ago and agreed the number 27 with a family's surname would signal an urgent plea for help. Enough was enough, we all agreed." Brown eyes framed by puffy skin tinged red by worry and smoke seemed to have aged him ten years since our arrival. "They came, Señor Morales. They helped save my family."

"They also helped save a group of strangers. We are indebted." We hugged awkwardly, weighed down by private burdens.

"It's time for us to leave. To get Eduardo medical attention."

Minutes later, soldiers transferred Eduardo to the copter transporting Rick and Sylvia. With his family gathered outside the sliding main cabin door to say goodbye for what they hoped would be a brief separation, Arturo projected an expression imploring *Please save my son.*

Lucia would travel to America in my helicopter. Mexico was no place for her today—and maybe ever. Marco Delgado, the man responsible for so much suffering, was bound tighter and strapped to his seat, arrogant defiance etched across his face.

Before lifting off, I demanded ample handguns and ammunition be left behind to help the Miranda family counter any La Buena Familia reprisal. It was an order General Taylor would find wholly unacceptable. The Army active-duty contingent balked at my command but ultimately looked the other way, likely out of respect for what the three of us had just accomplished.

Two Black Hawks resembling slanted futuristic insects rose amid a whirling flurry of reddish-brown dust, flying northward to complete their mission.

Chuff chuff chuff chuff chuff.

Rays of sunshine stretched across the high desert landscape and penetrated our windows. The survivors in the cabin squinted. I wondered if that was due to the intense glare or disbelief that they'd survived. No one spoke.

It had been one hell of an evening.

CHAPTER 42

Our Black Hawk pilot called out, "Captain Morales, urgent call. Grab the headset." I adjusted the fit while peering into Lucia's eyes. My heart warmed after glimpsing faint hints of hope within her gaze, which momentarily halted me. Taking a deep breath, I spoke into the mic. "This is Captain Morales."

"General Taylor here. Agent Washington is on the line. Can we get a quick brief?"

"Yes, sir." I questioned whether my report might be judged impossible. "We emergency landed the Black Hawk on a farm. Immediately took fire from La Buena Familia, including their .50 calibers. The farmer's family fought alongside us." Recalling the battle, it sounded like I'd insufficiently described the Mirandas' contributions. *Bravely.* The family fought heroically. One of them had his shoulder exploded by an AK-47 round." I grimaced at the severity of Eduardo's wound. "Then the plane tracking us blew the tail rotor off our bird. It fired a second missile, which lodged into one of the main cabin's sliding doors." *Come on, did this really happen?*

Neither Washington nor Taylor interrupted.

"We ran out of ammo just after one of your Black Hawks destroyed the bogey. General Taylor, if the reinforcements had shown up minutes later, we'd all be dead." We kept Delgado alive, too, but I knew everyone else wanted him dead. "Anyway, here's what matters. Army Captain Rick Bonham and a brave Mexican named Eduardo Miranda are in bad shape. They are barely holding on. Be ready for them."

"We'll be prepared," Taylor said.

Washington interrupted a long pause. "Remarkable journey, Mr. Morales. We'll debrief further, but congratulations on extracting Delgado."

I glared at the man responsible for inflicting so many emotional scars. "Thank you. The monster responsible for the killings of my wife and mother and the caging of my father for thirty years is lying right next to me." My voice trailed off. I remained somewhat disbelieving of how everything played out.

General Taylor barked orders to someone. It sounded like his hand covered and muffled the phone's mic. One or two garbled voices replied to the officer's demands. "So it's all set?" Taylor asked someone in his vicinity. I overheard a *Yessir* followed by another stream of rustling noises before the general continued, "Captain Morales, prepare yourself. Your father is now on the line."

A man struggling with emotions said in Spanish, "How do I begin? Dear God. I love you, son. I've never stopped loving you." The emotional words overcame the headset's white noise and the helicopter's constant clattering.

Feeling apprehensive and paralyzed, I gathered myself. "Father?"

Samuel pleaded in a broken, high-pitched tone, "Jaime, my son, light of my life." He pushed himself to continue despite his catching voice. "I'm sorry for your pain. For my being so close inside a guarded bunker, yet excruciatingly distant. Dreaming of this day kept me alive." He wept but forced himself to regain composure. "I just wish your mother were here to share it. And of course, your wife, Brooklyn."

"Oh God, I'm so sorry for everything you've gone through. Maria never stopped talking about you. *Never!* She missed you desperately."

"My dear Maria," Samuel said in a whisper.

"She said you and I look very much alike. I saw a recent photo of you on Marco Delgado's laptop. Mom was right. We're mirror images."

Samuel's tone changed. "Jaime, please listen carefully. Marco Delgado is evil personified. Do not trust anything he says or does."

"I know this, so don't worry. Samuel, I just can't believe you're alive." I leaned back against the cold, hard steel of the fuselage. Nothing could diminish my feelings of pure love, happiness, and hope.

General Taylor interjected, "Captain Morales, your father will depart for Fort Bliss from Camp Pendleton in minutes. He'll be very safe until your reunion."

"Thank you, sir. And Samuel, Dad, *Papi*, I'll see you soon."

"My dear Jaime, only hours separate us. *Te amaré por siempre.*"

I told myself he could call me Jaime, Jamie, Captain, or anything else he wanted for the rest of our lives. After ending the call, runaway emotions raged through my body and mind. The father and son who'd endured wrenching loss could now reunite to build a lifetime of beautiful memories together.

Lucia peered through her side window and screamed, *"Jets!* They're going to shoot us down!"

Grabbing my wrist as I scanned the horizon, her complexion turned white with fear, and blood drained from veins below her skin. She attempted to stand, forgetting a harness restrained her body. Just as

I noticed the two planes, a pilot twisted from his cockpit seat and screamed, "Captain Morales! Those are ours—Raptors."

Of course General Taylor would have delivered air support. Sitting beside Lucia, I explained the jets were American, advanced F-22 Raptor fighters ensuring safe passage to Fort Bliss. Color returned to her face.

The next hour of the flight was an opportunity to reflect. Stretching an arm toward my rucksack, I reached inside and pulled out a silk bag containing the Emerald Cross. Lucia grew intrigued by the captivating relic and smiled. Gripping the cross and massaging its molded gold, I stared at embedded emeralds that appeared too large to be genuine.

I eagerly anticipated returning the cross to its rightful owner—my father. Delgado insisted *he* was the lawful heir, but a wicked human could never legitimately claim something so beautiful and holy, even if his more respected ancestors had once owned it. Maria and her radiant smile were gone forever, but the man she loved was about to reclaim something beautiful bestowed by Marco Delgado's father.

My thoughts drifted to the man we were shuttling to the US, overlord of the most powerful cartel and heroin smuggling enterprise on earth. The DEA dossier described him as a man of vast contradictions, raised by a loving and respectable family, well-educated, and lauded by poor Mexicans as a charitable man who built schools and medical clinics. But any philanthropy was a pretense, a way of endearing himself to locals while simultaneously endorsing brutal retribution for defiance of his cartel's demands. I thought his paradoxes were best left for psychiatry PhDs to analyze. Regardless of academic opinions about who and what influenced him, I measured his savage rule in terms of people tortured and lives destroyed.

Was I wrong to keep him alive? There were no easy answers. I remained adamant death was too easy an end for Delgado. Shooting him in his den would have been simple, but that's how Brooke and Mom met their end. Drug lords deserve sentences of confinement that render hopeless misery for a lifetime.

Because every soldier lives affected by the horrors of war, to some extent, conflict was their constant companion. Were Delgado and I so different? The simple answer is, of course. He killed for sport and perverted retribution. But how could the man mesmerized by the religious artifact he now possessed deny the ugly truth people were killed to claim it?

The night before the attack on Delgado's compound, Sylvia, Rick, and I acknowledged having our psyches burdened by the slaying of enemies, even those vilest of humans. We each struggled randomly, questioning whether our victims might have possessed redeeming qualities as measured by decent relatives. We'd counter that Delgado and La Buena Familia were just despicable humans. Ultimately, no matter the circumstances and justifications, killing always took its toll.

Following the firefight on the Miranda farm, after the Black Hawks and Special Forces arrived to save the lives of the "good guys," at the last possible moment, I watched Sylvia walk alone to a peach tree, bend over, and heave repeatedly. Taking lives is a kind of sickness, humankind's greatest arrogance, for any soldier or person. One learns to cope, but one never forgets. I understood Sylvia better than most, including Rick, and always looked past her *badass* exterior, knowing she is fundamentally more reflective and sensitive than others might imagine.

SAC Washington remarked that numerous Marco Delgados would vie for control of La Buena Familia if the cartel boss were ever permanently incarcerated in the United States. "Power, riches, and beautiful women. These are mighty intoxicants for men striving to be the next king of kings in the drug realm." He added, "The cycle won't end in my lifetime. But if the DEA and others don't stand up to them, who will?"

We stood up to them! And now, that success might become another burden. Rick and Sylvia questioned why I didn't exterminate the unrepentant murderer of my wife and mother. I stood in his den with my gun pointed at his head. Would Samuel also find it disappointing I hadn't evened the score when given that chance?

I wasn't joyful, proud, or mollified by the prospect of Delgado living caged like an animal as he forced Samuel to survive. But there was great satisfaction knowing victims of his hellish reign might soon share the more hopeful bonds of a beleaguered community . . . the revenged.

CHAPTER 43

WE MADE IT HOME. SCANNING THE TARMAC BELOW, ANOTHER Bach instrumental stirred my emotions. Our two Black Hawks landed at Fort Bliss simultaneously, the odyssey completed. Strangers peered inside our windows, and multiple Army vehicles circled our copters. "Why do the soldiers have machine guns?" Lucia asked. I told her it was just a precaution. The helicopters' doors slid open, and anxious voices amidst frenzied activity consumed us. Lucia visibly relaxed after no one pointed a weapon at us.

After catching up with Sylvia as two medics rolled Rick into one of two waiting ambulances, I grew alarmed by her gashes. From shoulder to fingertips, she was a swollen and bloodied mess. "Damn it, Sylvia, your arm looks horrible."

"It can wait. I'm riding with Rick to the hospital."

"No, ma'am, you are not," said a lead medic nearby. "Not yet. Two more ambulances are in transit. We're stretched thin due to a big training accident."

"Those two men," said an evaluating doctor while pointing at motionless Rick and Eduardo Miranda, "don't have much time. Surgical teams are waiting. *Go! Now!*" He slapped the side of one of the idling ambulances, and it took off for the base hospital. The doors to Rick's transportation slammed shut just as Sylvia yelled, "I love you!" She stood frozen with squinted eyes fighting the rays of late afternoon sun, tracing the speeding vehicle's route.

"He's held on this long, Sylvia. He's got no intention of dying." I nodded, silently pleading for her brave fiancé I'd met only three days earlier to make it. She stretched her injured arm and studied it. The discoloration had worsened. "Why aren't you in an ambulance? That looks worse than five minutes ago."

"I know. The swelling exploded. Doesn't feel great. Something's not right."

"*Medic!*" I bellowed to a soldier tapping data into a laptop placed on the hood of an SUV. He was logging data regarding injuries and care during the mission. "Why wasn't more done for Captain Sokolov's arm while we were en route? Look at it!"

Sylvia shook her head to protest my questioning but didn't cut me off.

"I wasn't on that flight, sir. The medics on board were thorough. They infused her with antibiotics. Cleaned, sterilized, and rewrapped her arm and fingers. She'll get transported to Beaumont on the next ambulance."

I pointed to the right side of her body. "She's blowing up like a blimp! Those wounds are from a baboon attack. Could she have gotten rabies? Would that explain the bloating?"

Creasing his forehead as he internalized surprising information, he finally replied, "Unlikely, sir. It's too early for symptoms to manifest. But she's got a temperature of 103°, indicating a raging infection. I don't have time to argue with you." He pointed to his right. "Tell her to lay on the gurney until the next ambulance arrives. We'll infuse more antibiotics."

"Do it *now*," I snapped at Sylvia. She nodded with resignation and strode toward the gurney. Minutes later, she was wheeled into the first arriving ambulance. She stared at the ceiling with a pained expression and deep worry lines across her face. Dirt and fatigue gave her eyes a ghoulish look. Rick had been unconscious for the last few hours, barely breathing. She mouthed words I knew weren't meant for her but Rick.

I embraced Lucia and tipped my head to the bilingual nurses standing nearby. "Take good care of her. She's special." A male and female MPO escorted the women toward a single-story green home amid the officer's quarters.

General Taylor arrived and barked commands to have Delgado bound more securely. I suspect the directive was intended to send a message to the cartel king, as his existing constraints would've intimidated Houdini. While transferring Delgado to an SUV, three eager soldiers aimed their gray M4s at his chest, appearing hopeful of actions that would justify pulling their triggers.

The general motioned to me, and I stepped in his direction, fronting him with a salute. The chain-of-command formality seemed to have annoyed Taylor. He said, "I understand you have reservations about VA medical care." That was true. Unimpressed with certain VA hospitals my fellow soldiers and I had spent time in, I hoped Rick, Eduardo, and Sylvia would get transported to the best facility in the city, military or private. "Beaumont's not Stanford Medical, but it's one of the better VAs. Your injured heroes will receive excellent care."

"I can only hope so, sir. Your people made it clear I don't have any say in the matter."

Taylor noted antagonism in my response, but I was running on fumes, and the general didn't call me out. He caught me off guard with his words: "I know you're not in the mood to hear it, but what you and your team just pulled off will live in the warfare annals of my mind for the rest of my days. It's extraordinary. You've achieved something governments couldn't. I'll leave it at that."

"I had no choice, sir."

A Staff Sergeant interrupted to speak with Taylor. "DEA Special Agent Washington has just landed on base with two associates. As requested, they'll be shuttled to Room 2 and prepped for debriefing."

The general nodded to the soldier, then gazed thirty feet away at Delgado for a long pause before locking eyes with me. "Debrief. Interesting word. I'm guessing Agent Washington has more than a debriefing in mind. You'll be impressed by the leverage Washington has on your drug lord. We'll lose our opportunity to lean on him once Mexican bureaucrats and the rat's lawyers arrive. You brought him in, Captain. The DEA must ensure your efforts mattered by incarcerating him and pushing La Buena Familia into disarray."

His assistant told Taylor, "Base security precautions have been deployed, sir. Drone surveillance has been activated. Gates are on highest alert."

Taylor turned to me. "Best to take precautions. I'd put nothing past La Buena Familia. Or President Valdes, based on what you'll be shown shortly." He grabbed his driver's attention by pressing his fingers to his lips and whistling. "Shuttle us to Room 2."

Minutes later, upon stepping from a long hall lined with florescent ceiling lights and gray tiles into Room 2, General Taylor and I found Washington seated with two other DEA agents at a white table cluttered with laptops and digital devices. All three DEA men quickly swallowed mouthfuls of donuts they'd been heartily devouring. One comically spilled coffee over his chin while unsuccessfully attempting to wash the snacks down his throat. Washington stepped forward and extended his hand. "Mr. Morales. I'm sorry to hear about the casualties in Mexico. And I pray your team recovers."

His words appeared genuine, but their tone was unexpectedly dire. *Does he know something about Rick and Eduardo's condition that I don't?* I envisioned all three casualties getting poked, sliced open, sutured, and infused with countless medications. I took a deep breath and swept those images away. "I appreciate your concern."

Washington approached Taylor and introduced himself. They'd spoken over the years but had never met. Washington said, "We need to be efficient with our time. Mexican government officials have channeled urgent demands for Delgado's return. Surprise. They promised a trial and incarceration in their country," he said with a face reflecting absolute doubt.

"Of course they did. President Valdes needs him completely out of the picture," Taylor replied.

My blood boiled. "Hand him back? Over my dead body." Washington patted my shoulder to emphasize *relax*. "Where is the lunatic right now?"

"Across the hall in Room 3," Washington said. "None of us has any intention of releasing him. My comment about the Mexican government's request just highlights variables out of our control."

"Does our president know we've got Delgado on base?" I asked.

"He does," said the general. "We're required to give prominent foreign nationals access to their government's legal representatives. But the president has *no intention* of ever letting Delgado return to Mexico."

Taylor's comment bemused Washington. He wondered if he were the only person in the room who grasped the irony of the US president's stance on not returning the Mexican national. He cleared his throat after scanning every face around him and observing nothing but muted reactions. "Let's move ahead."

Taylor spoke measured words. "The man across the hall is unhinged and dangerous. I spent five minutes with him in a secluded area behind the tarmac. He suggested I facilitate his return to Mexico, or my family would be in danger. I had a bit of a visceral reaction." He held up a clenched right fist marred by abrasions atop four knuckles. "After his threats, you can imagine my thoughts on the prospect of his release."

Washington nodded and glanced around the room. "So let's get a more detailed accounting of your mission, Mr. Morales. Some of our questions may annoy you, but we have our process." The general, the DEA team, and I sat around the table, within reach of the stale food and beverages. "Tell us what your objective was. Provide hourly play-by-play details on the battle within Delgado's compound, absconding with the Mexican Marines helicopter, and the firefight on the farm in Chihuahua."

"My objective?" I asked, emphasizing the absurd question. "You're serious?" Leaning back in my seat, I tossed the remaining half of a donut onto a tray atop the table. "To grab Delgado and bring him to justice. Make him pay for filling our streets with drugs, leading to ruined lives and countless deaths." I looked around the table and quickly read their minds: *There's a much more personal reason you did this, Captain Morales.* Taking a measured sip from a red coffee cup, I shuffled my chair closer to the table. "And as retribution for La Buena Familia's murders of my wife and mother." I received affirming nods from Taylor and Washington. "I'd hoped the DEA, FBI, or Mexican government would take Delgado down." Washington and I glanced at each other. "I respect the DEA, but after three failed attempts to get him, they forced me to act."

"Based on your results, you obviously made the right decision," General Taylor said, like a proud father.

Washington exhaled long and loud before reaching for his coffee, his face colored with embarrassment or angst. I understood. The DEA's job was to get Delgado, and Washington was the point man. He failed.

I narrated my story, from the decision to fully commit while standing next to Brooke and Mom's ashes to our landing at Fort Bliss thirty minutes ago. Everyone grew mesmerized by a journey that seemed more Hollywood than real life. "So that's what happened. Here we are." All eyes darted from person to person. No one spoke for seconds.

Following additional minutes of discussion and fact-finding, Washington asked his Assistant Special Agent in Charge to join him and me in the room holding Marco Delgado. Taylor wasn't invited but followed as if he had been. *My Black Hawks, my base, my rules.*

Delgado's face was a farcical mess. The deep abrasions from Sylvia's fingernails were more evident since his blood had dried in what looked like frozen rivers of thick oil paint. His nose was swollen and crooked. One cheekbone had indentations matching the size and spacing of General Taylor's knuckles. The abrasions above each eye, delivered by Sylvia and me the night before, remained swollen. "You are all dead men," were Delgado's first words. He locked eyes with General Taylor. "Your family, as I promised—will suffer horrific deaths. Especially your daughter, Melissa. I will give the orders soon, perhaps tomorrow. Coordinate my return to Mexico—*now!*—and I may reconsider."

Taylor glanced at me. I reflected on meeting his daughter Melissa at the Santa Monica pier months earlier. Then I felt sorry for him having her pulled into a psychotic killer's realm.

"You enjoy threatening innocent people," Taylor said. "You're a sad little drug lord. If you keep threatening my family, you'll wish you were dead."

Delgado said in English with only a slight accent, "General Taylor, you make those comments because you fear me." He released a sadistic, deep-throated howl and flashed a devilish grin. "Please be assured I speak the truth. You have all messed with the wrong Mexican. You are right to be afraid."

Washington stood for effect. "As an agent of the United States Drug Enforcement Administration, I am placing you under arrest for murder, illicit drug manufacture and distribution, bribery, and—"

"Shut the hell up. And fetch me a cigarette, negro."

Neither Agent Washington, his team, nor the Black sentry standing against a wall reacted. General Taylor imperceptibly rotated his right wrist to stare at the swelling and blood caused by his earlier blow to Delgado's head. He wanted to slug him again. I think Washington's restraint heightened Taylor's respect for the agent. Washington replied calmly, "Get him a cigarette."

A sergeant left the room and returned three minutes later with a pack of Marlboros and a University of Texas lighter. Washington pulled one of the cigarettes, placed it between Delgado's lips, thumbed the lighter, and obediently raised the flame as his nemesis drew in, igniting its tip.

Puffing on the burning Marlboro, Delgado tipped his head at the UT lighter and effortlessly spoke with the cigarette dangling. "I am a Duke man, myself. A Dukie. Big basketball fan." Faces around the room scrunched up in disbelief, but no one interrupted. "President Valdes will demand my release. He is an honest man respected by global leaders. Your G.I. Joe here," he scowled at me, "murdered innocent Mexican Marines last night. You are all accessories to those deaths. These truths will deliver me home within forty-eight hours. I will never spend a day inside an American prison."

Talk about the perfect segue, Taylor thought. Flashing a look of victory, Washington said, "This thing's ready to go, right?" His Assistant SAC nodded, and everyone anxiously awaited what was to come. "Press enter." Just as Delgado exhaled and blew smoke toward Agent Washington's face, the senior agent pushed the button.

Delgado's expression initially appeared relaxed. A minute later, he grew visibly affected watching video footage of his $20,000,000 bribe hand-delivered to the President of Mexico, with gloriously implicating quid pro quo from both men. Defense lawyers thrive on ambiguities; this case was just won with unequivocal proof and made-for-TV drama.

Burning ashes from the tip of Delgado's cigarette were purposely flicked onto Washington's lap. General Taylor rushed from his seat and thrust the palm of his muscular right arm into the cartel boss's chest, hurling him and his chair across the floor. I remained seated and calm. Washington barely reacted. I guessed that watching Delgado panic was an unexpected and satisfying event for the career DEA agent.

Delgado regained his bravado after being lifted from the floor and helped into his seat. "I am, if nothing else, a man of my word. Each of you sitting here knows that to be true. For the sake of your families' futures, I *strongly* urge you to destroy this video. Doing so will make each of you wealthy." His shifting stare moved from me to Taylor to Washington. With furrowed brows and expressive intensity, he continued, "Here is the deal: If I spend even three days in your country, you will all be dead within a month. But before you die, everyone you love will be slaughtered. Spouses, children, aunts and uncles, nephews and nieces. Gone. I go free—none of that happens."

More than anyone, I understood these were not idle threats. This guy was frighteningly unhinged and more powerful than many governments. I suspect we all silently pondered the same question: Was Delgado *more* dangerous in jail than in the mountains of Sinaloa? Should I have shot him in Mexico?

Finally, Delgado turned and spoke to me in Spanish. "I ordered Brooklyn and Maria's deaths. It was a just decision. I have a special end in mind for Samuel. Ashley will wish she were never born. And your execution will be the most artistic of all. We had a deal, *Jaime*. You broke it."

If your job is battling cartel madmen, you speak Spanish. Washington gazed at me sympathetically. Although the SAC never captured Delgado, I considered him an honorable man.

Delgado's threats directed at everyone I loved and, in the case of Ashley, felt obliged to protect, inflamed my anxieties. Had I made a terrible decision by letting him live? My opportunity to remove Marco Delgado from this earth had passed.

CHAPTER 44

Warming rays of early afternoon sunshine blanketed Fort Bliss. General Taylor, SAC Washington, and I stood below the canopy of an old Rio Grande cottonwood. My mission debriefs and Marco Delgado's interrogation had just wrapped up. The grilling of the cartel boss had devolved into another threat-fest. His graphic warnings affected everyone in Room 3, but any concerns for their loved ones remained private.

The general's phone vibrated, and he stepped away for a brief conversation. After hanging up, he turned to me. "Important updates. Captain Rick Bonham is recovering after surgery. His vitals are stable, and he'll live. Captain Sokolov is responding well to whatever drugs they're pumping into her. She received seventy stitches in her arm and hand. Inflammation is abating, and she wants out of Beaumont. Keeps asking about Captain Bonham and the injured Mexican national."

"That would be Eduardo Miranda. Please tell me he survived."

Taylor nodded sympathetically. "I'm told he flatlined on the table. Doctors brought him back from the brink. Like I said earlier, we've got great nurses and surgeons on this base."

Staring at the horizon, I heard people calling my name but continued dissecting the health updates. Someone squeezed my arm, bringing me back to the conversation. Washington said, "We've all seen too much death and suffering in our lives, Mr. Morales. Your pain has been especially tragic." He was right, and I stood numb with recollections of Brooke and Mom. "But amidst that pain, you have a reason to smile. Samuel Morales has arrived and is waiting to reunite with his son."

My face must have radiated because Taylor and Washington smiled genuinely. I was about to meet the only remaining link to my direct family. "I'm stunned. This is all . . ." They watched me shake my head.

"Happening, Captain Morales. This is all happening. A remarkable moment," said General Taylor. "These men will escort you and Agent Washington to your reunion. I'll catch up with you both later." He looked at Washington. "As you requested, Delgado's transfer to federal custody is set for 1900 hours sharp."

The five-minute walk to meet my father was spent debating what I should say to a man who had not existed for three decades. My breathing grew louder as we rounded a curve leading to the guarded officer's quarter. I couldn't help it.

"My father was killed when I was six," Agent Washington said, placing one hand on my bicep and halting me. "It would be mind-numbing to have him back in my life. The only suggestion I have is to start with a simple embrace. Your conversation will just happen."

Thank you, sir. That's just what I needed to hear. I nodded but remained quiet. Washington purposely lagged as we approached Samuel's front door, which two sentries protected. I stood and stared through a window into the kitchen from the doorway until Agent Washington nudged me inside.

Samuel rose from his wooden chair. I'm sure he was struggling with his own thoughts of despair, joy, love, and hope. After setting my rucksack on the floor, we hugged without speaking. We grieved and wept for lost years, a wife and mother taken, and a daughter-in-law Samuel would never meet.

We took the first steps toward fixing broken lives as afternoon sunshine stretched shadows visible through front-room windows. My father's face was colored with unbounded affection. The moment seemed impossible, yet here it was, poignant and permanent. We emptied a pitcher of iced tea, and Samuel never released my free hand.

I reminisced about my wonderful childhood with a mother who spoke glowingly of her murdered husband and showered me with unconditional love. While chatting longingly of Maria, Samuel remarked that none of my praise surprised him: *This* was the woman who'd stolen his heart as a young man. He revealed spending years praying for a family reunion, which sustained him as he lived caged like an animal inside a bunker.

Samuel listened intently to my condensed version of the events triggering Brooke and Maria's murders. As I explained that the Emerald Cross Ashley attempted to sell Delgado triggered their deaths, I thought he might chastise my sister-in-law. Instead, he said Ashley was ignorant of the risks of trying to broker a deal but that the subsequent murders were an unthinkably harsh price to pay for her actions.

"It was a mindless thing to attempt," Samuel said, his throat catching. "But decent people, especially decent greedy people, have no clue about what a Marco Delgado is capable of. I forgive her, as it sounds like you have." With a face expressing pain and sadness, he wiped his eyes with a tissue. "You've retrieved the Emerald Cross. I look forward to seeing it someday."

Stepping away, I lifted my desert camouflage rucksack and returned to the table. Pulling the Beretta out, I laid it aside, clutched the cloth bag containing the cross, and handed it to Samuel. I placed his pistol back inside the rucksack. Having a gun nearby during our first sit-down in three decades felt unacceptable and ugly. "Samuel, Maria never mentioned the cross to me."

"Maria was perceptive and intelligent. She recognized possessing it was a blessing but also potentially a curse. Some history: Marco Delgado's father, Mauricio, endowed the cross to me. It had been in the Delgado family for over two centuries, a gift from a Spanish bishop for their ardent financial support. They'd always been a wealthy but pious family until three of Mauricio's four sons became narcos."

"Delgado believed you stole the cross. He blamed Mom for owning it."

"Dear God, son. That's heartbreaking. I should have anticipated that and never accepted it from Mauricio Delgado."

"Oh, Samuel. I shouldn't have said that. You could not have known what the future held. Please don't blame yourself for accepting the gift. I would have done the same. I'm honored Mauricio considered you a worthy keeper of the cross."

My father reached for the sweating glass of iced tea and swallowed a mouthful. It struck me that Brooke, Maria, and I consumed copious amounts of sun-drenched tea on lazy afternoons. Samuel and I could continue the desperately missed ritual.

"During my investigative reporting, I uncovered the genesis of La Buena Familia. Surprisingly, I learned Delgado's father kept a penthouse in Mexico City, not far from where we raised you." He lowered his eyes and said in a quieter voice, "I mean, where your mother and I raised you for two years. Well, I asked Mauricio Delgado for a confidential interview. He agreed."

"Samuel, we've only been reunited for hours. Don't feel obligated to delve into anything else Delgado. It's clear these are painful memories."

He raised his palm. "It is important, son. This man is responsible for our separation and your precious wife's murder. The daughter-in-law I'll never meet." He suppressed a fit of anguish, which produced strange sounds now escaping through a tightly clenched mouth. He rubbed his eyes with a palm. "I need to finish. It all leads somewhere."

I thought he appeared momentarily lost in thought. He sipped more tea and continued, "Mauricio Delgado and I had met perhaps five times over ten months. We became true friends. Son, he was such a *good* man. But the increasing violence and death toll wrought by La Buena Familia destroyed him. Every month, I watched him grow weaker and more troubled by the cartel's evil deeds, perpetuated by sons he still clearly loved. Mauricio disclosed everything he knew about Marco's burgeoning cartel empire during our visits. The months of detailed accounts, augmented by father-son letters, were critical in building the case of political bribery and rampant corruption between Mexican senators and the cartel."

But why, Samuel, is it so important to reveal all this today? Our first day together? I don't understand.

He stared out the window for a long pause, rigid with a look of resolve blanketing his face, then he turned back to meet my gaze. "In my last meeting with Mauricio, he laid a briefcase on the table, turned two combinations, and presented the Emerald Cross. He divulged its history and insisted I take it. Of course, I was awestruck by the relic, but I told him I could never accept it. *He insisted!* He considered me a better person than I probably was, repeating that he wanted the cross to remain with a decent man and protector. He felt if he donated it to the Church, Marco would steal it within weeks."

"Samuel, he understood you were honest and admirable. It's probably as simple as that. Also, the person Mauricio Delgado admired was the father Maria told me I had. She not only loved but venerated you."

"I must continue," he asserted without dwelling on my sentiment. "Mauricio revealed that Marco had recruited two of his three brothers into the cartel. He appeared a broken man during this final conversation." Samuel again peered outside, gently gritting his teeth, looking as if he were shouldering the weight of the world. "He couldn't take what his sons were doing anymore—threatening, bribing, torturing, killing. They had become monsters who wiped out centuries of a noble family's reputation in less than five years. So, I accepted the gift you now hold in your hands." He pushed himself from the table, steepled his fingers under his chin, and grew quiet. After mentally stepping back into the *now*, he said in a barely discernible voice, "The next day, authorities found Mauricio murdered inside his penthouse. I believe Marco executed his father after discovering he met with me. And perhaps for gifting me the cross."

"It's obvious you cared deeply for Mauricio."

"I did. Thank you. Weeks later, I presented my corruption findings implicating five Mexican senators to President Cornesa. And two weeks after that, La Buena Familia abducted me. That was the last day I ever saw Maria. And I assumed it was the last day I would ever see my son." He pressed his palm to my tired and stubbled face.

"Just out of curiosity," I asked, "did Mauricio provide a deeper history of the Emerald Cross?"

"I memorized most of what he told me. He also handed me a written history, which I hid within the frame of one of our paintings. From what I understand, when Maria hurriedly emigrated from Mexico, she left her belongings behind, so I assume the written account is gone. As for its history, Mauricio explained that a Franciscan friar stole emeralds and gold Inca relics from a Spanish galleon he was serving aboard, the *Santa Sofia*, sometime around 1530. The ship moored off what is today the western coast of Central Mexico before sailing northward and disappearing from recorded history."

"Incredible."

"The thieving friar repented as an old man, delivering the religious artifacts to Father Junipero Serra, whom the king of Spain had chartered with converting indigenous peoples in the New World up the western coast of what is today Mexico and California. After passing from bishop to bishop for decades, the gold figures were melted down and formed into a cross, during which artisans inlaid the emeralds. And voilà—the Emerald Cross was born. Mauricio Delgado claimed the Catholic Church later gifted the cross to his family's ancestors in appreciation for organizing laborers and helping to finance the construction of churches throughout the region." He smiled, "At least, that's the story."

Leaning back, I adjusted my eyepatch, faintly nodding. "And what a story it is. You have quite a memory." I stared at the cross as Samuel reached and pulled it from my grasp. "I'm curious. What was the painting you tucked the history of the cross into?"

"An oil painting of Our Lady of Guadalupe."

Smiling, I said, "Then you'll be happy to learn it was the only piece of art she ever really cared about. It's hanging on the wall of her casita on our property." I caught myself. "I guess it's just my property now."

Samuel rested a hand on my knee. "Wonderful. You can test my memory further, comparing what I just recounted to what the written words attest." Samuel took another sip from his tall glass and then rubbed his forearm. He tilted his head back, his gaze cast onto the ceiling, before lowering his eyes with a worried look. "Jaime, Delgado might try to kill again to avenge his capture. And he'll certainly want to repossess the Emerald Cross. You must heed the threats of this madman. I'm *very* worried, son."

"The days of a Green Beret during combat duty are tinged by periods of absolute terror. I'll be fine. Delgado's an intimidating man, but his power and influence will diminish after he's languishing in a high-security prison cell."

"I wish I could believe that. But I think he'll attempt to act on every threat. He's a dreadful man with conviction and no conscience. Terror and death are his *modus operandi*. His signature. We are all in great danger."

"I've done what I can, Samuel. It's out of our hands now. Are you thinking I should have killed him?"

He stayed quiet for a long pause. And then he never answered the question.

"As I've told my comrades recovering in the hospital, death is too easy an end for evil bastards like Delgado."

With a tone of admiration for his hero son, he said, "I hope you are right."

CHAPTER 45

After our fourth hour of a reunion I deemed impossible two days earlier—*how does one reunite with a murdered father?*—I apologized leaving to visit Lucia, Eduardo, Rick, and Sylvia. We were excited to reconvene over dinner at the same table, catered by Buffalo Wild Wings, compliments of the US Army.

The civilian clothes Taylor had delivered didn't fit me well, but this was a day for ignoring trivial matters. I returned the Emerald Cross to my rucksack at the foot of my bed. Samuel was concerned about our safety, so I reiterated Fort Bliss was teeming with soldiers and security, including the sentries standing watch outside. Stepping out the door, I yelled to my father, "Try to get some rest!"

Lucia would be my first stop. After presenting a white Armed Forces identification to gain entrance to her quarters, I found her wet-headed, freshly attired, and deep in conversation with a bilingual Army nurse. She rushed forward with arms held wide and hugged me tightly for seconds that felt like minutes. After our discussion, I grew consoled, realizing Lucia had already found seeds of hope for her future.

Wiping away her tears, I kissed her forehead and promised to check in tomorrow. Her parting words caught me off-guard: "Why didn't you shoot the devil?" It was a fair question from any of his victims, but it required time I didn't have to navigate a proper response. We tabled the issue. I recalled Sylvia informing me she wouldn't let this stranger get mauled to death by Serengeti lions and tigers, hideous entertainment for Delgado's sicarios. Now here she was, alive and recovering—a victory.

As I walked toward Beaumont Medical Center, someone called my name. SAC Washington and his associates surprised me from inside their vehicle. Glancing at my watch, I curtly waved and kept walking. I didn't want interruptions to delay my visits.

"Headed to the hospital?" asked Washington.

"Good guess," I replied with a wink.

"Let us give you a lift."

"You guys are busy. I don't mind walking."

"Nonsense. We'll get you there in half the time."

After obliging, we drove in a green Army SUV toward Beaumont, a sprawling complex lying on the northern perimeter of Fort Bliss at the foot of the Franklin Mountains. Washington said, "We just spent another hour with Delgado. Access to him will be more difficult after he gets transferred tonight at seven."

"'More difficult' translates to 'accompanied by scum lawyers who'll tell him not to utter a word.'"

"Precisely." The perspiring SAC glanced at the other agents. "This is way out of bounds to divulge, but you've earned the right to hear it. Our conversations with Delgado have grown increasingly disturbing."

"Let me guess. He's reiterating our extended families will die within days or weeks."

"Essentially, yes. That surprises no one, but he says it with great conviction. It's quite unsettling." He scratched his chest through his black DEA long-sleeved shirt as the bustle of a military base flashed through their windows. "General Taylor tried to pull strings to detain him on base for two more days. He was unsuccessful."

"It doesn't surprise me he tried or failed. What was his plan had his superiors granted the request?"

"He wanted more time to assess Delgado's threats before demanding resources to coordinate precautions."

"That's a waste of time, sir. Keep him locked up, put him on trial, get him convicted, and throw away the key. His threats and influence will wane."

"That's a best-case scenario." Washington pressed a button to lower his window, inviting an annoying wasp to exit the SUV. One of his agents slapped and bounced the insect hard against the dashboard, which only enraged the yellow and black passenger.

"General Taylor's a patriot who finishes jobs," I said. "He wanted to buy time for a final tête-à-tête with Delgado, where he'd turn the tables and make his own threats. He could only do that before his law dogs got their dirty paws on him."

"The general and I see the world through similar lenses," said Washington. "But we diverge on how to act once we've read the tea leaves. I follow most protocols and believe everyone should. Taylor's more prone to act like a vigilante. Damn the torpedoes. Do what's right. To hell with the consequences."

"I'd likely fall somewhere between you two. But one thing I now know—protocols don't mean shit when dealing with psychotic, murdering cartel despots. Too many people don't understand that."

It may have been a clever dig to imply the DEA was clueless about people like Delgado. Maybe it was my way of reemphasizing that Washington and his team failed to apprehend the drug lord three times over the past year. Whatever my intent, he sat unperturbed. I wondered if he silently accepted primary blame for those failures or was annoyed that a one-eyed retired Green Beret who'd overcome his PTSD succeeded where authorities and militaries couldn't.

"Drop me off here, and thanks for the lift. Do whatever you can to ensure Delgado spends the rest of his life behind bars."

I stepped toward the entrance of Beaumont Medical Center. Washington flung his passenger-side door open, and I heard him jogging in my direction. The shadow of his profile grew visible, and he said, "Mr. Morales, a final word."

I turned around, and we faced each other. "I've met heroes in my life, but I've never met one like you. You've somehow achieved the impossible. You made the world a better place, a cliché but it's true. I stand in awe."

"It was a team effort. Sylvia Sokolov, Rick Bonham, DEA, Army, the Miranda family, Mexican farmers—everyone played a role. I never could've done this alone."

It appeared he disagreed.

We shook hands. There was nothing else to say. "I should go, Agent Washington. Stay well."

I made my way to Rick's room, one of about two hundred in the ugly Modernism building. He lay prone in his bed, two hours post-surgery, hooked up to machines I recognized from surgical post-op care in Germany. A nurse flashed a faint smile as she left the room. Sylvia sat beside Rick's mending body and held vigil. Her right arm was tightly bound with gauze and tape. A heart monitor beeped in the background. I thought neither injured soldier looked fit for conversation, but Sylvia had a habit of defying expectations.

"He'll make it," she said with words strained by a tightened throat. "I should've never doubted. But you know, Jamie, we've each seen soldiers who looked better than Rick did, who never made it. You really never know." She leaned forward to gently run the fingers of her uninjured hand across Rick's moisture-beaded forehead, tenderly combing his dirty hair with her fingers. "I'm just so happy," she said haltingly. "And so *damn* proud of him."

"Roger that." I leaned forward with a hand on her knee. "General Taylor says he will pin Medals of Valor on both of you. Even though it wasn't an 'Army sanctioned' mission." We quietly chuckled.

"I don't care about medals."

"I know you don't. It's because you have too many," I said with a smile while glancing at her arm. "Wow, it's hard to believe how quickly your swelling subsided."

"Damn straight. Watch this." She bent her bandaged arm at the elbow, back and forth, tight angles. "No pain. They must've pumped medical magic into my veins."

"Come on, that must hurt. Never mind. You'd lie even if it did just to make a point."

"That's true. Hey, give me an update on Lucia. I hope she's holding up. What a trooper."

"I met with her twenty minutes ago. She's exhausted but hopeful. What you did for her was extraordinary, Sylvia."

"What we *all* did. I do feel maybe God placed me in that moment for her sake."

"Anything's possible. Truth is stranger than fiction." I reached for her hand and squeezed.

"What about Eduardo Miranda?"

"He made it through surgery. The doctors somehow saved his arm. He was out cold when I stopped by."

"Fantastic news. The guy battled sicarios we brought to his front door. He fought like hell. Delgado and his minions couldn't take him out." She adjusted her hospital gown and looked at me with relief. "I prayed you wouldn't have to tell Eduardo's wife, 'Sorry, ma'am, your husband's dead.' Or, 'My sympathies, Señor and Señora Miranda. You've lost another son.'"

"Yeah, a little less guilt for both of us. So, Delgado will be transferred to federal agents in forty-five minutes. The President of Mexico wants him back. So does La Buena Familia. He's a popular guy."

"Unlike you, I just want him dead. Like that Iranian general who just got whacked. Certain wicked people need to die so the rest of civilization can live in peace." We changed the topic and discussed matters having nothing to do with drug lords and cartels but everything to do with optimism and hope for us and our loved ones.

Exiting the hospital, the physical and mental strains of not just the past two arduous days but a lifetime of emotional burdens caught up with me: a father allegedly executed, Wes Berkeley getting blown up, my torture in Afghanistan, and finding Brooke and Mom. Knowing Samuel and I would share our futures, everything felt a little less painful. I had found light at the end of a long, dark tunnel.

CHAPTER 46

As we neared our housing, I checked the time; it was 6:55. Unlike the earlier two, only one sentry was posted at the front door. The fit sergeant saluted, and I returned the formality. "Looks like you drew the short straw, soldier. The other grunt gets to enjoy a social life tonight."

"Maybe later, sir," he replied. "Your father asked to take a short walk minutes ago. Sergeant Muncy's accompanying him. They should return by 1920."

I'm sure I looked confused.

"Your father said he left you a note inside."

With that comment, my body, mind, and senses grew hyper-aware. *Take a deep breath, buddy. Everything's fine. You know you overreact sometimes. He just needed fresh air.* I stepped inside the house and beelined for the kitchen, where no note was visible. Dashing into my bedroom, a white piece of paper lay beside my rucksack at the foot of the bed. I read the note in blue ink: *Dear son, Delgado will follow through on his threats. My love for you is eternal.* I thrust my hand into the rucksack—my Beretta was gone.

Exploding out the front door, I screamed *Follow me!* without a glance at the sentry. We exited the area marked Officers Quarters and dashed over a cement walkway toward the building housing Delgado.

Approaching the building awash in waning Texas sunshine, I saw a contingent of DEA and Army personnel. Washington and Taylor were directing Delgado's official transfer. Samuel was nowhere in sight, but this premonition was more than a hunch.

Armed soldiers led the uncuffed and calm Delgado toward a pair of SUVs. In my peripheral vision, I discovered Samuel rushing the group from another angle. He stopped, pulled out my Beretta, aimed at his nemesis, and screamed, *"No more murders and threats, Delgado!"*

He was about to get shot by one of the DEA or Army personnel. Or one of the American cartel trash lawyers packing heat for protection. That thought drove me to move with even greater reckless abandon. I must tackle Samuel before he gets filled with lead. Then a sickening awareness enveloped me—there was too much ground to make up.

Samuel squeezed the trigger three times, but no shots rang out. The clip had been emptied during the firefight on the Miranda property. The group transferring Delgado froze, assessing the chaos, while two Army soldiers raised their M4s to eliminate the danger—Samuel. A moment before their merciless weapons fired on the unidentified aggressor, Washington and Taylor screamed at their soldiers not to open fire. But the soldiers were trained to act and aimed their lethal carbines. Out of nowhere, Sergeant Muncy, the sentry trailing Samuel, caught my father from behind and took him violently to the ground. No M4 triggers got pulled. No one died.

The people surrounding Delgado moved fervently to get him into the idling SUV. But the drug lord recognized Samuel and was in no hurry to miss a wonderfully theatric moment. The lawyers barked at him to jump inside his transportation. He brushed their hands off his body and snickered. "Let me watch Samuel Morales realize he has lost his opportunity." He yelled out in Spanish, "I am still alive, you bumbling fool. You and your son shall soon be dead. *As God is my witness!*" He stepped forward, disregarding his handlers' pleas to get inside the idling SUV. Again, he shoved the lawyers' hands and arms aside. Delgado stepped forward and separated himself from those who protected and despised him. He stood defiantly and glared like a boxer chiding a reviled opponent he'd just knocked out. Washington raised his arm to shield his eyes from the blinding sunset.

I watched it before I heard it. It all played out in slow motion, as epic moments on the battlefield often do—a single shot from an unknown shooter. It was a large round capable of ending a man's life if it grazed his skull, but this was not a grazing. Supersonic high-caliber bullets decimate their target before the booming sounds of discharge and reverberations reach their mark. Two seconds later, the boom arrived.

No one could be sure, but I thought it sounded like, and looked like, a direct hit from a US Army M24 sniper rifle, essentially a modified Remington 700 used for hunting big game. Most eyes turned toward the Franklin Mountains standing behind Beaumont Medical Center, but the rumbling echoes made it impossible to know for sure. At least, at this point.

But one thing was certain.

Marco Delgado was no more.

ACKNOWLEDGMENTS

To the early readers who offered invaluable critique and constant support, you have my deepest gratitude:

Karen Cruickshank, Peg Schuetz, John Busch,
Kris Curry, Kirk Rozman, Kevin Luby, Beth Groshans,
Dan Groshans, Miriam Long, Steve Long, Leslie Heinrich,
Paul Younkin, Bart Adams, Mark Marcantonio,
and Karen Shorr

AUTHOR BIO

Due to multiple sclerosis and an accident, Ken Cruickshank uses speech-to-text software to write groundbreaking thrillers, fiction, and memoirs. *The Emerald Cross* is Ken's second novel. *Eagle Bay* was his debut psychological thriller, released in 2023. Both stories take readers on surprising journeys, and he hopes their endings are unguessable. *Stand Up: a memoir of disease, family, faith & hope* was released in 2017. Ken appreciates every reader who commits precious leisure time to his books. After thirty years in Oregon, he and his artist wife, Karen, now call Arizona home.

Visit Ken online at:
kencruickshank.com
instagram.com/authorkencruickshank
facebook.com/KenCruickshankAuthor/

Printed in the USA
CPSIA information can be obtained
at www.ICGtesting.com
CBHW021602260624
10521CB00052B/311/J